Malcolm Richards crafts stories edge of your seat. He is the auth mystery novels, including the PI nominated Devil's Cove trilogy, Many of his books are set in Cornwall, where he was born and raised.

Before becoming a full-time writer, he worked for several years in the special education sector, teaching and supporting children with complex needs. After living in London for two decades, he has now settled in the Somerset countryside with his partner and their pets.

Visit the author's website: www.malcolmrichardsauthor.com

BOOKS BY MALCOLM RICHARDS

PI Blake Hollow

Circle of Bones

Down in the Blood

The Devil's Cove Trilogy

The Cove

Desperation Point

The Devil's Gate

The Emily Swanson Series

Next to Disappear

Mind for Murder

Trail of Poison

Watch You Sleep

Kill for Love

Standalone Novels

The Hiding House

DESPERATION
POINT

THE DEVIL'S COVE TRILOGY: BOOK TWO

Malcolm
Richards

StormHouse

First published in 2018 by Storm House Books

ISBN 978-1-9993384-5-9

www.stormhousebooks.com

For Victor

PROLOGUE

THE SCREAM WAS piercing and racked with pain. Ross Quick's eyes snapped open and stared into darkness. He sat up, his head spinning. Somewhere below him, Meg's barking was angry and urgent. Ross had fallen asleep in his clothes. An empty bottle of gin lay next to him on the bed. He was still drunk. Nausea and disorientation climbed his throat.

It took him a moment to remember the scream. He turned to look at the bedside alarm clock. It was just after 2 a.m. Had he been dreaming? Meg's incessant barking said no.

Swinging his legs over the side of the bed, Ross took a moment to find his balance. Cold air bit his feet as he staggered through the darkness to the window.

He had left the curtains open. This far out in the countryside darkness was absolute, and now winter had settled over the land like a death shroud, there was no escaping it. Darkness greeted him in the morning and whispered him a goodnight. It made the solitude of his existence on the farm even more of a void; made the allure of alcoholic oblivion much more tempting.

The scream.

Pressing his face against the glass, Ross stared into the yard. It was too dark to see anything. Downstairs, Meg was growing frantic.

"All right, girl!" Ross bellowed. "Settle down!"

The dog's barking continued as he stumbled from the room. The cold was worse out here, attacking him through his clothes, freezing his breath in frosty plumes. Shivering, Ross flipped on the light switch and squinted at the low-ceilinged landing. A dull throb had started at the base of his skull and was now reaching up to drag nails across his scalp.

Taking the stairs two at a time and yelling at the damn dog to shut up for a minute, Ross descended into darkness. Mistiming the last step, he slipped.

His feet went out from under him. His right temple slammed against the wall. Ross lurched forward and hit the floor.

He groaned as pain shot through his body. The dog's barking grew to an unbearable crescendo.

Ross pushed himself up to a sitting position and checked for damage. There was no blood, but a lump on his temple was already surfacing.

The drinking needed to stop. It had been getting worse lately; this need to lose himself at the bottom of a bottle each night. But what would he replace it with? He was alone out here. His evenings felt vast and empty, as if he were lost in darkness and waiting to die.

Allowing a minute for the farmhouse to stop spinning, Ross hauled himself back onto his feet.

He staggered along the hall in the direction of the kitchen, Meg's barking driving nails through his skull.

Throwing open the door, he flipped the light switch and stared across the cluttered kitchen.

Cold seeped through the flagstone floor and gripped his bones. The black and white Border Collie was at the back door, her nose pointed upward as she filled the room with noise. Lurching across the floor, Ross laid a clumsy hand on the dog's head.

"Easy, girl. Calm yourself."

Meg's barking came to an abrupt halt and was replaced by a deep, guttural growl. Pulling back the curtain of the kitchen window, Ross peered into the yard. Still unable to see anything, he reached across and flipped a switch. The exterior light blinked on. Shadows receded, hovering at the edges.

Ross cocked his head, trying to listen above Meg's growls. The yard was still. He heard no more screams.

Perhaps it had been a fox that had woken him. It would explain Meg's behaviour—she hated the animals. Ross wasn't fond of them either; last year, one had broken into the coop and slaughtered half of his hens.

He'd since made the coop more secure. But foxes were sly. If there was a way in, no matter how imperceptible, they would find it.

As Ross stared into the backyard, he was struck by a sudden realisation. With all the noise Meg was making, the sheep were being unusually quiet.

Pulling back the locks, he opened the door.

Cold rushed in. Meg bounded out, shooting across the yard and disappearing into the darkness.

Ross yelled after her. That damn dog was going to be the death of him. Grabbing a wax jacket from the back of the door, he slipped his feet into a pair of boots then stepped outside.

Motes of dust and frost drifted through the air. His teeth chattered. Very quickly, he was sobering up.

He turned his head, staring into the night. Meg was still barking somewhere in the near distance. If there was a fox on the property, the dog would chase it away. But if it was something else . . .

An uneasy feeling reached out from the darkness and coiled around him. Returning to the house, Ross grabbed a torch from the kitchen window and his shotgun from a locked cabinet in the hall. It was already loaded with two shells, but he filled his pockets with more.

Now completely sober, he switched on the torch, and with the shotgun perched over his right arm, he crossed the yard.

A narrow beam of light illuminated his mud-splattered Range Rover and an abandoned shell of an old harvester.

Meg's barking echoed in the night.

Passing outbuildings, Ross pointed the torch in the direction of the chicken coop. He could hear the chickens clucking anxiously inside, unsettled by Meg's barking, but the coop looked undisturbed and the ground was clear of feathers and blood.

Perhaps the fox hadn't been able to break into the coop, after all. Perhaps Meg had scared it off.

Stumbling forward, Ross reached the large wooden barn. Meg appeared in the light. She glanced back at him, acknowledging his presence, then returned to growling.

After a day of bitter cold and rain, the sheep were inside for the night to dry off. They were eerily silent.

Meg's head was down low, her teeth glittering in the torchlight.

"Easy, girl," Ross said. "Easy now."

Foxes rarely bothered with sheep, unless it was lambing season. Perhaps a stray dog, then?

His brain caught up with his vision. Ross tightened his grip on the shotgun. Once, last week, he'd been drinking before bringing the sheep in and hadn't closed the barn doors. The sheep had wandered all over the farm and it had taken him and Meg most of the next morning to herd them back to their usual field.

The barn doors were shut now. There was no stray dog. No animal of any kind.

An intruder?

It was unusual. People didn't tend to trample through the countryside at night, especially mid-winter.

Unless they meant to cause trouble. Unless they meant to steal.

Staring at the barn doors, Ross remembered the scream that had woken him. He felt the sudden urge to wrench open the doors and rush inside.

The sheep were his livelihood. The food that he put on his table. The clothes he wore on his back. No harm could come to the sheep because if it did, harm would come to him.

Unnerved by the silence, he watched as Meg sniffed the bottom of the barn doors and scratched the ground with a paw.

Brushing her to one side, Ross tucked the torch under his arm and removed the latch. The doors swung open.

His breaths came fast and heavy. Ross aimed the shotgun into the darkness.

Meg immediately began barking. But she wouldn't go in.

"Someone there?" Ross called out. "You're trespassing. I'll give you ten seconds to leave or I'll fire."

The shotgun trembled against his forearm as he spread his

feet and waited. There were no sounds. No bleats. No shifting of wool or bodies.

He stepped forward.

The smell hit him; deep and coppery like rusted metal. Lowering the shotgun, Ross lifted the torch and pointed it into the barn. Meg's barking grew to a skull-splitting crescendo.

"Dear God!"

The torch shook in Ross' hand. The shotgun swung limply by his side.

The sheep lay scattered across the barn, unmoving. The blood was everywhere, splattering their white wool, soaking the ground, painting the walls.

They were dead. All of them. Every last one.

And not only dead. Parts of them were missing.

Ross stared at the massacre, his head swinging from side to side, his lips twitching up and down.

The stench of death was overwhelming.

A hundred sheep. Dead. Mutilated.

Meg barked and growled and scratched at the ground. Ross staggered back. The world spun around him. An anguished, guttural sound climbed his throat and shot from his mouth, shattering the night.

1

AARON BLACK SWITCHED off the engine of the silver Peugeot and stared through the windscreen. In the distance, heavy charcoal clouds rolled and churned above a foaming slate ocean. In the foreground, the beach was colourless and barren. A beach bar called The Shack was currently closed. Blustery winds battered its walls, flinging sand, dried seaweed, and shell fragments.

Bleak, Aaron thought as he leaned forward to observe the towering cliffs that flanked the cove. The Mermaid Hotel sat on top of the left cliff, its blackened exterior encased in construction scaffolding. On the right cliff, a rusty looking lighthouse stood like an ancient guardian, while behind it, the coppery-green canopy of Briar Wood was effervescent against the brooding sky.

Aaron's gaze returned to the left cliff and slipped down to the arch of rock jutting into the ocean.

He shivered. *Bleaker than bleak.*

And cold.

The temperature inside the car was already beginning to drop, leaving icy tendrils to seep through the cracks. Buttoning his dark winter coat up to his neck, Aaron turned his attention to the rear-view mirror. His was the only vehicle taking up space in the seafront car park. Behind him was Cove Road, which circled the town of Porth an Jowl like a hangman's noose, providing the only way in and out by land. A row of old stone cottages sat on the other side.

No one was around. It was as if Aaron were the only person in the world.

A blast of wind hit the car, howling and whistling as it hurtled by. Aaron winced as he stared at his reflection in the rear-view mirror. There were faint shadows forming beneath his dark brown eyes. Days' worth of stubble covered his usually clean-shaven face. His hair was a straggly mess, well overdue a cut.

He turned away, suddenly feeling decades older than his thirty-seven years. As soon as he got back to the hotel, he would have a hot shower, take a razor to his face, perhaps pop a sleeping pill and sleep for fourteen hours straight.

But right now, he had a job to do.

Pulling his long coat tightly around him, he grabbed his bag from the back seat and opened the door.

The cold hit him like an open-handed slap. The wind howled. The sea roared. The sky grew dense and black; rain was on its way. In an hour, maybe two, darkness would fall.

Exiting the car park, Aaron stepped onto the faded pink promenade and stopped short of the protective iron railings. The beach lay below. Stone steps led down to the sand. Aaron thought about heading down there, but the cold was already eating into his skin and chewing through his bones.

From his bag, he pulled out a digital SLR camera, slung the strap over his neck, and removed the lens cap.

Adjusting the aperture, he snapped pictures of the beach and the cliffs, the hotel and lighthouse. He lowered the camera for a second, mesmerised by the view. He'd read Emily Brontë and the Poldark novels, and had expected to find a rugged, romanticised wild beauty. Perhaps at any other time of the year, such a view would have been possible. There were traces of that beauty still lingering, but Cornwall in mid-December, as he was quickly learning, was harsh and brutal; a world away from the sunny pictures found in tourism brochures.

Turning his back on the crashing surf, Aaron gave his attention to the town.

Porth an Jowl was a small community with a population of four thousand people, most of whom lived in rows of two-hundred-year-old cottages that climbed all the way to the top of the cove.

His research revealed that the town had started life as a busy fishing port, but as the years had gone by larger towns had sprung up, and Porth an Jowl had been unable to compete. Its fishing industry had gradually receded, and the place had morphed into what it was today: a reasonably popular tourist destination that sold surfboards and ice creams in late spring and summer, and became a veritable ghost town for the rest of the year.

Aaron took pictures of the stacked rows of cottages. The town was picturesque, he supposed, which seemed ironic considering the horrors that had taken place here just three months ago.

When he was done, he followed the promenade with his eyes. At the far end, below the right cliff, he saw a small harbour and a handful of boats. He considered walking down there to get more pictures, but now the cold had seeped into his marrow.

Movement pulled his attention to the road.

Three youths, dressed in loose jeans and dark hoodies, were rolling through the car park entrance on skateboards. They moved in tandem, turning in a half circle, then coming to a halt a few feet away from his car. They stared at the vehicle, then across at Aaron, their faces masked by their hoods.

Aaron eyed them suspiciously. If they touched his car, he would break their hands. But only if it came to it; confrontation was not his way of doing things.

The youths were still staring at him, muttering to each other.

Aaron waved a hand.

"How are you doing?" he called out.

The trio stared. One of them whispered something, provoking sniggers from the other two.

Aaron narrowed his eyes. It didn't matter where in the world you found yourself, teenagers were always the same—stubborn, moody, self-involved little shits.

But maybe these little shits could be useful.

Quickly slipping the camera inside his bag, he made his way back to the car. "Kind of cold to be out here skateboarding, isn't it?" he smiled.

The trio, two boys and a girl, he couldn't be sure, stared at him. Aaron smiled again, closed-mouthed this time.

"Hey, do you know Jago Pengelly? Or where I can find his mother, Tess?"

The trio turned to each other. Something was muttered. They turned back. One by one, all three dropped their skateboards to the ground. Aaron watched them roll out of the car park and onto Cove Road. None of them looked back.

"Thanks for your help," he muttered.

A blast of wind roared across the tarmac, making his jaw

clench. High above his head, a flock of gulls appeared, screeching as they soared towards the tide.

Following in the direction of the skateboarders, Aaron exited the car park. Crossing the road, he cut through a narrow alley nestled between the cottages.

Moments later, he emerged in the town square, which was small and paved with cobblestones. At its centre, a circle of seats surrounded a stone plinth, from which a Victorian style street lamp protruded.

Shops lined all sides. The more touristic stores had banners taped across their glass fronts, all conveying the same message: *Closed for Winter.* The rest were closed for Sunday and would resume business tomorrow.

One shop caught his eye. Pressing his face against the glass, he stared through the window of Cove Crafts. Empty shelves peered back at him. Taking out his camera, he took a photograph, then turned and snapped a few more of the empty square.

Porth an Jowl really was a ghost town.

But there was one shop open, he noticed, as he crossed the square and headed away from the direction of the seafront, his shoes slapping against the cobbles.

Aaron nervously licked his lips as he entered Porth an Jowl Wine Shop. He was greeted by a welcome blast of heat. It was a small shop, crammed with shelves of alcohol and snacks.

An old man stood behind the counter, wiry white hair protruding from his scalp. He stared at Aaron and offered a polite nod. Aaron nodded back. For a moment, his eyes pulled away from the man to stare at the shelves of bottles behind him.

"Afternoon," the man said. "Surprised to see your face in here."

Aaron stared at him. Had he met this man before? He was certain he hadn't.

"I know a tourist when I see one," the man smiled. "We don't get too many of your kind this time of year."

"I'm not a tourist," Aaron said, moving to the counter to offer his hand. "I'm Aaron Black."

"Jack Dawkins." The man shook his hand then recoiled. "You're freezing, boy. Need to get yourself a decent pair of gloves."

Aaron's eyes lingered over the rows of whiskey bottles on the shelf behind. "You're probably right."

"Where did you come from, then?" Jack asked, eyeing him.

"London."

"Never much liked the city. Prefer the peace and quiet. On holiday, are you?"

Aaron shook his head. "Work."

Jack regarded him for a second longer. "Oh? I hope it ain't any kind of outdoor work. You ain't dressed right for that. Anyway, what can I get you, Mr Black?"

Aaron pulled his gaze away from the shelves and back to Jack. "Actually, just some information. I'm looking for someone. Tess Pengelly. Do you know her?"

A strange expression fell over Jack's face. His smile faded.

"Tess Pengelly?" he repeated. "I know her. She don't live here anymore, though."

Shit. Aaron's mind raced. "She moved?"

"Last month. After all that terrible business."

"You know where to?"

"A friend of hers, are you?"

Aaron smiled. "Not exactly."

The old man's brow crumpled into a frown. "I can't say

where she's got to. All I know is she took her boys and left. Don't blame her, neither."

Aaron felt a jab of frustration. This was going to make things difficult. But not impossible. Someone would know where she could be found. He turned back to Jack.

"How about Carrie Killigrew?"

Jack folded his arms across his chest, his initial friendliness now gone. "What are you? A journalist or something? Because you're about three months too late for that story. We've had enough of reporters writing rubbish about Porth an Jowl. So, if you don't mind, if you're not buying anything, I've got things to do."

Aaron flashed the old man a disarming smile. He was a tricky one, this Jack Dawkins. He liked him. But he still needed to tread carefully. It was far too early to be making enemies of the locals.

"I'm not a journalist," he told him. "I'm an author. A mystery writer. Maybe you've heard of me."

"A mystery writer, eh?" Jack raised his eyebrows. "Aaron Black . . . Nope, can't say I have."

"What about the Silky Winters Mysteries?"

"I like to read the newspaper. Leave all that hokum to the wife."

Ignoring the sting of his ego, Aaron laughed. "So, you're a facts man? In that case, you just might be interested in my latest project. It's why I'd like to speak to Carrie Killigrew and Tess Pengelly." He paused, waiting for Jack Dawkins to look up. "I'm researching a book, you see. Not a mystery this time, but a true crime account of Grady Spencer's horrific legacy. Did you know him?"

Across the counter, the old man raised his eyebrows. Then

narrowed his eyes. "Everyone knew Grady Spencer," he said. "And I don't know what you're doing writing a book about the awful things he done, but I'll tell you this for free, Mr Black— no one in this town is going to help you with that. All we want is to be left alone. For the world to forget all the terrible things that happened here."

"Surely you know that's not going to happen. Not for a long time. Maybe not ever."

Aaron turned for a second, distracted by light bouncing off bottles of amber liquid. A wanton thirst was growing inside him. Pushing it away, he turned back to the old man.

"Look, I'm not here to cause trouble, Mr Dawkins. My intention is to write an accurate account of what happened. No embellishment. Just the facts. People need to know the truth, to understand exactly what went on here."

"People need to mind their own damn business," Jack Dawkins said. "Now, you buying anything or what?"

Sighing, Aaron shook his head. "Can you at least point me in the direction of Grady Spencer's house?"

Jack leaned across the counter, his eyes cold and steely.

"That's easy. It's the last row on the left, on your way out of Porth an Jowl." He leaned back again, folding his arms across his chest. "Do yourself a favour, Mr Black. Go back to London. That can of worms has already been opened. You go stirring things up again, no good will come of it. I promise you that."

Aaron held his gaze for a moment longer. He felt a smile tugging at his lips and quickly pushed it away.

"I'll bear that in mind," he said. "Thank you for your time, Mr Dawkins."

The cold attacked him the moment he stepped outside. Pulling his coat around his body, he hurried back to the car and started the engine. He could no longer feel his hands, so he rubbed them together as he waited for the heaters to kick in.

His first encounter with the locals had gone as expected. But now he knew where to find Grady Spencer's house of horrors. Turning the car onto Cove Road, Aaron shivered as he wondered what was waiting for him inside.

2

AARON TURNED LEFT onto Grenville Row and parked the car. He stared out the driver window at the line of quaint homes and neatly kept gardens. Grady Spencer's house stood on the corner like a tumour.

Unlike the other dwellings, it was faded and cracked, as if time had accelerated, leaving it to crumble into ruin. Windows were boarded up. Graffiti covered the walls: CHILD KILLER. DEATH HOUSE. GHOSTS INSIDE. Aaron's throat went dry. His heart raced.

He could feel negative energy pulsing from the walls of Grady Spencer's house in nauseous waves. Horrors had occurred inside, many of which had only recently come to light.

Climbing out of the car, Aaron looked both ways along the empty street. He turned ninety degrees and glanced over the rooftops of the houses below. From here, the beach was a smudge of grey-brown; the ocean, a charcoal froth.

He turned back to the Spencer house, then shifted his gaze two houses along to the left, where a FOR SALE sign was staked in the front garden. Reaching for his camera, Aaron took a picture. News reports had said the Pengellys lived just two doors away from where four-year-old Noah Pengelly, had been held prisoner for months.

No wonder they moved, Aaron thought.

Wherever they had fled to, there were resources he could use to track them down—phone directories, electoral registers, social media—but finding them wasn't the issue; it was getting them to agree to be interviewed.

Still, finding the Pengellys could wait for another day.

Letting out a nervous breath, Aaron crossed the road, heading for the Spencer house.

The rusty hinges of the gate moaned as he entered the garden. He walked along the path, noting dead and dying plants and the weed-choked lawn.

Someone had spray-painted the words KIDDY FIDDLER in red across the front door.

Aaron raised the camera and snapped away.

The door had no handle, only a key latch. He pushed against it and was unsurprised to find it locked.

What he really wanted was to get inside. A true crime book was nothing without pictures. Sure, readers lapped up every grisly detail, but photographs of where the terrible things happened took their imaginations to a whole new, depraved level.

Following the garden path, Aaron turned the corner of the house and made his way towards the backyard. As he walked, he glanced over the fence at the property next door, observing the neat lawn and floral print curtains in the windows.

Grady Spencer's backyard was empty.

Images he'd seen on TV had shown a dangerous maze of junk; old refrigerators, car batteries, broken cabinets and chest freezers. According to news reports, Grady Spencer had been a hoarder his entire life. The rooms of his house had been piled to the ceiling with boxes, newspapers, and other artefacts he'd collected over the years.

Most of the human remains uncovered by police had been found in the basement, but some parts had been sealed in airtight bags or stored in containers and tucked away among the rest of Spencer's hoarded possessions.

Aaron couldn't hide his disappointment as he stared at the dark stains of the now empty yard. No doubt it had all been taken away to be examined for evidence.

Did that mean the house had been emptied, too?

He stared at more boarded-up windows then rattled the locked back door. Frustrated, Aaron scuffed the ground with his foot. It was then he noticed the grille in the ground.

Dropping to his knees, he twisted his neck and strained to see through the bars. There was a window down there. One that hadn't been boarded up. Perhaps it was a way in—if he could get past the grille.

Wrapping his fingers around the bars, he pulled. Freezing metal bit into his fingers. The grille held fast. Frustration turned to irritation. There had to be a way of getting inside.

As far as was known, Grady Spencer had no living relatives, which meant his house would have been deemed *bona vacantia* —ownerless property—and would duly become property of the Crown. Aaron thought it unlikely that the current Duke of Cornwall would lend him the keys for the afternoon.

His other option was to ask the local police force for help, but their jurisdiction over the property would have ended with their investigation. The police could still prove helpful in other ways. Due to his death, Grady Spencer's heinous crimes had not been brought to trial, which meant crime scene photographs had not entered the public domain. Perhaps, if he spoke to the right person, he could gain access to those photographs, perhaps even receive permission to feature them in his book.

But crime scene photographs weren't going to get him inside this damn house.

Irritable and frozen, and aware he was fast losing light, Aaron snapped a few images of the house and yard, then returned to the front garden. He felt his mood sinking. With the Pengellys gone and Grady Spencer's house locked up, he wasn't getting very far.

Screw it, he thought. He'd head back to the hotel, take a hot shower, then write up his observations. Maybe he'd go down to the hotel restaurant for dinner.

His mind made up, he headed for the gate. He was halfway down the garden path when he stopped in his tracks.

Someone was watching him.

He turned to see a teenage girl with cropped dark hair standing in the adjacent garden and sucking on a cigarette. She wore an oversized parka jacket, black skinny jeans, and military boots that looked like they could crush skulls with minimal effort. She stared at Aaron as she smoked. It was not a friendly stare.

Aaron raised a hand and set his teeth chattering by smiling.

"Hi, how are you doing?"

The girl continued to stare as she blew out streams of smoke and frosted breath.

"Got a spare one of those?"

The girl sucked on the cigarette, blew out more smoke. "Not for you."

Her eyes wandered up to Grady Spencer's house and, for a

moment, grew very dark. Aaron watched as she took one last drag on the cigarette, dropped it on the garden path, and crushed it beneath one of her large boots.

She turned to go inside.

"Wait a second," Aaron called. He stepped off the path and moved up to the fence separating the properties. "Did you know Grady Spencer?"

"I don't talk to the press," she growled.

Jesus, this girl had serious anger issues. He glanced down at her boots again, imagined them pulverising his head like a pumpkin.

"I'm not the press," he said.

The girl stopped still, staring at him. "Then what are you? Another thrill seeker hoping to get off over a few dead bodies?"

"Actually, I'm an author."

"Really." There was no admiration in her tone, only deep-rooted cynicism.

"Really, yes. My name is Aaron Black. I'm researching a true crime account about your deceased neighbour, Grady Spencer. The Pied Piper of Cornwall."

The girl raised an eyebrow and snorted. "The Pied Piper of Cornwall? That's what you're calling him?"

Aaron shrugged. "It's work in progress. The press didn't come up with a name for him. Every serial killer needs a name."

"Sure, if you want to turn a child killer into a celebrity."

"It's not about celebrating what they've done. Giving a mass murderer a moniker allows us to distance ourselves from the terrible acts they commit. It gives them mystique, turns them into legends. Monsters from horror stories. And a monster from a story, even if it's a really scary one, is much less terrifying than a real-life monster, don't you think?"

The girl shrugged but made no move to leave. "Maybe. But still, it's different when you live next door to one."

She was silent for a moment, contemplating. From her jacket pocket she pulled out a pouch of tobacco and a sheath of cigarette papers.

"What books have you written?" she asked him as she worked.

Aaron shivered in the cold. He could no longer feel his hands, but he was intrigued by this girl. And now that she had relaxed a little, he wondered if she might be of use.

"Mysteries, mostly. I write the Silky Winters series."

The girl smirked. "Silky Winters?"

"You've heard of them?"

She shook her head. The cigarette rolled and sealed, the girl tucked it behind her ear and began rolling another. She nodded at Grady Spencer's house. "Were you trying to get inside?"

Aaron nodded. "Just to look around. But it's all boarded up. I thought you kids would have found a way to sneak in already."

The girl's eyes narrowed. "Watch who you're calling a kid. I'll be eighteen in three months. Then I'm out of this hell hole."

"Forgive me. Where are you escaping to? University?"

"Nope. London."

She finished rolling the second cigarette. Glancing at Aaron, she let out a little sigh, and held the cigarette over the fence.

Aaron took it. "Thanks."

"So why do you want to write a book about Grady Spencer?" She lit her cigarette, then held out the lighter.

Aaron lit his cigarette and inhaled. He held back a cough. He hadn't smoked a cigarette in three years. The acrid taste reminded him why. Then the instant high made him forget.

"I have a fascination with true crime; it informs my writing.

Besides, it's not every day we have a serial killer in Britain. Someone will write about it eventually, so I thought, why not me?"

"So, it's about money?" The girl's eyes were cold steel.

Aaron smiled. "Everything's about money, isn't it?"

"Not everything."

"Well, when you're older, you'll see that—" One look from the girl and Aaron cut himself off. "What I mean to say is, yes, it's about money. But also, it's about giving an honest and accurate account of the events. Grady Spencer murdered eight children. At least, eight that we know of. And he did it right in that house, in this tiny little town, without anyone noticing. Until Cal Anderson washed up on the beach." He paused, staring at the graffiti-covered house next door. "Eight innocent victims. Don't you think they deserve to have their stories told?"

"You don't think Cal was a victim?" The girl was staring at him with an intensity that made him feel uncomfortable. "How about Noah?"

"Noah Pengelly's a survivor. If it wasn't for his brother, he would have been Grady Spencer's ninth victim. Or perhaps Cal Anderson's first."

Aaron paused, noting the girl's pained look at the mention of Jago Pengelly. Was there something there? Had they been friends? Living next door to each other, it was possible. She was staring at him again. Aaron wondered if he should ask her about the Pengellys. She would help him, or she wouldn't. Either way, it was too damn cold to be standing around for a minute more.

But then the girl surprised him. She nodded at the Spencer house. "I can get you inside."

Aaron followed her gaze. "Really? But I looked; there was no way in."

"Maybe you were looking in the wrong places."

He stared at her. Was she playing him? "Well, that would be great. Lead the way."

"Fine, I can do that. But it depends on one thing."

Here we go. "And what's that?"

The girl took one last drag on her cigarette then crushed it beneath her boot. "How much you're willing to pay."

She was sneaky. Sly. Aaron immediately liked her.

"What's your name?"

"Nat Tremaine."

"Well, Nat Tremaine, I'll give you ten," he said.

"Don't insult me."

"Twenty, then."

Smiling now, Nat shook her head. "Fifty."

Aaron's mind was filling with nicotine-spun cotton. He stared down at the cigarette, feeling dizzy. "Fifty? I bet if I look a little harder I'll find a way in for free."

"Okay, good luck with that." Nat shrugged and turned to go inside. She turned back. Desperation flashed in her eyes. It was only for a second, but Aaron saw it clearly. "Look, I can get you inside for fifty. But for a hundred, I can give you something even better."

"Really." Aaron smiled, curious now. "And what's that?"

"A first-hand account of my escape from the evil clutches of Grady Spencer."

"Is that so?" Aaron said, raising an eyebrow. There'd been no such story in the newspapers or on the TV, and he'd been thorough with his research.

Nat nodded. "And I happen to be Jago Pengelly's best friend."

That got his attention. A hundred was a lot, but if she was

telling the truth, he'd happily pay. Besides, once his book became a bestseller, a hundred would be a drop in the ocean.

"Deal," Aaron said, reaching across the fence.

Nat stared at his hand for a second, then shook it. "Deal."

"Great." A gust of wind whipped around them, numbing what feeling Aaron had left in his extremities. "So get me inside Grady Spencer's house before this cold fucking kills me."

3

THE DOOR JAMB SPLINTERED. The door flew inward. Nat straightened, a crowbar swinging in her hand and a smile spreading across her lips as she stepped to one side.

Aaron's mouth hung open.

"I thought you knew a way in," he said, staring into the gloom as nerves fluttered in his stomach.

Nat shrugged a shoulder. "You're in, aren't you?"

"Jesus, what do I get for two hundred? Plastic explosives?"

Glancing nervously over his shoulder, Aaron stepped inside Grady Spencer's house. He was in the kitchen. Appliances remained, all from a bygone age and possibly hazardous. The rest of the room was empty, covered in unspoiled layers of dust.

Hooking his camera strap around his neck, Aaron changed the flash setting then signalled to Nat.

"I believe my hundred covers entry *and* information, so get yourself in here."

He turned back to the gloom and began snapping pictures, lighting up the kitchen in bright bursts.

Nat, who had taken a few steps inside, shielded her eyes.

"You want to close the door?" Aaron said as the camera whirred and flashed.

"Why?"

"I don't fancy getting arrested for breaking and entering."

"No one's around to see," Nat said, closing the door and shutting out the failing daylight. "Besides, I hear the next-door neighbour is easily bribed."

"You're hilarious. You ever considered a career in comedy?"

The camera hanging from his neck, Aaron took out his phone and switched to torch mode. Pale blue light pushed back the shadows. There was another door at the far end. It was open, but darkness masked what lay beyond.

"I need more light," he said.

"Scared the ghosts will get you?"

Smirking, Nat pulled her phone from her pocket and activated the torch. More cold light spilled over the room.

Sucking in a nervous breath, Aaron stepped through the door.

The hall was damp and musty smelling, the air filled with dust that coated the inside of his nose and the back of his throat.

Coughing, he swung his phone from right to left.

Up ahead, two open doors stood on opposite sides. He checked the first, then the second.

His heart sank.

Both rooms were empty. It was as Aaron had expected— everything had been seized by forensics.

"Might as well take pictures, anyway." Pocketing his phone, he lifted the camera. "Hey, Nat, where are you? I need light."

He turned back to find her still standing in the hall, just outside the kitchen. She was staring at a closed door Aaron had missed before. Even in the poor light, he could see fear in her eyes.

"Everything okay?"

Nat's expression quickly hardened. She nodded.

"Well, let's see if the police left anything for us upstairs."

The steps felt rotten beneath Aaron's feet. The stink of mould burned his nostrils.

The first door revealed a bathroom that was cramped and dingy with nothing to show. Aaron snapped a couple of pictures and moved onto the next room.

The master bedroom had also been cleared. All that remained was an empty bed frame. In the far corner, a dark stain spread along the floor and across the wall.

Aaron took more pictures while Nat remained on the threshold. "Tell me what happened between you and Spencer. Did you know him well?"

"I only knew him as my creepy next-door neighbour," Nat said, digging her hands into jacket pockets. "He was old. Grumpy. Walked with a stick."

"Old age or an injury?"

"No idea. To be honest, I'd never given the psycho much thought until Honey went missing."

"Honey?"

"Rose's cat. Rose is my—she's a foster carer."

Aaron stared at her. *Interesting.*

Nat turned away. "There'd been other animals going missing. Margaret Telford found her dog hacked into pieces and left in a sack in her backyard."

"She was the one who found Cal on the beach? The papers say he did that to her dog. You think that's true?"

"Don't know. Maybe." She paused for a second, fear making

her eyes glisten in the dim light. "Anyway, Rose was scared something had happened to Honey, so I went looking for her. I knocked on Grady Spencer's door, asked if he'd seen her. He got me to come inside. Tried to get me to go down to the basement to look for her. He stood so close I could feel his breath on my neck. I knew something was wrong, then. That I should get out. Now I know why."

She visibly shuddered.

"What about the cat?"

"What do you mean?"

"Did you find her?"

Nat glared at him in the shadows. "Yeah, she showed up a few days later."

"That's good. I like cats." Aaron took another picture. "Grady Spencer had a dog, didn't he?"

"Yeah. Caliban. That sick fuck fed it parts of that journalist he murdered. I wonder what happened. To the dog, I mean."

It was a good point. Aaron couldn't imagine anyone wanting to adopt the animal, considering it had tasted human flesh. More than tasted, he thought, with a shudder.

"Let's keep moving."

A quick search of the rest of the floor revealed two more empty rooms and a growing stench of mould that made the air hard to breathe.

"What about Jago?" Aaron asked as they returned downstairs.

"What about him?"

He detected a frostiness there. Not aimed at him, it seemed. "You said you guys are best friends?"

Nat shrugged. "I haven't heard from him in a while. Not since he moved away with his family."

"You have a fight or something?"

He felt her eyes burning into him. "He's probably busy taking care of Noah, that's all."

"That makes sense. It's not every day your little brother winds up inside a cage in a serial killer's lair."

Aaron made his way back towards the kitchen then came to a standstill.

"You know where they moved to?"

Nat came up behind him, her eyes fixed on the closed door Aaron had stopped outside. "Yes. But don't ask me for their address because I'm not giving it to you."

"Let me guess. Not until I pay you another hundred?"

"It's not about money. They don't need any more trouble."

"It's not my intention to cause trouble." Aaron tried the door. It swung open. Impenetrable blackness greeted him. "But if I were to ask politely?"

He could hear Nat's breaths in his left ear, quick and thin.

"I said no."

Aaron shrugged. He would work on her. Holding up his phone, he counted the steps that led down into darkness. He could just make out another door at the bottom. A chill crept up from there to sink claws into his flesh.

It was down in the basement that Grady Spencer had done much of his killing. The police had found all manner of terrible torture instruments, along with an old workbench that had been adapted into a crude surgeon's table, complete with restraints for hands and feet.

The basement was also where he'd kept Cal Anderson captive for seven years, and where young Noah Pengelly had been found locked in a cage. Who knew what kind of horrors the young child had witnessed or had been subjected to. Or how long the psychological damage would last.

Aaron shivered.

Behind him, Nat scraped her boot against the floor. "Well, are you going down there or what?"

A voice in his mind told him to turn and run. To go back to his car and give up this ridiculous notion of writing a true crime account.

Staring into the darkness, he slowly nodded.

"Sure. But you're coming with me."

"Whatever."

They took the stairs, one behind the other, gripping the rails.

There was more light in the basement than in the entire house. The window Aaron had spied through the metal grille in the backyard was like a beacon. The light made him feel safer. Less afraid. Grady Spencer was dead, killed in this very basement, but there was something invisible left behind; a residual energy from all the pain and death and torture that the old man had inflicted upon his victims.

The basement was L-shaped, and like the rest of the house, its contents had been seized, including Grady's torture table. The cages, too. Aaron swung his phone to the left, directing the light towards the far end of the room.

"The tunnel," he breathed.

The door frame was still visible, but the entrance had been bricked up.

"They sealed it to stop kids wandering up from the beach." Nat stayed close to the stairs, clearly afraid despite her steely expression. "Did you see the hotel? They're planning to tear it down and use the rubble to fill in the tunnel."

Raising his camera, Aaron snapped pictures of the bricked-up door. The flash lit up the basement.

"Jesus!"

Startled, Aaron turned.

"There," Nat said, pointing in front of him.

Aiming the phone light at the ground, Aaron peered down at a large black stain. Crouching, he ran fingers along it then held them up to the light.

Believing his brother was dead, Jago had opened up Grady Spencer's throat with a scalpel and left him to bleed out. So ended a legacy of abduction, torture, and murder.

"I'm glad he killed him, even if Noah was still alive." Nat's voice was barely a whisper. She moved up beside Aaron and stared down at the long-dried bloodstain. "That bastard had it coming."

Straightening, Aaron took pictures of the bloodstain, then explored the other side of the room.

"What about Cal?" he asked as he checked the empty shelves.

"Didn't meet him. Then he ran off, so . . ."

"Jago must have told you about him."

"A little. Did you know he attacked Jago? Bit him right in the neck. Almost ripped his throat out."

Aaron glanced at her silhouette. "No, I didn't."

Following the shelves to the far end of the room, he came to a halt. There were marks on the ground—old rust stains from cages.

He shuddered. As exhilarating as it was to be inside Grady Spencer's house, he was only too aware of the depraved acts that had taken place here. The rusty marks of the cages were a stoic reminder. He photographed them. Then, the camera swinging from his neck, he lifted his phone and directed the light at the wall.

Aaron crouched down, drawing closer.

Nat followed him. She squinted. "What is that?"

Aaron ran a finger along the wall. There were crude drawings scratched into the surface. Childlike images of people, buildings, and animals, all lined up in vertical rows like ancient Egyptian hieroglyphs.

Etchings made between bars, Aaron realised.

One caught his attention. Next to a rectangle house with a triangle roof and broken windows was a Christ-like figure crucified on a large cross, its outstretched arms ending in two claw-like hands.

Aaron took pictures. These would be great for the book; powerful images showing the innocent side of a tortured, corrupted mind. There was no evidence that Cal was guilty of murder. There had been the animal killings, although his guilt was only based on conjecture.

But three questions remained unanswered.

One: why had Grady Spencer kept the boy alive for seven years, instead of killing him as he had done with all his other victims? Two: why had Cal fled after witnessing the death of his abductor? Three: where was he now?

The police had spent three fruitless months searching for him. At first, speculation had been rife. Some believed he was hiding out in the countryside, living off the land like an animal. Others believed he'd taken his own life, thrown himself off a cliff and his body washed out to sea.

Now, in mid-December, public attention had already begun

to wane. Cal's name was fading from their minds. Even the police had dialled back their search, citing further budget cuts and a lack of resources.

Aaron ran fingers along the etchings on the wall.

He imagined Cal would not be forgotten by the people of Porth an Jowl. Not for generations to come.

"You seen enough?"

Nat's voice startled him. She shifted her weight from foot to foot as she glanced over her shoulder.

Aaron eyed the drawings one last time. This was a terrible place, and he and Nat were breathing in every drop of blood that had been spilled between its walls.

Neither of them spoke again until they were out of the house and standing in the backyard.

"What are you doing about that?" Aaron pulled the broken back door behind them, only for it to swing open again.

Nat shrugged. "Not my problem."

"Thought as much."

He stared into the darkness seeping out through the door. For a second, he was back in the basement, surrounded by tortured ghosts.

The daylight was almost gone. Rain clouds were growing thick and heavy above their heads. While they'd been inside, the temperature had dropped a couple of degrees and was continuing in a downward spiral.

Aaron glanced at Nat. She stared back expectantly. Of course. She wanted her money.

Fumbling with his bag, he took out his wallet. Turning his back on Nat, he stared at the fat wad of cash inside. His fingers hovered for a moment. Nat was difficult and borderline aggressive, but he could already see she had her uses. Including her connection to the Pengellys. If he gave her what he owed her now, he might lose that connection altogether.

"Here," he said, handing her a few notes then snapping his wallet shut.

Nat flashed him an unimpressed look. "That's only fifty. We agreed a hundred."

"It's all the cash I have on me." Aaron held up his hands, half expecting her to swing a fist at him. "I'll get the rest to you."

Nat muttered something under her breath, folded the notes, and slipped them inside a pocket. As they walked back to the road, Aaron watched her drag her boots sulkily against the ground. It had to be dull as hell growing up in a town like Porth an Jowl, especially if you didn't fit in, and he had a feeling Nat fitted in like a square peg in a round hole.

"Thanks again for your help," he said, stopping outside Nat's house. "Perhaps we could keep our little excursion between the two of us for now?"

Nat shrugged but made no move to go inside.

"If you give me your number, I'll call you the next time I'm back in town."

Aaron held out his phone. Nat glared at it, then at him.

"Don't you want the rest of your money?" he said. "I'm sure every penny counts if you're planning to leave."

He waved the phone in his hand, feeling like he was coaxing a wild animal with a tasty treat.

Her eyes fixed on him, Nat reached out and took it.

"Wonderful." Smiling, Aaron watched her tap in her number before handing the phone back. "I'll be in touch."

Once he'd crossed the road and made it to his car, he turned and watched Nat disappear inside.

"Never play a player," he said, then shivered. This cold was going to be the death of him.

4

The Lemon Quay hotel was located in Truro, a large town masquerading as Cornwall's only city. It was a nondescript building with four floors of guest rooms that, if they were anything like Aaron's own, were in dire need of refurbishment. But the place was cheap, the staff friendly, and, importantly, it was warm. Stopping at the front desk, he greeted the young male receptionist.

As he waited for the man to check for any messages, he looked around the small foyer. No one else was here. A quick glance at the key board behind the desk suggested he was the hotel's only guest.

"There's nothing for you, Mr Black," the receptionist said.

Aaron nodded, arranged for a hot meal to be delivered to his room, and headed for the lift. Halfway across the foyer, he paused and trained his eyes on the smoked glass doors of the hotel bar. He hovered for a moment before continuing on.

His room was on the third floor. It was a cramped affair, but it had a bed, a bathroom, and a small writing desk—all that he needed. There was also a mini-bar, which, as requested, had been emptied of alcohol and restocked with soft drinks.

Making a mug of instant coffee, Aaron drank it and then undressed. After taking a hot shower, he slipped into a pair of jeans and an old blue hoodie.

Room service arrived. Aaron ate a bland-tasting dinner of fish and potatoes at his desk, then set about connecting his camera to his laptop. As he waited for the images he'd taken to upload, he crossed the room and peered through the window at the dark city street below. The wind had died but the rain now fell in heavy sheets. No vehicles passed. No pedestrians hurried by. A sudden loneliness surged through him.

He picked up his mobile phone from the bedside table and saw he'd missed another call from Taylor. There was a voicemail too, but he hit the delete key without listening to it.

Guilt grew heavy in his chest. Suddenly, he wanted nothing more than to return Taylor's call and beg for forgiveness.

He turned away, resisting the urge. To call Taylor would mean a fight. And not only a fight. Taylor was likely angry enough to involve the law.

The photographs had finished uploading. Aaron returned to his position on the bed. Despite the police having emptied Grady Spencer's house, he was surprised to find the images had managed to capture the insidious atmosphere that still lingered there.

It was not the first murder house he'd entered in the name of research, but it was the first belonging to a serial killer of children. He'd created his own fictional psychopaths over the years, all of whom had eventually been brought to justice, but it was a far cry from standing in a darkened basement where very real, unspeakable acts had occurred. The experience had left him marked somehow, like Billy Bones being given the Black Spot in Treasure Island.

Ignoring his unease, Aaron spent the next thirty minutes examining the photographs and writing up notes. He'd already made a rough outline of how he wanted the book to flow, but until he'd interviewed key witnesses and learned more about Grady Spencer's past, he had little to go on.

His thoughts turned to Nat Tremaine. She was an interesting character. He'd been surprised to find out she was in foster care, but he supposed it explained her defensive behaviour.

Despite her not-so-latent anger issues, Aaron had instantly liked her. She'd proven useful, too; not just by getting him inside Grady Spencer's house, but because she clearly knew a lot more about September's events than she'd mentioned. And while she hadn't exactly been forthcoming with her secrets, Aaron was confident that once he'd gained Nat's trust, she'd eventually give him the Pengellys' location.

It was getting late. Shutting down the laptop, Aaron gloomily readied himself for bed.

Today had been a good first day, he supposed. But he needed to steel himself. Because tomorrow he was determined to interview Cal Anderson's mother.

5

Monday morning was cold and bitter, the wind whipping up from the sea to stalk the streets of Porth an Jowl. Aaron stood on Clarence Row, his coat doing little to keep him warm. Yet another sleepless night had left him tired and irritable, and the three cups of coffee he'd downed for breakfast had done nothing to clear his foggy mind.

It had taken him just two minutes to find Carrie Killigrew's address in the local telephone directory. Now, he stood outside her garden gate, wishing he'd remembered to shave before leaving the hotel, and wondering if showing up unannounced was the right approach. He'd considered telephoning ahead, but it would have given Carrie an opportunity to say no before he'd had a chance to work his charm in person.

"Here we go," he muttered to himself as he pushed open the gate. He could tell the garden had once been lovingly tended, but winter had killed most of the plants and those that remained had been left to grow wild—a sign that all was not well in the Killigrew household.

The front door was just ahead. Aaron slid to a halt, doubt

flooding his mind. Carrie had been hounded by the press not once, but twice in her life. And although Aaron was not the press, would she see him as any different?

He would have to convince her that he was.

Carrie's interview was crucial to the book. Sure, he could write it without her and enjoy moderate success, but to have an exclusive interview with Cal Anderson's mother, to have her personal thoughts and words about what had happened to her son—it would be the magic sauce that shot his book into the stratosphere and finally make *Aaron Black* a household name.

He pressed the doorbell, stepped back, and held his breath. Moments later, he heard a chain unlatch. The door opened a crack. Aaron flashed his most charming smile.

"Yes?"

The woman in the doorway was not Carrie Killigrew. She was older, perhaps in her early sixties, but she did have more than a passing resemblance to Carrie. Her mother?

"Good morning, my name is Aaron Black. I was wondering if I could speak with Carrie," he said, keeping his smile friendly.

The woman stared at him, her eyes narrowing.

"Aaron Black?" she said. "Are you a friend?"

Aaron shook his head. "Actually, no. We don't know each other. But I would like to speak to her about—that is, I was wondering if . . ."

The woman's expression hardened.

"No journalists." She moved to shut the door.

Aaron held up a hand. "I'm not a journalist. I'm an author. I'm writing a book and I'd like to interview Carrie about—"

"No authors, either!"

The door slammed shut in his face. Aaron stumbled back. Further along the street, a dog started barking. Pulling his phone from his pocket, he checked the time. It wasn't even ten in the morning and already he'd wrecked his chances of his book hitting the number one spot.

"Well done, asshole," he muttered.

Angry with himself, he returned to the street. Movement from an upstairs window caught his eye, and he turned in time to see a curtain fall closed.

She was up there, watching him.

He stood for a long time, waiting for the curtain to open again. When it didn't, he stalked back to his car.

There had to be another way of reaching Carrie Killigrew. All he had to do was find it.

6

CARRIE HOVERED in the darkness of the bedroom. She had watched the man come and go, observed him pause in the street looking defeated before driving away in his car. She wondered who he could be. Another journalist? But they'd stopped coming around a month ago.

Her curiosity passed. All she wanted was to be left alone.

She thought about returning to bed. Somewhere inside her conscience, a voice told her to shower, put on some clean clothes, return to the world. But she couldn't.

A voice called to her from somewhere below.

"Carrie, love? I'm making tea. Are you coming down?"

Carrie heaved her shoulders. She didn't want tea. She wanted alcohol. It was the only medicine that could numb her pain and erase her memories.

Now, she heard feet on the stairs.

"Carrie? Are you awake?"

Carrie glanced at the alarm clock on the bedside table. It was almost ten a.m. She'd slept through most of yesterday and it was her intention to do the same today. Before her mother had hands up in defeat. Leaving the bedroom door open and the light flooding in, she returned downstairs.

Carrie heaved her shoulders. Ever since her mother had arrived, she'd been trying to make things better between them. But you couldn't fix five years of absence in two weeks, no matter how much tea you made.

Rubbing her eyes, Carrie leaned forward. Guilt pressed down on her. "Fine," she grumbled. "Anything to shut you up."

Besides, all the alcohol was in the living room cabinet and the bottle stashed beneath her bed was empty.

She found her mother buzzing around the kitchen, pouring tea into a teapot and setting cups on the table.

She'd cleaned again. The dish rack was empty. The surfaces sparkled.

"There you are!" Sally beamed. "Now sit yourself down and let me finish making the tea."

Carrie slipped into a chair. She was tired and sluggish. Her bones ached. The voice in her head warned her again about the dangers of mixing alcohol and sleeping pills. She should probably stop taking the pills, she thought. The problem wasn't that she couldn't sleep. The problem was that her dreams were filled with *him*.

Cal. Her son.

The pills made him disappear, leaving Carrie's sleep dark and empty, as if she ceased to exist. Just the way she wanted it.

Sally poured tea into cups. She laid out slices of fruit loaf on a plate, which she offered to Carrie, who shook her head but accepted a mug of tea.

"You have to eat something." Sally's face wrinkled with concern. "You've lost too much weight already."

"How would you know?"

arrived two weeks ago, she'd hardly bothered with getting
bed at all.

A soft rapping on the door.

Carrie grumbled and gave a cursory glance at her cru
bedsheets.

The door opened, letting in light from the landing.

Sally Nance stood on the threshold, peering into the
ows. Carrie and her mother shared many physical traits.
wild hair. Dark, intense eyes. Both small in stature but st
Except Carrie didn't feel strong. Not anymore.

"There you are," her mother said. "Didn't you hea
calling?"

Carrie nodded.

"Then why didn't you answer? And are you going to
the dark like this again all day? It's not good for you, love. `
disappear into nothing. At worst, you'll get Rickets."

Carrie rolled her eyes. It was like being a teenager a
her overbearing mother scolding her over her latest m
meanour. But Carrie was thirty-six and in no mood
lecture.

Her mother hovered in the doorway, wanting to come in
seemingly afraid of what her daughter was becoming in
darkness.

"Come on, darling. Come down. I'll make something to
We can talk, if you like. Maybe watch some television."

Carrie's focus moved from her mother to the window.

"Who was at the door?" she asked, her voice dull and life

"No one important." Her mother was still hovering,
wringing her hands. "Well come on then, get yourself on
feet."

Sally stood for a few moments longer before throwing

Sally flinched then looked away. "I meant since I've been back."

Carrie stared at the loaf. Her stomach tightened. It would not let her eat, even if she was starving.

Mother and daughter sat at the table in silence as Sally made quick work of spooning sugar into her mug. Carrie watched her, half resenting her still being here, half relieved that she still was.

"I'm defrosting a chicken for dinner," Sally said, when the silence had become too much. "Thought I'd make a casserole."

Her gaze moved down to the uneaten fruit loaf, then back up to Carrie.

Carrie nodded. She'd force a little of her mother's casserole down later, if only to stop her from calling the nearest mental hospital and having her committed.

More quiet.

"Tomorrow, I thought we could go to the supermarket. We're running low on everything." Sally cleared her throat. "And then on Wednesday, Joy's invited us over. Do you remember?"

Carrie stiffened.

"Melissa will be excited to see you."

The name was a blade sinking into Carrie's heart. She winced but stopped short of clutching her chest.

"I don't think so," she said, once she was able to breathe again.

Sally's brow wrinkled. "Oh, Carrie, don't say that! Of course Melissa will be excited to see you. You're her mother. She misses you very much."

"I meant I don't think I'll be going over."

"But she'll be expecting you. Joy and Gary, too. And Dylan . . ."

Carrie stayed quiet. Just the mention of her daughter's name made the void she was tumbling through feel even more vast.

She shook her head. "I can't see her. Not right now."

Across the table, Sally gripped her mug. "Your daughter needs to see you. She's four years old. She doesn't understand what's going on, or why you sent her away. It's not fair."

"What's not fair would be to keep her here. For her to see me like this."

"If you don't go, you'll only disappoint her. It'll make things more difficult for when you're ready to be a family again."

Carrie lifted her mug to her face and pressed the porcelain against her cheek. She welcomed the burning sensation. Images of her daughter's young face filled her mind.

It had been over two weeks since they'd been in the same room. She knew it was wrong, that refusing to see Melissa was hurting her and making everything more confusing. And it was doing nothing to heal Carrie's relationship with Dylan.

But what could she do? She couldn't be a mother to Melissa right now. She'd already failed one child. It wasn't her intention to fail the other.

She just needed more time.

Carrie sipped some of the tea, which was bitter and unpleasant. She stared at her own mother, who had failed her. Who was now trying to make amends.

"You go," she said. "I don't need to be there."

Anger flashed in Sally's eyes. Carrie could tell she was struggling to keep it out of her voice. "Melissa's still getting to know me. She's shy, scared to be with me without you there. Besides, I'm not sure Joy and Gary are particularly fond of me. Please Carrie, if you can't do it for me, do it for your daughter. She needs you."

"I—I can't." Carrie stood, almost tipping the chair.

She felt the darkness reaching for her again. Calling her name. And then Cal entered her mind. She tried to push him out. To cast him away. But his face remained, his eyes burning into her brain. Searing her unconscious. He would never leave her thoughts. And she could never let him.

That was why she couldn't see Melissa—despite everything Cal had done, despite all the atrocious things he'd been accused of, she still loved him. She could still forgive him.

She was still his mother.

"Tell Melissa I'm sorry," she said, backing away from the table. "Tell her I'll see her soon. I promise."

She glanced at her mother one last time before ducking into the hall. She slowed as she passed the living room door. Memories assaulted her. She was back in Grady Spencer's basement, tied down to his torture table with Cal staring blankly at her, scalpel raised. Instantly, the scar on her right shoulder began to throb.

Alcohol. She needed it now.

Bursting into the darkness of the living room, she headed straight for the cabinet. Grabbing the closest bottle, she unscrewed the cap, filled a glass, then swallowed its contents in three desperate gulps. She filled it again and drank.

The basement faded from her mind, taking the pain and blood with it. Carrie sank to the carpet, her back resting against the cabinet. Tears came. She refilled her glass and drank some more.

The tears went away.

7

THE RAIN PERSISTED throughout the day, adding to Aaron's sinking mood. He spent the rest of the morning sat in a dingy tea room by the harbour, battling an ailing phone signal and hostile stares from the locals as he worked through a list of potential interviewees.

With Carrie temporarily out of the picture, his next key witness was Margaret Telford. Her daughter, who was visiting from Penzance, told Aaron that Margaret's health had been in decline since discovering her poor dog's remains in the backyard, and that any kind of interview was out of the question. That left Aaron circling back to the Pengellys. He'd already tried searching local directories, both physical and online, but it was too soon for their change of address to be registered. He'd also searched social media and come up empty.

So far, the family's whereabouts remained a mystery, which meant he would need to somehow convince Nat Tremaine to give up their address.

Moving on to his secondary list, the families of Spencer's other victims, proved almost as fruitless until he spoke with

Anthea Baker, mother of Toby Baker, who agreed to be interviewed and would be free this coming Friday; which was something, at least. Finally, with some disdain, Aaron moved onto his third list of interviewees; a ragtag cohort of neighbours and residents who'd either been name-checked or quoted by the press. Predictably, almost everyone he called agreed to be interviewed.

He spent his afternoon navigating the narrow, windswept streets of the cove and drinking several mugs of tea while repeating his list of questions and recording the answers. Not one of his interviewees had had any direct involvement with September's grim events, but all had something to say on the matter.

Mabel Stevens, manager of the local post office, emphatically declared a curse had been placed on Porth an Jowl by Grady Spencer, who was almost certainly a deranged practitioner of the dark arts. A Satanist, no less.

"That's what happens when you name a place Devil's Cove," she declared. "You invite evil in."

Old Peter Pascoe, proprietor of Porth an Jowl Newsagent and Stationery Store, was also convinced the town had been gripped by malevolent forces.

"There's a cancer growing in this place," he said, jabbing a finger across the shop counter. "And it ain't finished with us yet."

By four o'clock, the sky was aglow with sunset embers and Aaron's head was teeming with bad omens and strange folklore. His research into Cornwall had revealed a culture long steeped in tall tales of faeries and goblins, witchcraft and dark magic— and he'd assumed that such stories had been kept alive to entertain the tourists. But here, in Porth an Jowl, it seemed that a belief in dark forces was still very much alive.

Perhaps it was these so-called dark forces that were hindering his progress. All he had to show for days of research were photographs of empty rooms and a bunch of interviews that had only served to waste his time. With the last of the day fading above him, he found himself back at Clarence Row and standing outside Carrie Killigrew's house. The curtains were all closed but he could see light seeping through the cracks of the living room window. He was tempted to knock on her door again, but he had a feeling that, with his present luck, a second encounter with the woman he'd met earlier wouldn't end well.

Instead, he moved on to his final pointless interview of the day, just a few doors down. Five minutes later, Aaron was sitting at Dottie Penpol's kitchen table, sipping hot tea, and doing his best to look interested in what the elderly woman had to say.

"I knew that boy was trouble as soon as he washed up on that beach," Dottie said, waving a crooked finger. "I could tell just by looking in his eyes. There was something dark there. Something unnatural. Like you couldn't see his soul."

"You met Cal?" Aaron asked, sitting up. "You spoke with him?"

Dottie shook her head. "Not exactly. But I seen him through the window, and I swear to you, it was like the devil himself was staring right at me. Lord, I ran home and prayed that night, I can tell you!"

Aaron forced a smile to his lips as he drank more tea. *Another lunatic.* He wasn't going to glean anything useful here, just more wasted time.

"It's a tragedy, really, if you think about what that poor woman's been through," Dottie went on. "First, she has to deal with the guilt of not watching over her son and letting him drown. Then she has to deal with the shock of him being alive all this time, never mind all the terrible things that happened since! I tell you, it's no surprise to anyone in this town that poor Carrie's lost her mind."

"Is that right?"

"Had some sort of breakdown, she did, supposedly. Not that I listen to rumours or anything, but Dylan, that's her husband, he's had to take that poor daughter of theirs to live with his folks on the other side of town. Carrie can't cope, apparently. You'd think now Sally's back in town, she'd be doing better."

"Sally?"

"That's Carrie's mother. Turned up a couple of weeks ago. I expect Dylan called her because it's not like Sally ever won Mother of the Year herself. She and Carrie were estranged, you see. Ever since Cal was thought drowned and Sally and that husband of hers took off on their fancy pants yacht."

Dottie paused for a moment to catch her breath and take a sip of tea. Aaron picked up a pen and jotted down some notes. It was a strange thing to do, he thought, to leave Carrie when she needed her parents the most. But grief made people behave in all sorts of strange ways. When his father had died, his mother's reaction had been to book herself in for a face lift.

"It's a crying shame," Dottie said, with a sad shake of her head. "That boy used to be such a happy child, all smiles and laughter. Polite, too. I hope Grady Spencer is burning in hell for what he did to him and all those poor little kiddies. Lord knows where that boy is now! Dead, I expect. That don't stop Carrie from looking for him every night, though, does it?"

Aaron stared at the woman, who smiled as she leaned forward.

"Oh, nothing much gets past Dottie Penpol! I see her, I do. Every night, after dark. Waits till everyone's in their homes, then off she goes walking the streets. Looking for that boy of hers."

"Every night, you say?"

Dottie nodded. "Like clockwork. It's a sad thing to see, poor dear. She'd be better off concentrating on the family she has left because if Carrie don't buck her ideas up soon, that little girl will forget she even had a mother."

Aaron nodded, masking his excitement. He cleared his throat and smiled warmly at the woman.

"Tell me, Dottie, what time do you usually see her?"

8

Carrie slipped on her coat then stopped by the front door and cocked her head. She could hear her mother's hushed tones drifting down from upstairs as she made her nightly call to Carrie's father. Quietening her breaths, Carrie strained to hear what was being said. She quickly regretted it. Words like *drinking* and *getting worse* and *not helping* made her wince.

So, she had already become a burden to her mother in just two weeks. The truth was she *had* been drinking a lot lately. She wasn't exactly sober now. But considering what she'd been through in the last few months, she thought her mother should have been exercising a little more empathy and a lot less judgement.

Sinking further into a pit of misery, Carrie slipped out of the house. It was just after seven. The street was dark and cold. Coastal winds pulled at her clothes, but the rain had finally stopped.

There were lights on in people's houses, where normal lives were playing out. Carrie felt a pang of envy deep in her chest as she stood there, lost in memories, until the chattering of her teeth got her moving again.

Heading right, she turned onto Cove Road. She paused for a minute, staring down at the beach. A thick sea fog was rolling in, devouring the sand. She had no desire to visit the place where her son had been found that day, face down and half dead, the tide washing over him. A small part of her wished that Margaret Telford had not thought to pull him away from the water but had left him to be swallowed into the ocean's depths. She turned away, ashamed that she could think such things.

The wind stinging her face, Carrie climbed the hill. If she kept walking, she could leave this town. She could go somewhere far from here, where no one stared at her with pity, or worse still, blame; as if what Grady Spencer had done to her son was somehow her fault.

Grady Spencer. The monster who had stolen her son.

His house loomed on Carrie's left. She didn't mean to come this way, yet here she was drawn each night, poised at the edge of Grenville Row, staring up at the graffiti-covered building. She was still having trouble processing that Cal had been held captive just a stone's throw from where she had stood at her living room window, night after night, month after month, hoping to see him come running through the garden gate.

Her son had been kept prisoner for seven years while Grady Spencer had slowly chipped away at his mind, destroying his memories, his emotions, his foundations. And then Grady Spencer had built him back up again, training and shaping him into something barely human, little more than an attack dog.

Rage flowed through Carrie's veins like hot lava, threatening to erupt. How she longed to tear the boards from the windows of Grady Spencer's house, to smash every pane of glass! But she knew she wouldn't be able to stop at the house. Like a forest fire, her anger would burn out of control. She would raze this town to the ground. She would incinerate the world until all that remained was a pile of white hot ash.

Because her son was gone. And he'd left behind a gaping, empty hole that could never be filled.

Unable to stand here for a second longer, Carrie pushed on. Soon, she reached the top of the cove. The road flattened out. Briar Wood was on her left. Opposite, Cove Holiday Park sat in shadows, closed until spring. Melissa's school was further along the road.

A twinge of guilt pinched Carrie's chest. *Melissa.* She couldn't think about her right now. She couldn't think about anything. All she wanted right now was to disappear. To let the darkness take her.

Turning off the road, Carrie entered Briar Wood.

As she stumbled along the dirt track, she got her wish. Streetlights disappeared. The evergreen canopy blotted out the stars. The darkness became absolute.

Carrie ploughed forward, unafraid, moving deeper into the wood. There was no birdsong. No sounds of nocturnal animal life. Only the rustle of wind through branches and the soft squelch of her boots on wet mud.

And then a flash of bright light illuminated the trees in a wide arc. Moments later, it swung round again, forcing Carrie to shield her eyes. It wasn't until the light had passed by a third time that she realised what it was.

Quickening her pace, Carrie continued along the dirt track, until the trees began to thin out and the smell of sea salt grew stronger. And then she was stepping out of Briar Wood and onto a stony cliff.

The lighthouse towered above her, its beam of light revolving through the night sky. Parked next to the lighthouse was an old Range Rover, which she knew belonged to Ben Ward, the lighthouse keeper, who would be inside somewhere, no doubt smoking the pipe that was always hanging from his lips.

Tucking her hands inside her coat pockets, Carrie strode past the lighthouse, spongy, wet moss beneath her feet, until she was just a few paces away from the cliff edge.

Desperation Point; that's what the locals called it.

For years now, suicidal individuals had come here to end their lives. After so many deaths, a petition had been created to demand a barrier be erected, but so far nothing had been done about it.

Carrie edged nearer, the wind blasting her hair and making her eyes sting. She moved as close to the edge as she would dare. Then looked down.

Below, the fog had thickened, covering the ocean. Carrie heard angry waves smashing against the rocks that had claimed so many lives. It would be so easy, she thought. Just a few more steps and the world would fall away, taking all her pain, all her guilt, all her anguish.

She would no longer wake up having to remember that Cal was gone. She would no longer have to remind herself of what had been done to him. Or of what he had done. He'd almost killed her because Grady Spencer had commanded it. If Jago hadn't rushed in at that moment, would she even be here now, teetering on the cliff edge, wondering if she should end it all?

A voice whispered inside her head—the same voice that spoke to her each night she was drawn to Desperation Point.

Do it. End it. Make it all go away. Above her, the beam of the lighthouse travelled another cycle. *Go on. Step off. What are you waiting for? You'll never have to feel hurt again.*

She leaned further forward and wondered how long it would take for her falling body to smash against the rocks.

Would she be killed instantly? Or would she feel immeasurable pain as her body was torn apart?

One more step and it'll all be over. Do it. Do it now.

From the trees came a powerful gust of wind.

Do it!

Carrie toppled forward.

HIDDEN in shadows at the edge of Briar Wood, Aaron watched in horror as Carrie Killigrew approached the cliff edge. After leaving Dottie Penpol's, he'd parked his car just down from Carrie's house, ducked down in the driver's seat, and waited.

He'd watched Carrie leave the house around nine, walk to the end of the street, and begin climbing Cove Road. Keeping his distance, he'd followed on foot. Now he stood, frozen in fear, wondering if he was about to bear witness to Carrie's death.

This was not part of the plan. The plan had been to follow her until they were a safe distance from her mother, then casually introduce himself and request an interview. And he was going to, until Carrie had stopped outside the Spencer house. Even from the shadows of his hiding spot, Aaron had seen the fury and despair in her eyes. And when she had marched with determination into Briar Wood, he'd had no choice but to follow.

Now he knew why she'd come here. And he had to do something about it.

But what? If he came running from the tree line, hands

waving like a mad man, the surprise might send Carrie tumbling to her death regardless. But if he did nothing, merely stood and watched, her death would be on his hands. It wouldn't matter that she'd chosen to end her life, he'd live the rest of his days knowing he hadn't tried to stop her.

Aaron drew in a breath, just as Carrie leaned dangerously forward and looked down into the abyss. Above her, the beam of the lighthouse swung around and delved through the trees, illuminating branches.

From the corner of his eye, Aaron saw a flash of movement. He turned his head sharply to the right. The beam swung past, cloaking the wood in darkness once more.

Aaron stared into the trees, momentarily distracted. He had seen something. He was sure of it.

Before he had time to register a second thought, a gust of wind burst through the trees and rushed towards Carrie. He watched her topple. He heard her cry out. He tried to move, to run and lunge and pull her back.

But Aaron's feet were paralysed.

Carrie fell forward. Her arms shot out.

The lighthouse beam swung around again.

Something moved on Aaron's right. And in that split second, he smelled dirt and sweat and fear in the air.

His eyes shot back to Carrie, in time to see her body buck wildly as she fought to keep her balance.

She tumbled backward, landing heavily on the ground, then scrambled away from the edge on her elbows. When she was at a safe distance, she pulled her knees up to her chest and grew still.

Aaron had stopped breathing. Not because he had just witnessed Carrie almost die. Not because, like a coward, he had done nothing to help her.

But because there was someone else here.

The lighthouse beam swept by and he saw the figure standing just inside the treeline, watching Carrie cry uncontrollably into her hands. The figure was small in stature and lithe like an animal.

It was a boy.

A boy with eyes that glinted like black tar pools as the light flashed across his face. There was no emotion in his expression. Only cool, primal observation; a snake, hiding in the undergrowth, waiting to strike—or perhaps, a boy filled with the night, watching his mother come apart at the seams.

Aaron's heart smashed against his ribcage. The lighthouse beam swung towards him, pitching the figure into darkness.

"Cal," he whispered.

Carrie's sobs grew louder. Aaron stared wide-eyed into the darkness, waiting for the beam to come around again, half expecting it to fall on empty trees.

But there he was. Cal Anderson.

Only he was no longer staring at Carrie. He was staring straight at Aaron, his glittering black eyes igniting with fire. Then just as the light was about to plunge him into darkness once more, Cal bolted towards him.

Terror exploded in Aaron's veins.

Somewhere at the edge of his panic, he saw Carrie jump to her feet and spin around to face the trees.

"Who's there?" she called.

Aaron turned and ran.

Branches whistled past him, scratching his skin as he plunged into the darkness of Briar Wood. He could hear Cal's footfalls tearing up the foliage, getting closer by the second. Aaron pumped his arms and legs, adrenaline blazing through his muscles. Light cut through the trees, briefly illuminating his way. He saw the dirt track that led back to the road and he threw himself onto it.

He ran, on and on, without looking back.

It wasn't until he saw the protective glow of streetlights up ahead that he realised he could no longer hear Cal chasing him.

Clearing the trees, Aaron slid to a halt. His chest heaved and his lungs burned as he stared back at the darkness, waiting for the boy to appear.

But stillness had resumed in Briar Wood.

Turning on his heels, Aaron half ran, half skidded down Cove Road until he reached Clarence Row and the safety of his car. Jumping in, he locked the doors and slipped the key into the ignition. The engine roared to life.

He had left Carrie up there. Alone. After she had almost jumped. What kind of a person was he?

She'll be fine. Cal won't hurt her. She's his mother.

Perhaps he should wait. Just to make sure Carrie was safe. Just to make sure she made it home unharmed. Shame hit him like a slap to the face.

You're a coward, Black. You watched a woman almost end her life tonight and you did nothing to intervene. You ran for your life from a boy half your size because you were afraid he would hurt you.

But it wasn't just any boy, was it?

It was Cal Anderson.

Son of Carrie Killigrew. Deranged protege of renowned serial killer Grady Spencer. Mutilator of animals.

And he was right here, in Devil's Cove, stalking through the trees of Briar Wood while everyone believed him gone forever.

Aaron's body trembled with fear and excitement.

Cal Anderson was alive, and that changed everything.

Sitting in the darkness of the car, Aaron's mind raced. What did he do with this newfound revelation? More importantly, how could he use it to get what he needed?

He wondered if he was the only person to know Cal was still haunting Devil's Cove? Because it was clear Carrie didn't have a clue. It explained why Cal had remained hidden from her. It explained why she had been tempted to take her own life.

He sat up, peering through the driver window into the empty street. Had Cal been watching his mother all this time? Surely that meant he still possessed a shred of humanity. That his bond to Carrie was keeping him attached to his old life and the possibility of returning to it. Aaron wondered how he could use that to his advantage.

10

WHAT HAD SHE DONE? Carrie stood at the living room window, watching Sally battle with an umbrella as she exited the garden, heading for the supermarket in town. She had tried to persuade Carrie to go with her but had eventually given up and left in exasperated silence. Now alone, Carrie listened to the ticks and creaks of the house, and the rain dashing against the window panes.

She had only slept a few hours, her mind replaying last night's events. She was scared of herself. *For* herself. One minute she'd been walking, the next teetering on the cliff edge, moments away from leaping off and plummeting to her death.

Had she sunk so deep into her despair that life had suddenly become so worthless? What did that say about her love for Melissa? For Dylan? Had she become so empty that she thought them better off without her?

Guilt crushed the breath from her lungs. What if she'd gone through with it? How would Melissa feel to know that her mother hadn't cared enough about her to live?

But Carrie did care. It had been a momentary, desperate

lapse, nothing more. She loved Melissa more than anything on this earth. *Except for Cal,* a voice whispered from the shadows. *You've always loved him more and you always will.*

Tearing herself away from the window, Carrie eyed the cabinet against the far wall, her mouth running dry at the thought of the whiskey decanter inside.

"Stop," she gasped to the empty room. "Just stop."

Clutching her stomach, she fled from the room. Sleep was what she needed, not inebriation. But sleep did not want her, and so the next best alternative was coffee. She set about making a pot, humming to herself to shut out the taunts.

And then she was back at Desperation Point again, staring down at the fog bank, waves crashing in her ears.

What about the other sounds she had heard? Someone had been in the woods, hadn't they? At first, she'd thought it was a startled animal. But the largest animal one might encounter in the Cornish countryside was a fox, or in rare circumstances, a wild deer—though she was certain deer hadn't been spotted in Briar Wood for hundreds of years.

No, the footfalls she'd heard had not been made by an animal. They'd been distinctly human. Someone had been watching her. They'd seen what she'd tried to do.

But who?

A name formed on her lips, one she dared not say aloud. She forced it from her mind.

What if it had been someone from the cove? Gossip spread like wildfire around here. All it would take was a whisper or two and soon, the whole town would know that Carrie Killigrew had tried to kill herself. What would happen then? How would Dylan react? Her mother? What if she was deemed a risk to

Melissa's wellbeing? She was dangerously close to becoming a negligent parent as it was.

Anxiety coiled around Carrie's ribs. Did this nightmare have no end? The electronic tone of the doorbell answered her question. Carrie tensed. Leaving the kitchen, she stole through the hall and came to a halt by the living room door. Whoever it was, they would go away if she didn't answer.

The doorbell sounded again, followed by the rap of knuckles on wood. Entering the living room, Carrie crept up to the window and peeked out. It was the man who had come by on Monday, the one who'd looked so disappointed when Sally had shooed him away. She watched him standing on the garden path, a look of urgency on his face as the rain soaked into his clothes.

She wondered who he was and why he looked so desperate. The man stepped forward, disappearing as he pressed the buzzer again. Then, to Carrie's surprise, she heard his voice calling through the letterbox.

"Mrs Killigrew, I'm sorry to disturb you, but I need to speak to you urgently."

Carrie froze. He didn't sound like a journalist. Besides, the press had grown tired of her silence weeks ago. Backing away from the window, she moved to the living room door.

"Please, Carrie," the man called. "Please, open the door. It's about your son."

The breath caught in her throat. Carrie leaned forward and peered into the hall. She saw the flap of the letterbox propped open and the man's round eyes peering in. They shifted, meeting her gaze.

"Please," he said again.

Carrie stepped into the hall, her arms wrapped around her

ribcage. "What about my son?" Perhaps he was a journalist after all, and this was nothing more than a ruse to get her to talk.

The man's eyes blinked. "I've seen him."

A flash of hope lit up Carrie's insides, but was quickly snuffed out by anger. So, it was a journalist after all. They'd tried all sorts of tricks to get her to open the door, but none had stooped this low.

Carrie clenched her jaw as she spoke. "You need to leave. Now. Before I call the police."

The man's eyes disappeared and were replaced by his mouth.

"This isn't a joke," he said. "I'm telling the truth, I promise. I saw him last night. Up at Desperation Point."

The world fell away. Carrie shot out a hand and grasped the wall. She struggled for breath.

"I don't believe you," she gasped. "You're lying."

"I swear to you, I was there. I saw Cal. He was watching you."

Before she could stop herself, Carrie threw open the door with such force it bounced off the wall.

Aaron stared at Carrie with something approaching awe. Standing this close, he could see the dark shadows of sleepless nights lurking beneath her eyes and the fresh new lines that had appeared at their corners, carved in her skin by untold horrors. This was the face of a woman who had experienced terrible things, who had stared into the abyss and seen her own reflection staring back.

And last night she had tried to end her anguish. But something had stopped her. A remaining glimmer of hope, perhaps.

Or the pull of the cord that connected her to her children, one innocent, the other snatched away and corrupted by evil.

Staring into Carrie's haunted eyes, Aaron saw terror and loss, anger and guilt. But he also saw underlying strength. Carrie was a survivor. She had survived seven years of believing her son was dead. She had survived the shock of his return and the knowledge of what he had become. Now she was facing the loss of her son for a second time, and she was standing on a precipice, wavering. He wondered if he was about to push her over the edge.

"Who are you?" Carrie growled.

Aaron cleared his throat, wiped the rain from his face, and introduced himself. He told her who he was and why he was here, and what he had seen up at Desperation Point, and as he spoke, his words spilling over each other in excitement, he realised that his book was not to be an account of the heinous crimes of a psychotic serial killer, but the heroic struggles of a desperate mother, fighting to survive the type of unimaginable nightmare that most parents only dream about.

This was how he pitched it to her, and when he'd finished, he stood back, oblivious of the rain, and triumphantly waited for Carrie to say yes. But Carrie didn't say anything. Instead, darkness swept across her eyes.

"You followed me," she said, her voice deadly quiet. "It was you I heard running away."

Aaron shook his head. This was not how it was supposed to go. "It was your son, I swear."

"It was you."

"Okay, yes, I did follow you, but only to introduce myself. Your mother wouldn't let me see you, I didn't know what else to do. I followed you and I was going to speak to you, but then you walked up to that cliff and I realised what you were going to do."

Carrie's eyes were ablaze. Her body trembled as she spat out words. "So you thought you'd just watch, did you? Sit back and take notes—an eyewitness account for your book?"

"No, I—"

"You followed me up there and when you realised you weren't getting the show you wanted, you took off!"

Aaron held up his hands. "Carrie, please, that's not how—"

"How dare you come here, talking to me about my son! You didn't see him—you're lying to make me help you with your damn book!"

Aaron was losing her. This was all going wrong. He stared at her, pleading with his eyes. "Cal was watching you. I startled him and he came after me. I got to the road, but he didn't follow. I'm telling you the truth, Carrie! Your son is still here. You could have a life with him again!"

Carrie's complexion was sickly pale. Her teeth mashed together. Her face contorted into an expression of pure rage.

"Get out!" she screamed. "Get out or I'll call the police!"

"Please, Carrie. I'm telling you that your son is—"

"Leave! Or so help me God I'll tear your throat out!" She lunged forward, slamming her hands against his chest. "Get out!"

Aaron stumbled back, almost slipping on the wet path. He watched as Carrie's body heaved and trembled, as her tears bled into the rain.

"Please," she begged. "Please, just leave me alone."

Nodding, Aaron pulled open the gate and staggered into the street. Neighbours had heard the shrieking. Doors were opening. Curious, alarmed faces were peering out.

Aaron stumbled to his car. He turned back to see Carrie standing in the rain, her face twisted with grief and fury. Then he climbed in and drove away. This was not the plan. This was not how his meeting with Carrie was supposed to end.

As he sped away from the cove, he couldn't tear the sight of Carrie screaming in the rain from his mind. Neither could he shake off the realisation that any chance of saving his career from leaping off Desperation Point and crashing onto the rocks below had just been lost.

11

BACK IN HIS HOTEL ROOM, Aaron stood at the window watching the rain lash down and feeling despair wash over him. There was no way Carrie was going to help him now. Without her, the book he wanted to write—that he *needed* to write—was nothing more than a fruitless dream.

Which meant he was screwed.

He briefly wondered if he should call his publisher—ex-publisher, he reminded himself—and beg them to sign him for another Silky Winters novel. He recalled his final meeting in their plush offices and the expletive-filled tantrum he'd thrown when they'd not only turned down his book proposal but announced they were terminating his contract. So long, thank you for your time, please shut the door on your way out.

Anger seethed beneath Aaron's skin. Six years he'd given them! Six years and hundreds of thousands of sales. Didn't that count for anything? So, the last Silky Winters hadn't sold anything like the others, but was it his fault *they* hadn't promoted it? And was it his fault that his newly ruined career had *forced* him to start drinking again after months of sobriety? If only Taylor had understood that, maybe Aaron wouldn't have found himself homeless and sleeping in his car. Maybe he wouldn't have been forced to empty their joint savings account and head down to this godforsaken place in a final desperate bid to make something out of his abysmal, fucking life!

Aaron slumped on the bed and eyed the mini bar. At least he'd capped the drinking again before it had spiralled out of control.

"Doesn't that earn me a second chance?" he muttered, his shoulders sagging. Except that he'd lost count of the second chances Taylor had given him, and he had a feeling that clearing their bank account and promptly vanishing had pretty much slammed the coffin lid on their relationship.

His eyes returned to the mini bar. His tongue ran over his lower lip. This book was supposed to be his salvation, not his downfall. He'd pinned his last shred of hope to it. Now he'd have to go grovelling on his knees back to his publisher, back to Taylor, begging to be forgiven and granted one last chance. Again.

Because what was the alternative?

The alternative, he knew, was rotting in this hotel until the money ran out, then sleeping in his car until he either drove it straight into the sea, or froze to death in the back seat, starved and penniless. Because there was no way in hell he could ever return to the nine-to-five grind. Never on this green earth!

The room pressed down on him, sucking out the air. He had to get out of here. Clear his head of all the noise, so he could think of a way out. Besides, he was hungry. How was he supposed to think when he was hungry?

And there was always a solution. There had to be. Otherwise, he might as well get in his car and drive into the ocean right now.

Riding the lift down to the lobby, Aaron breezed past the front desk and smiled at the bored-looking receptionist. The restaurant was off to the side, shrouded in darkness. He stooped and peeked through the glass door.

"We've had to close it," the receptionist called. "Chef's sick."

Aaron returned to the desk. "What's a guest supposed to do for dinner, then?"

The young man looked him up and down. "The bar's open. They have snacks. Or, if you like, I can make you a sandwich. Alternatively, there's a selection of restaurants nearby if you don't mind braving the weather."

Aaron glanced across the foyer at the soft light filtering through the bar's smoked-glass front. Piano music floated on the air. It was a recording, something old and bluesy. He listened to a few bars while he debated whether he should go in.

Perhaps there would be people inside. He wasn't sure he wanted to engage in conversation, but there was still company to be had in the presence of strangers. And just because you happened to enter a licensed establishment didn't mean you were contractually obliged to drink alcohol, even if you had hit rock bottom. Besides, they had snacks.

Aaron wavered. Then he nodded to the receptionist, sucked in a breath, and stepped through the doors.

Considering the ailing state of the rest of the hotel, the bar was surprisingly slick. Red velvet booths lined the sides of the room, while tables and chairs filled the centre. The bar itself was lit with strings of colourful lights.

The only occupant was the barman, who stood behind the bar, absentmindedly polishing glasses. As Aaron approached, he looked up and flashed him a smile. Probably pleased to have something to do, Aaron thought, before nervously glancing at the illuminated bottles behind.

"Good evening, sir," the barman said. "What can I get you?"

He was younger than Aaron, in his early twenties, with dark hair slicked into a side parting and a clean-shaven face free of lines and wrinkles.

Aaron sat on a bar stool and rested his hands on the counter. His eyes scanned the rows of bottles before him. Hypnotised, he ran his tongue over his lower lip. Perhaps it was a mistake to come in here. Too soon.

The barman was waiting, his smile warm and pleasant.

"Peanuts, please."

"Nothing to drink?"

"Lime and soda." The words felt alien on his tongue. "No ice."

The barman raised an eyebrow.

"Lime and soda, it is." He reached beneath the counter for a glass. "Freshly squeezed or cordial?"

"Cordial will do just fine."

Aaron could feel his face heating up. It hadn't been so long ago that he would have laughed at the idea of ordering lime and soda, unless the glass was already half filled with gin. But those days were behind him now. Yes, he'd slipped after his meeting with the publisher. Yes, he'd suffered the consequences. But when it came to booze, he was a changed man now. And he'd made that change without help from anyone.

"So, you're here on business?" the barman asked as he reached for the soda. "I can't imagine anyone being here on holiday at this time of year."

Aaron nodded, not wanting to make conversation. But the barman was clearly bored of his own company.

"What kind of business?"

"Research."

"Oh? For what?"

"A book."

The glass was set before him, along with a bowl of peanuts. Aaron stared at them. Perhaps instead of drinking himself to death, he could eat his way to a massive coronary. Or perhaps he'd take up smoking again. He briefly recalled the headiness of the cigarette Nat had given him a few days ago.

"You're a writer?" the barman asked, suitably impressed.

Aaron nodded, momentarily buffered by the young man's awe. He could at least pretend for a moment that life was wonderful.

"What's your book about?"

"The life and crimes of Grady Spencer."

The barman's expression soured. "That old psychopath?"

"The one and only. You know much about him?"

"Only what I heard on the news. Really nasty business. Didn't do much for the tourist trade either, apart from bringing all the weirdos and freaks out from under their rocks." He looked up suddenly. "Present company excluded, of course."

Aaron smiled. He shovelled peanuts into his mouth, then glanced up at the barman. "What do you know about Devil's Cove?"

"I know the locals don't like it being called that for a start. Especially now." The barman began picking up polished glasses from the counter and returning them to a shelf below. "You interviewing the locals?"

"Trying to. You know anyone from Dev—from Porth an Jowl?"

"Nope. Never been there."

"How about Grady Spencer's victims?"

"Sorry. Can't help you."

Sipping his drink, Aaron turned and glanced around the empty bar. His thoughts returned to Cal Anderson.

Finished with the glasses, the barman leaned his elbow on the counter. "What kind of sick-minded individual murders little kids?"

"A sick-minded one," Aaron said, with a wry smile.

"I've said it before and I'll say it again—it's a nasty business." The barman shook his head. "There's been too much of that going around lately."

Aaron studied the young man's face. "What do you mean?"

"I mean all the satanic stuff that's been happening."

"Satanic stuff?" He set down his glass with a smile and stared at the young man. Clearly, superstitious hysteria wasn't relegated to Porth an Jowl alone.

The barman grimly nodded. "A couple weeks back, a farmer found his entire flock of sheep butchered. Bits of them hacked off and taken. Ritual sacrifice, the papers said. There's been a whole spate of it. A horse mutilated, its hooves cut off. A goat decapitated, its guts ripped out."

Something was signalling to Aaron from deep inside his brain, like a flare shooting through the dark.

"Satanists?" he said. "Are you sure?"

"Said so in the papers." The barman shook his head. "Who would have thought of such a thing in this day and age?"

It sounded preposterous to Aaron. Were there really clusters of Devil worshippers roaming rural Cornwall, sacrificing live-stock under a full moon? Or was it something else?

Despite the warmth of the bar, Aaron's skin prickled.

Cal Anderson had been accused of mutilating animals, hadn't he? Including Margaret Telford's dog, who'd been hacked to pieces and left in a sack for her to find.

The barman nodded at Aaron's empty glass. "Something else?"

But Aaron didn't hear him.

You could find him.

He laughed. What an idea! He closed his eyes for a second, imagining himself emerging from the wilderness with Cal in tow. He imagined jostling news crews, cameras rolling as the world wondered how he'd achieved something the police could not: the capture of Cal Anderson. But he would not tell them. Not yet. Only within the pages of his book would he detail exactly how he'd done it. And then would come the seven-figure publishing deal, the celebrity TV guest spots, the awards, a Hollywood movie.

Aaron snapped out of his fantasy. He stared at the barman, at the rows of glinting bottles that all seemed to be singing his name.

This was real life. A life in which he was doomed to fail, over and over. Unless he did something rash to change his fortune *now*.

Something like finding Cal Anderson.

Aaron sat up, eyes glittering as he stared at the barman.

"The stories were in the paper, you say?"

12

Briar Wood was still and quiet. The rain had stopped an hour ago and now, as the temperature plummeted, tiny ice particles formed on branches and the ground began to freeze.

He stood at the treeline, shivering as he watched the road, waiting for her to come. He'd been waiting for an hour now.

Something was wrong. Something to do with that man, perhaps. Who was he? Why had he been watching her? What did he want?

Somewhere deep inside Cal's chest, an anxious feeling unfurled its wings. It couldn't be a coincidence that the man had appeared and now his mother hadn't shown up on her nightly walk to Desperation Point. He didn't trust that man. He had hidden in the trees like a hunter stalking its prey, and he had watched Cal's mother step up to the cliff edge without doing anything to stop her.

But hadn't Cal done the same? Rubbing his hands together, he edged closer to the road.

Where was she? Her absence felt like a hole inside him that was growing wider. It scared him. It made him angry.

I told you, boy, a voice whispered inside his head. *That stinking bitch never cared about you.*

Cal replayed last night's events in his mind. His mother had almost thrown herself into the ocean. Why had she done that? On all the other nights, she'd walked up to the cliff but she'd stayed back from the edge, as if she had been afraid to get any closer.

Cal had watched every night. When he'd first found the courage to return to the cove, he'd waited until the early hours and stolen through the streets, until he'd found himself standing outside his childhood home. The curtains had all been closed, the lights turned out, but he could feel her inside. He could sense her pain as acutely as he experienced his own.

That was back when Dylan had still been at the house. Now, Dylan was gone and he'd taken Melissa with him. Cal thought that was a good thing. Their absence gave him hope.

After they'd left, Cal had started coming to the house more and more, earlier and earlier, watching the closed curtains of the windows, hoping to see a glimpse of his mother.

Then Sally had turned up. At first, Cal hadn't recognised her, but then a memory had floated up from deep down. A memory of being small, maybe four or five, and sitting on his grand-mother's knee as she read him a story. The memory had surprised him—he'd thought all those recollections had been lost.

But it hadn't surprised him as much as when his mother had started leaving the house, night after night, passing him by just on the other side of the street. The first few times, she'd suddenly stopped a few metres along the road and looked back, as if she'd known he was there. Then she'd walked on and Cal had followed.

It had become a habit, although now he waited for her up at Briar Wood. Despite the camouflage of dark winter evenings, sneaking through the cove came with risks, especially if his mother left the house before the rest of the town had fallen asleep. It would only take a single person to spot him through their window and to call the police, then Cal would be sent away. Maybe locked up forever. That scared him more than Jacob finding out where he was going every night.

But it didn't scare him as much as the thought of losing his mother forever. Even though she'd left him to rot in Grady Spencer's basement, even though she'd replaced him with a new family, he knew she was filled with regret. He'd seen how lost she looked without him—how bereft—and it gave him hope that they would one day be together again.

But not yet. Not while there was still anger in him. Not while Jacob and the rest of the farm were breathing down his neck. Not while there were others forming a human barrier between mother and son.

Where was she?

You're wasting your time. Forget about that whore. After all, she's forgotten about you.

Cal shook the voice from his head.

Stepping out from the tree line, he checked the caravan park, then glanced both ways down the road. Satisfied he was alone, he darted forward, crouching down like a cat as he descended into the cove, heading for his mother's home.

The streets were empty, but lights were still on in houses. He stole by each one, silent as a shadow, and turned onto Clarence Row.

His breaths grew thinner as he came up to his mother's

house and ducked down behind a stationary vehicle. Frosty air pinched his skin, but he was oblivious to its sting.

The living room curtains were open and the lights were on. His grandmother was sitting on the sofa, television light flickering across her face. There was tiredness in her eyes. Tiredness and worry.

His gaze drifted up to the top floor towards his mother's bedroom window. The curtains had been drawn but a light was on. Cal closed his eyes, trying to sense her presence, to pull on the cord that connected them. He opened his eyes again. A silhouette was projected on the curtains as a figure moved inside.

She was there.

Cal's chest grew hot and tight. Why hadn't she gone walking tonight? What had changed? Had she rejected him again? Changed her mind about wanting him back?

She never wanted you in the first place, boy.

Cal frowned. *That's not true.*

No, something else had kept her indoors tonight. Something else that was trying to come between them.

Or *someone* else.

Like that man. The one who'd been spying on her in the trees.

His mother's silhouette was still at the window. Then it was moving away, vanishing into the room.

Nausea churned Cal's stomach. Now he felt the night air's icy touch and he shivered. Confused and anxious, he watched the house until Sally switched off the television and drew the curtains. He watched until the light went out in his mother's bedroom. Until the cold pierced his flesh and numbed his bones.

Until he felt something small and lithe rub against his leg.

Glancing down, Cal saw the shadowy form of a cat curling

around his feet. He stooped down and stroked its head with icy fingers. The cat purred contentedly.

Cal thought about the man. Darkness penetrated his body, puncturing his heart. He thought about his mother coming close to death at the cliff edge. He thought about how he would wait for her again tomorrow night at Briar Wood, and about what he might do if she didn't show.

You should stick her like a pig. Open her throat and shower in her blood.

No, I can't. She's my mother.

Somewhere at the edges of his thoughts, he felt fur and muscle writhe in his hands, and sharp claws scratch at his skin. Hot blood spilled over his fingers, warming him against the night chill.

Cal smiled a strange smile.

You're mine, boy, Grady Spencer whispered in his head. *You're all mine.*

13

CARRIE WAS SILENT, her eyes fixed on the ground in front, the hood of her jacket pulled over her head as she walked through the Wednesday morning rain. Beside her, Sally grumbled about the British weather and how she longed for long, hot days like the ones she and Carrie's father, Jeff, had spent sailing around the Mediterranean. Not that it meant she wanted to leave. No, of course not, she was staying right here for as long as she was needed, but wasn't this constant rain just a weight on a person's happiness and enough to drive anyone to despair?

She continued her strained monologue as they entered Trevithick Row, its fifties style housing a stark contrast to the rest of the cove's two-hundred-year-old architecture.

Carrie remained oblivious of her surroundings. Inside, her mind was trapped in a tornado of fury and panic. That writer, Aaron Black, had followed her to Desperation Point and watched her almost end her life! Worse still, he'd tried to convince her that Cal had been watching, too. But it was a wicked lie. A cruel trick to get her to talk. She'd been too afraid to go walking last night, in case the man had been lying in wait again. She should have called the police and had him arrested. But she hadn't. And she'd kept Aaron Black a secret from her mother, too. Why was that?

Because there's a chance he's telling the truth.

She tried to push the thought away. But it was too late. She pictured her son hiding in the scrub of Briar Wood, watching her teeter between life and death. Was he really out there, hiding on the outskirts? If it was true, why hadn't he given her a sign? Why hadn't he come back home into her waiting arms?

Because Cal was gone forever. And yet it was as if she could still sense him. As if she could feel his loneliness like it was her own. Carrie shook her head. She didn't know what to believe or what to do about it.

A gentle squeeze of her hand brought her back to reality. She looked up to see her mother's concerned face. They had arrived at their destination.

"You look tired," Sally said. "But I'm glad you decided to change your mind."

The front door opened. Gary Killigrew greeted them with a solemn smile. "Morning," he said, standing to one side.

Sally went in first, immediately bursting into a flurry of nervous chatter as she disappeared into the living room.

"Coming in?"

Gary stared at her patiently. It was a familiar look, one she had seen on her husband's face several times. The phrase 'like father, like son' was very fitting for Gary and Dylan Killigrew; they were carbon copies in both looks and temperament.

Carrie nodded, avoiding her father-in-law's gaze as she entered the modern bungalow and made her way to the living room.

Thoughts of Cal momentarily melted away.

"Mummy!" Melissa barrelled forward, latching onto Carrie's thighs, her mass of blonde hair falling across her face.

Carrie gently removed her daughter's hands then crouched down and kissed her on the cheek.

"Hello, sweet pea. How's my little star?"

"Come and see the picture I'm drawing with Nana Joy," Melissa said, bobbing up and down. She tugged on Carrie's sleeve, pulling her towards Joy Killigrew, who stood up from the couch. She smiled at Carrie but kept her hands by her sides as the women exchanged hellos. Joy's gaze wandered to the side of the room.

"Melissa, aren't you going to say hi to Grandma Sally?" she said.

Melissa turned and glanced over her shoulder, to where Sally stood by the fireplace, arms wrapped around her ribcage.

"Hello," the girl mumbled.

"Well hello there, angel!" Sally said, a smile rippling across her face. "It's very nice to see you again!"

Melissa stared at her new grandmother, whom she'd only met last week, before refocusing her attention on Carrie.

"Come and see!" she said in a voice bright as sunlight.

Carrie remained where she was, watching her daughter race to the couch and pick up a sketchbook.

"I'll make some tea," Joy said. "Everyone want some?"

Carrie nodded.

"I'll help." Sally sprang to life and followed Joy out of the room. Gary, who was still hovering in the doorway, stepped to one side.

"Look, Mummy!" Melissa held up her sketchbook. "I drew you, me, and Daddy."

Carrie took the sketchpad and studied the picture.

To her relief, she saw a park scene. Trees and flowers glowed in bright colours. Carrie and Dylan stood to one side, stick figures with cherry red smiles. Unlike a certain picture her daughter had drawn not so long ago, their heads were still attached to their bodies. Melissa had drawn herself leaping through the air like a ballerina.

Cal was not in the drawing.

Carrie wondered if Melissa had already forgotten him, or if she was consciously attempting to erase him from her memories so that normal life could resume once more. It seemed to Carrie that her entire family wanted her to do the same. But she couldn't. Especially now that Aaron Black had offered her more false hope to cling to.

Melissa was up on her tiptoes, desperate to be acknowledged.

"It's lovely, sweet pea."

"I drew it for you. So you can take it home."

A crease appeared in the centre of the girl's forehead. Her large blue eyes stared up at her mother.

Carrie turned away. "Where's Dylan?"

Gary, who was busy staring at the floor, shifted his weight. "He'll be home soon."

A tug on Carrie's sleeve pulled her attention back to Melissa.

"Mummy, are we coming home today?"

The weight in Carrie's chest grew heavier.

"Not today, sweet pea. But soon, I promise."

"Grandpa Gary said you're sick."

Carrie glanced at Gary, who cleared his throat but kept his gaze fixed firmly on the carpet.

"You don't look sick," Melissa said, studying her.

Carrie opened her mouth. She closed it again. How did she

explain to a four-year-old what was going through her mind? What *sick* meant in a situation like this?

Gary broke the silence. "Your mother just needs a little time to figure things out, that's all," he said. "You'll be home before you know it. In the meantime, you've got Grandpa Gary and Nana Joy to run rings around, haven't you?"

Joy and Sally returned with tea trays and welcome chatter. Her shoulders relaxing a little, Carrie watched as Sally picked up Melissa's sketchbook and fired questions at her granddaughter. Melissa replied in monosyllabic whispers. It would take a while for her to adjust to having another grandma, Carrie thought, but it would take Sally even longer to get over the guilt of staying away.

Her thoughts turned to her own guilt. To the hurt in her daughter's eyes when she was told she couldn't come home. To the look of betrayal on Cal's face just moments before he'd disappeared forever. *You should have found me years ago*, his expression had said. *You should have saved me from a life of hell with Grady Spencer.*

What if Aaron Black really was telling the truth? Did it mean Cal had been watching her all this time? That her son was still out there somewhere, longing to come home? If it was true, then all was not lost. If it was true, there was one last chance to save her boy. Was that why she had kept her encounter with the writer to herself?

"Daddy! Look, Mummy's here!"

Carrie pulled herself back to the room. Her heart raced as she saw her husband enter and sweep Melissa into his arms. Their eyes met. Dylan offered Carrie a cautious smile. She smiled back. Neither made a move towards the other.

"Hello handsome," Sal said and held up Melissa's drawing. "You're officially a work of art."

Dylan gave her a nod, his cheeks flushing as he eyed the picture.

"Gary, fetch another cup," Joy said.

Dylan held up a hand. "Actually, if you don't mind—Carrie, can I talk to you in private?"

Carrie's throat ran dry as she became aware of the sudden silence. She didn't want to talk. She wanted to go home, to crawl inside her bed and hide from the world.

But this was Dylan. Her husband. The man she'd asked to leave their home and take their daughter with him. Not because she didn't love them anymore, but because being around them reminded her of everything she had lost. The least she could do was listen to what he had to say.

Joy and Gary's kitchen looked as if it had been frozen in time since the fifties.

"How are you doing?" Dylan asked, staring at her from across the Formica table.

Carrie shook her head. "How are *you* doing?"

"Missing my wife. Wondering when we can come home."

"Dylan, don't."

She could see from his eyes that he had no idea how to handle the situation. How to handle her. Carrie looked away, noticing more of Melissa's sketches fixed to the refrigerator door.

"I'm sorry," Dylan said, his hands clasped together in front of him. "Melissa keeps asking. I don't know what else to tell her. She's so confused."

"I know. I'm sorry."

Silence fell between them. Dylan heaved his shoulders.

"She's having nightmares. Really bad ones."

More guilt. More pressure. Carrie gazed at Dylan's hands, suddenly wanting nothing more than to have them around her waist.

"Nightmares? About what?"

Now it was Dylan's turn to look away. He bit his lower lip.

"She says they're about Cal."

"Oh?"

"She says he comes into her room at night. That he climbs through the window and watches her. I've told her it's just a bad dream, but she's convinced it's real."

Carrie felt blood drain from her face. The air in the room grew thick and heavy.

I saw your son. He was watching you.

"It's a dream," she said. "Of course, it's a dream."

"*I* know that," Dylan said. "But how do you convince a four-year-old that her brother isn't coming to get her like some boogie man? I've even started locking her window at night but she's still terrified."

Their eyes met, and just for a second, Carrie thought she saw a flash of accusation.

As quickly as it had appeared, it was gone.

"I'll talk to her," she said.

"And tell her what? That she still can't come home and be with her mum? Because honestly, I think that's the only thing that's going to stop these nightmares."

They were both silent. A sick feeling took hold of Carrie. Sickness mixed with fear. She glanced at Dylan, who looked sad and alone, confused by what their family had become.

What if Melissa's dreams were not dreams? What if Aaron Black was telling the truth? The thought made Carrie shiver.

No, Cal was gone. Even the police had more or less given up looking. He had left Cornwall, gone far away. Or he had ended his life like the rumours suggested.

The possibility that her son was dead knocked the air from her lungs. She stared at Dylan, who placed his hand over hers.

"When will this be over?" Carrie said, tears glistening at the corners of her eyes. "How do we make it stop?"

Dylan shook his head.

"Perhaps you should both move back in and I should go somewhere. Rent a hotel room with my mother."

"No." Dylan was grave, insistent. "I'd be afraid you'd never come back."

"I'd never do that to Melissa."

"Would you do it to me?" The question hung between them like stale air, until Dylan could no longer hold Carrie's gaze. Until, slowly, his fingers slipped from hers.

"Anyway, Melissa's nightmares aren't the reason I wanted to talk to you," he said.

"Oh?" Unease crept into Carrie's voice.

"A few of the boys were talking down at the harbour. There's a writer in town. He's been asking questions, wanting to know about Grady Spencer . . . and about Cal. He's been asking about you, too. Apparently, the asshole's writing a book." Dylan's nostrils flared as he drew in a breath. "Has he been to see you?"

Carrie froze, staring hard at the table.

Your son is still here.

"Carrie? I need to know—I won't let some money-grabbing prick harass my family."

You could have a life with him again.

Carrie looked up, staring directly at Dylan.

"You know what Sally's like," she said. "She'd go down for murder before she'd let some journalist through the door."

Dylan relaxed a little. "Good, that's good. Because the past is the past, you know? We all need to leave it behind and start looking forward. That's how we make it stop, Carrie. That's how it all goes away."

She couldn't speak.

You're wrong. The words repeated, over and over in her mind. *You're wrong because it will never stop. Not if my son is still out there. Not if there's a chance to save him. I owe him that.*

Carrie forced a smile to her lips.

"We'll get through this," Dylan said, reaching out and taking her hand again. "You, me, and Melissa. The three of us. Together."

The smile wavered. Carrie fought to keep it steady.

14

THE BLUE CLAM café was all dark wood and silver trim, with clean, modern furniture and nautical murals on the walls. It was just after four and it was already growing dark outside. Aaron sat at a table in the far corner, nursing a watery black coffee and watching the customers dotted around the room; students meeting after class, he guessed, and a few old timers waiting for the rain to ease off. He had a feeling they'd be waiting forever.

His gaze moved to the glass front of the cafe, where people hurried by, their collars pulled up and their umbrellas colliding. It felt good to see something resembling city life, even if it wouldn't last. In a few hours, the streets would be empty again. Cornwall in winter really was one giant ghost town.

Aaron was tired. After a few hours of tossing and turning, he'd given up on sleep and given into curiosity, spending the rest of the night and most of the morning hunched over his laptop in research mode.

While scouring news websites for evidence of the barman's macabre tales, he'd been surprised to find an abundance of stories, detailing lurid acts of animal mutilation and dismemberment right across the county. Each story contained sensationalist phrases like *devil worship* and *satanic ritual*, with no real evidence to prove such outlandish claims. Some even contained images of the slaughtered animals, with the gorier aspects blurred out.

What had been most perplexing to Aaron, however, was that the majority of stories had been reported long before Cal Anderson had disappeared from the face of the earth.

Losing track of time, he'd gone over the stories again, this time looking for discernible patterns and discovering that several of the attacks had occurred under a full moon or during summer and winter solstice. Symbols, drawn in blood, had been found on the animals' bodies or on nearby trees and rocks. Research into the occult, and more specifically, satanic ritual, had revealed that these same attacks had occurred on specific dates of the Satanic calendar, notably St Winebald Day, Candlemas, Feast Day, and Lamass Day.

Feverish from lack of sleep, Aaron had come to the startling conclusion that it was entirely possible satanic cults were indeed roaming the Cornish countryside and sacrificing animals—which shocked him, even if it did nothing to sway his belief that the devil was not real but a form of control, dreamed up to scare people into behaving themselves.

Cal Anderson was very real, though. Aaron had seen him with his own eyes. And there had been no evidence—regardless of local beliefs—to suggest that he was in league with the devil.

No. Cal Anderson was a victim just like those other poor children; the only difference being that Cal was still alive.

Now, with his notebook in front of him, Aaron stared at the list he'd made. Taking his pen, he crossed out all the attacks that had occurred before September, and all those he'd linked to satanic rituals. This left five attacks, including the two the barman had relayed last night, and the killing of Margaret Telford's dog, Alfie.

Aaron drew a ring around each attack and wrote: *Cal?*

A cold blast of air pulled him back to the room. Nat stalked through the door, short hair wet and glistening, eyes darting from table to table. Aaron raised a hand and watched with amusement as Nat collided with an empty-handed waitress.

Scowling, she stomped her way to Aaron's table.

"Glad you could make it," he said, closing the notebook.

Nat slumped onto the opposite chair. "I have to catch a bus in thirty minutes. You look like shit."

"Thanks."

The waitress approached and lifted her order pad in silence. Nat ordered a coke, Aaron another coffee.

"Good day at college?" he asked, once the waitress was gone.

"It sucked."

"What are you studying?"

"Does it matter?"

Aaron smiled. "There's this thing called small talk. You should try it some time. You might make a few friends."

"I didn't come here to make friends. I came here to get the rest of my money."

Nat glared as the waitress returned with their drinks.

"So, I've had an interesting couple of days," Aaron said, spooning sugar into his coffee. "Turns out the only people in Devil's Cove who want to talk to me are raving lunatics. Did you know there's a curse on your town?"

Nat sipped her coke and eyed the room. "It's not my town."

"Oh, that's right. You're getting out. Just as well, or an evil spirit might take a bite out of you."

"Look, do you have my money or not?"

Smiling, Aaron reached for his wallet, pulled out some notes, then held them just out of Nat's reach.

"You know, you were very helpful the other day," he said. "And I can see you're desperate to save what you can and get the hell out of that godforsaken place. So, how would you like to earn a little more cash to add to your escape fund?"

Nat leaned across the table and snatched the notes from his fingers. Once she'd checked to see it was all there, she tucked the notes inside her jacket pocket.

"Doing what, exactly?"

"Research," Aaron said. "Something's come up, a development. Which means I don't have time to get it all done myself. Primarily, I'd need you to build a profile of Grady Spencer. There's been very little about him in the newspapers, so it'll require some asking around, searching public records, that kind of thing." He paused to slide a sheet of paper across the table. "I've made you a list. There are no reports of any family, so let's start with the basics. Where did he live before moving to Porth an Jowl? What did he do for a living before he retired? Any history of mental illness or previous criminal convictions? And see if your foster carer knows how he got that limp."

Nat's face reddened. "Her name's Rose."

"Of course. Rose." Aaron was suddenly tempted to ask how Nat had ended up in care, but her expression made him quickly change his mind. "So, what do you think? There's a few hours work there. Maybe more if you do a good job. Perhaps even a special bonus if you can help me get a certain interview."

Nat's eyes narrowed. "You mean the Pengellys? Because I already told you—not happening."

"We'll see." Aaron flashed her a smile, which Nat countered with a glare. "So, what do you say?"

"What kind of development?"

"Pardon me?"

"You said something came up. A development. What kind?"

Aaron stared at her, suddenly tempted to tell all about his encounter with Cal Anderson. But he couldn't. Not yet. All Nat had to do was tell a single person that Cal had been seen in Devil's Cove and it would be pitchforks and burning torches, and any chance of Aaron finding him first would be snatched away.

No one was going to steal this opportunity from him. Not the people of Devil's Cove. Not even Carrie Killigrew. She had called him a liar, but he had seen hope flickering in her eyes. If there was a chance of getting her son back, he knew she wouldn't waste it by going to the police. They would take Cal away from her. She would never see him again.

Aaron stared at Nat. He shrugged.

"I'm not at liberty to say. Anyway, you haven't answered *my* question. What do you say? Do you want to be my research buddy?"

He watched as Nat curled her lips into a grimace.

"Not if you call me your *buddy*," she said.

"Excellent. Any questions? No? Good. Then feel free to get started right away."

Nat stared down at the list of research tasks. "How much am I getting paid?"

"Enough."

"Enough? That's not exactly an enticing proposition."

"Neither is being stuck in Devil's Cove for the rest of your life. Take it or leave it. It's up to you."

Aaron watched Nat's face pull into an angry scowl. After a long silence, she picked up the research list, folded it neatly in half, and slipped it inside her jacket pocket.

"Good. Now, off you go before you miss your bus." Taking a business card from his wallet, Aaron handed it to her. "Call me when you have something."

Nat stood. "So much for small talk."

She hovered for a moment, as if unsure what to do, then stomped towards the exit. Alone again, Aaron opened his notebook. He was relieved Nat had agreed to take on the research. He still had the Baker interview coming up on Friday, but it meant he was now free to focus on his hunt for Cal Anderson.

He eyed the list of remaining animal attacks. He would start searching tomorrow, in the safety of daylight.

15

Rose Trewartha's kitchen was warm and cosy, with floral print curtains hanging in the window and a bumblebee-shaped clock on the wall. The heat was like a welcome hug as Nat entered and threw her backpack down on the floor. A large pot of stew bubbled on the stove, tantalising her taste buds.

At the counter, Rose was busy slicing a freshly baked loaf of bread. Nat took in her portly frame, flowery apron, and shock of grey hair. Sometimes Rose reminded her of the archetypal fairy-tale grandmother.

"Dinner's in an hour," the woman called over her shoulder. "You got any homework, you best do it now."

Other times, she was just plain annoying.

"It may come as a surprise but I'm almost eighteen years old," Nat said, crossing her arms. "I don't need to be told to do my homework."

Rose turned, her round, ruddy face pulled into a scowl.

"How could I forget? You only tell me a hundred times a day."

"Whatever." A smile tugged at Nat's lips.

Rose had a good heart, she supposed. She was certainly more understanding than the rest of the carers who hadn't been able to cope with Nat's anger. In fact, if she thought about it, Rose had been more of a mother to her than her own had ever been. She would miss her when it was time to go.

Nat heaved her shoulders, suddenly wanting nothing more than to smoke three cigarettes, one after the other. But all that would lead to was another lecture from Rose. She thought back to her meeting with Aaron. She had almost turned him down— he'd been deliberately vague about how much he was willing to pay, which undoubtedly meant not very much—but in three months, Nat would officially be an adult, no longer a ward of the state. She would be on her own, and that meant she needed money.

Beggars can't be choosers. That's what Rose would have said on the matter. And it was true. Ignoring the unease creeping up on her, Nat sat down at the table, pulled a notebook from her backpack, and turned to a clean page.

"Hey, do you know how Grady Spencer got his limp?"

"What's that?"

"He had to get around with a walking stick. Was it old age or something else?"

Rose turned to stare at her. "He used that stick for as long as I can recall. Ever since he moved next door when I was a teenager. What's that got to do with anything?"

Nat scribbled into her notebook. "And you're what, fifty-four? So, we're talking roughly forty years ago. Do you know if it was an injury or a birth defect?"

"No, I don't. Are you going to answer my question?"

"What about where he came from? He wasn't from the cove originally, was he? Did he have family?"

"Natalie Tremaine, what is this all about?" Rose said, throwing her hands in the air.

Nat stared at her, unblinking. "School project."

"And pigs might fly. Tell me the truth."

"Okay, fine. I have a job. A temporary one."

"What kind of a job involves asking about Grady Spencer?"

"Research assistant. For a writer."

"A journalist?" Rose said, her ruddy cheeks growing a shade darker. "You know better than to talk to those damn reporters. You seen for yourself what they wrote about this town. Made up stories, that's what! No one knew what that mad man was up to next door. No one!"

Nat held up her hands. "He's not a journalist, Rose. He's an author. A crime writer."

"And how did you meet this crime writer?"

"He wanted to get inside Grady Spencer's house to have a look around. I may have helped him."

Rose's eyes grew round and wide. "So, you're breaking the law now? Dear Lord! I can't tell if you're trying to get me struck off the foster care register or put in an early grave! What were you thinking?"

"I need the money," Nat said, folding her arms again.

"You don't need it so badly you have to go breaking and entering. Christ, girl! I've turned a blind eye on the drinking, I've ignored the mood swings and the bad language, but I refuse to sit by and do nothing while you behave like a criminal! What other illegal activities is this so-called writer getting you involved in?"

"It's not like that."

Nat was getting a headache, and now something else was pressing down on her. Guilt. She quickly explained who Aaron

Black was, why he was here in Porth an Jowl, and what he had hired her to do. "See? It's all legit. No more breaking and entering, just research."

Rose was quiet for a long while, her gaze somewhere off to the side. She shook her head. "No, I don't like it. I want you to stay away from that man. People are trying to get on with their lives. All that book is going to do is stir everything up again. Do you want to be responsible for that?"

Nat stared at Rose. She opened her mouth then closed it again.

"I know you're almost eighteen," Rose said, less angry now. "I know you think I don't have a right to tell you what to do, but I worry about you. Especially now that Jago's gone and you're—"

A sudden anger rushed through Nat's body. "And I'm what? Go on, you can say it—now that Jago's gone and I'm all alone."

Rose stared at the floor. "You're not alone. You have me."

"Only for a few more months."

"You can stay until you're twenty-one, they've told you that."

"And you'll get less money for me. I'm not having you pay for me out of your own pocket. Besides, they've probably lined up some other helpless runt for you to take care of."

The words hung there between them, filling the room.

Nat stared at the notes she'd written. She shut her eyes.

"It's just research, Rose," she said. "A few days' work sat in front of my laptop."

Rose was unmoving, her face turned slightly away.

"You better do your homework," she said in a whisper.

Nat picked up her notebook and got to her feet. "I'm going up to my room."

Rose held up a hand, then heaved her round shoulders and let out a long, sad breath.

"Invite him to dinner," she said.

"There's no need for—"

"Oh, yes, there is. As your foster carer it's my duty to make sure you're not being exploited in any way. Invite him to dinner."

Nat stared uncertainly at Rose.

"Fine," she said.

If a home cooked meal and interrogation-like scrutiny was what it took to get Rose on board, then Aaron Black would just have to deal with it.

16

THE HOUSE WAS alive with noise. In the dilapidated kitchen, Cal tossed a chunk of wood into the furnace of the ancient Aga oven. Flames sprang up, licking the wood and making shadows dance around the room. Basking in the warm glow, he listened to the children's turbulent chatter floating out from the back room. It was a rare sound at the farm. Usually, at this time, the only sound in the house would be Jacob's voice as he delivered his evening lesson.

But Jacob wasn't here.

He'd left this morning while the others had slept, taking Heath with him. A business trip, Cynthia had told them in her usual, vague way. But Cal and the older ones had all come to know what a business trip meant. Jacob would be gone overnight. Tomorrow, he would return with a brown package tucked beneath his arm. They all knew what would be inside. It excited them. But not Cal. What the package contained made him feel like he had no control, which was no good to anyone.

A squeal of laughter pierced the air, followed by a scolding adult voice. Playtime was over.

Somewhere down the hall, a door opened and the children came spilling out. He turned in time to see three of them dart past the kitchen doorway, lanterns swinging through the dark. A second later, two of the youngest ones appeared—a boy and a girl no more than four years old, gently carrying another lantern between them. They stopped and stared into the kitchen. Their faces lit up with smiles as they spotted Cal.

He stared back.

Cut off the fingers and cut off the toes. Cook the skin until it's nice and crispy.

A dark-haired young woman stepped into view. Barely out of her teens, she was tall and athletic, her features sharp and angry in the dim light. She shooed the children along then turned in Cal's direction, her eyes burning into him like two hot coals.

"Morwenna, come! It's too dark!" The child's voice was shrill with panic.

The young woman remained for a moment longer, glowering at Cal, silently challenging him, before following the children.

Another body hurried by in the darkness. Probably Alison, he thought, who could always be found chasing after Morwenna and the little ones like a lost puppy.

The hall was quiet then, the children's voices still audible but dampened by ceilings and walls. Cal moved to the kitchen window and opened the shutter. Darkness shrouded the yard. It called to him. He closed his eyes, feeling the pull. In an instant he was back at Desperation Point, watching his mother choose between life and death. Watching that man spy on her.

Checking over his shoulder, he moved up to the back door. Icy tendrils crept in from beneath. He would run, all the way to the cove. Just to take a look. Just to make sure she still wanted him.

Why don't you listen to me, boy? I should beat you black and blue. I should cut that heart from your chest and feed it to Caliban.

Silently, Cal drew back the bolt.

"Where do you think you're going?"

The voice startled him. He spun around.

A sturdy, middle-aged woman with short red hair and angry eyes stood in the glow of the oven.

"Well, spit it out, boy," she said, thrusting a hand on her hip. "You were sneaking off again, weren't you? Off to wherever it is you go at night."

Rooted to the floor, Cal stared at the woman.

"How many times has Jacob told you?" she said, stabbing a finger at him. "But still off you go, thinking we don't know about it. Thinking we're stupid. Don't you care about us no more? Is that it?"

Cal shook his head, lowered his eyes to the floor.

The woman let out a heavy sigh. "You probably think old Cynthia here is a walkover, don't you? Easy to pull the wool over her eyes. But I know you go out every night, Cal. I know sometimes you wait until Jacob is . . . busy with other matters. But no more. If you leave tonight, I'll have no choice but to tell him when he comes back. You know what will happen then." Her face softened, but there was fear in her eyes. "Haven't you been through enough without making it worse for yourself? Without making it worse for all of us?"

Cal stood, frozen on the spot, his chest growing tight around his lungs.

The woman held out a hand. "Come away from the door, boy. There ain't nothing and no one left for you on the other side. Your place is here with us, with the Dawn Children." She waggled her finger, coaxing him towards her like a nervous animal. "Come on. Come and help old Cynthia fold the laundry. You'll thank me for it when Jacob gets back."

One foot in front of the other, Cal stepped away from the door.

"That's it. That's my boy. Set the younger ones a good example by doing the right thing."

Cal felt her hand wrap around his, a little too tightly. He kept his face blank as she led him from the kitchen and through the shadows of the hall, but at the centre of his chest a fire was burning. He was struggling to keep it contained.

The streets were empty and dark. Carrie took her usual route onto Cove Road and past Grady Spencer's house, this time without stopping, until she crested the hill. As she walked, she threw furtive glances over her shoulder, hoping to see a shadowy figure dart behind a parked car or melt into darkness. But she saw no one.

The rain was icy against her face. Her hands were numb despite the gloves she wore. Above, the night sky was heavy with clouds that blotted out the stars, masking Briar Wood in impenetrable darkness.

Carrie ground to a halt, an invisible wall preventing her from going any further. But she had to keep going. She had to know if he was here, waiting for her.

Swallowing down fear, she stepped onto the path that led to Desperation Point. Darkness wrapped around her, pulling her into the wood. She walked slowly, keeping her step light and soft, her breathing quiet and shallow. She cocked her head, trying to hear above the pattering of rain on branches.

There were no other sounds, just the rain and her sodden footfalls.

The familiar beam of the old lighthouse cut through the trees. Carrie's eyes darted in all directions, hoping for a glimpse of her son. But if Cal was here, he was well hidden.

Carrie walked on, rain washing away hope. She reached the tree line and slid to a halt. The lighthouse was up ahead, a bright needle pointing to the heavens. The cliff edge lay just beyond.

"Cal?" Her voice was a whisper. She turned back to the wood and tried again, this time louder. "Cal, are you here?"

The rain answered her in drips and drops. Behind her, the sea crashed against rocks.

"If you're here, come out. Come home with me. We can put things right. Please, Cal, I'm begging you!"

She waited and listened. The lighthouse beam swung through the trees, illuminating branches.

Aaron Black had lied to her. He'd poisoned her with hope.

But he seemed so earnest. So convincing. What a fool I am!

Shivering, she glanced over her shoulder towards the cliff edge.

Perhaps Dylan was right. Perhaps the only way to make it stop, to make it all go away, was to keep her eyes forward.

To never look back.

Carrie turned her head and stared into the blackness of Briar Wood. Could she do that? Could she give up on hope?

She stood, eyes searching the darkness, feet pinned to the ground, feeling like a butterfly trapped inside an airtight jar.

Could she give up on her son?

17

FRANCES CURNOW's home was in Penwartha, a tiny hamlet of brick houses flanked by rolling farmland, two miles south of Porth an Jowl. In summer, Aaron imagined the place would be green and leafy; the epitome of idyllic country living. But now it was all grey hues and splattered with mud, the emptiness of the surrounding fields almost suffocating.

"Are you from the papers, then?" Frances asked.

They stood in an enclosed yard behind the house, Aaron hanging back at the gate as Frances scattered food pellets on the ground from a bucket and a horde of clucking hens swarmed around her feet. Frances was in her mid-thirties, tall and slim, and not at all how Aaron had imagined her when they'd spoken on the phone.

"Er, no," he said, spying a large red hen advancing towards him. "I'm writing a book."

Frances watched with amusement as he scuttled away from the curious bird. "A book, eh? About Satanists?"

"Something like that."

"I see. And you want to know what happened to Aunt Bessie?"

Aaron raised an eyebrow.

"Our goat," the woman explained, as she threw out another handful of feed. "Don't look at me, the girls named her."

Aaron nodded, his eyes fixed on the marauding hens. "Yes. Aunt Bessie."

"Right, well, you best come in, then."

The kitchen was clean and modern. Aaron sat at a large oak table feeling grateful they were now inside and warming up, while Frances set about making coffee. His phone buzzed in his pocket.

It was a text message from Nat: DINNER AT ROSE'S TONIGHT. 6 PM. SHE WANTS TO MEET YOU. BE THERE OR THE DEAL'S OFF.

Aaron smiled as he texted her back. Since arriving in Cornwall, his diet had consisted of junk food and hotel snacks. Some home-cooked goodness was just what his body needed. Besides, he was curious to meet the woman who had lived next door to Grady Spencer all those years, blissfully unaware of the horrors transpiring in his basement.

Frances Curnow handed him a steaming mug of coffee and sat down. Aaron activated a digital voice recorder and placed it at the centre of the table. The interview began.

"I still can't believe it happened," the woman said, staring curiously at the recorder. "I mean, one day she was here, the next . . ."

Aaron watched her shudder.

"What happened to it? I mean, to Aunt Bessie?"

"The girls found her. I wished to God it had been me. Poor Kelly hasn't slept since. She's my youngest. Her sister's Leila."

She nodded to a framed photograph hanging on the wall, in which two young girls, the eldest no older than eight or nine, sat on bright red bicycles, their smiles bright as summer.

"Anyway, it was their job to feed Aunt Bessie each morning before school. She wasn't supposed to be a pet, I thought keeping a goat would be a greener way to keep the lawn short, plus I always wanted to try my hand at making cheese. But the girls loved that daft old goat, treated her as one of the family. Which made what happened that much worse."

Aaron waited as Frances drew in a breath, her eyes reflecting the horror of that morning.

"It was a bloodbath. They didn't just kill her. There were pieces of her all over the lawn. My first thought was an animal had done it, a stray dog or something. But then I found poor Bessie's head."

"Where was it?"

Frances exhaled. The tips of her fingers turned white against the coffee mug. "It was inside the front basket of Kelly's bike. Someone had put it there, deliberately, as if they wanted to make sure she'd be the first person to find it."

Aaron swallowed, forcing the grotesque image from his mind. "Who do you think did it?"

"The police suspected teenagers, but you can see where we live—there are six, maybe seven houses here, and my girls are the only children around. Besides, I don't think teenagers these days make a habit of wandering the countryside, mutilating animals, do you?" She paused to rub her eyes. "And of course, the papers talked about Satanists. Devil worshippers making blood sacrifices."

"You don't believe that?"

"I know there have been other attacks. Horses found with

their bellies slit open or their throats cut. But what happened to Aunt Bessie feels different."

Aaron leaned forward. "Different, how?"

Frances was quiet for a long while, haunted eyes staring into space. Then she said, "Because of the violence. If you'd seen what was done to her . . . it was as if whoever killed her was filled with pure rage. As if they couldn't stop until there was nothing left to rip apart."

As Aaron drove along winding country roads, he replayed the recording of Frances Curnow's interview. Her final words echoed in his mind.

Without knowing it, she'd confirmed what Aaron believed to be Cal Anderson's state of mind: a maelstrom of pure rage. He had seen it in the boy's eyes that night, two white hot flames blazing in the dark. It had terrified him. The savagery Frances had described, even more so. The attack on Aunt Bessie had been brutal enough, but the head in the basket was an elevated level of cruelty.

Why had these poor girls been targeted for such a heinous, brutal attack? What had they done to deserve it?

Because they were loved, Aaron thought. *They were punished for being loved.* He wondered if his next destination would reveal a similar pattern.

Glebe Farm was a short drive from Penwartha, and about a mile and a half southeast of Porth an Jowl. The farm was cold and wet, the yard a dirty stretch of concrete littered with old machinery and bordered by outbuildings and a granite farm-house that was slowly falling into ruin.

Closing the car door, Aaron shouldered his bag and slipped his voice recorder into his pocket. He grimaced as farmyard smells assaulted his senses.

He was unsure about turning up unannounced, but the farmer, a man named Ross Quick, hadn't responded to any of Aaron's calls or messages. Any other person would have taken it as a sign that Quick wanted to be left alone, but Aaron's curiosity was piqued—the attack on his farm was not only the most recent but also the most vicious.

Crossing the yard, he headed for the farm house and knocked on the door. He recoiled, wiping his knuckles against his jacket. Everything out here was covered in a glistening sheen of filth.

He waited, growing colder with each passing second. He knocked again. When there was still no answer, he wandered over to some farm equipment rusting in the corner and took a few pictures with his camera, then turned and pointed the lens at the dilapidated house. He couldn't imagine being a farmer, especially one like Ross Quick, who, according to the news story, lived alone. What a sad isolated life, Aaron thought, as he stared at the windows of the house.

Ross Quick was either hiding or elsewhere. It was possible he was out in the fields, but unlikely—the farmer had nothing left to farm. Circling the house, Aaron soon located the fields; barren stretches of earth sloping over a slight hill.

A barn stood off to the right. It was the old-fashioned kind, constructed from wood, with small windows high up near the roof, and a large pair of doors slick with mud. There was no padlock. Instinctively, Aaron glanced over his shoulder, then grabbed one of the looped handles and pulled. The door swung open a few inches.

The sharp odour of blood and death hung in the air, like the echo of a scream. Checking he was alone, Aaron pushed the door open further and stepped inside

The barn was empty. Empty except for the dark stains and splatters that covered much of the floor.

They were dry now, almost black in colour. Scraps of blood-soaked straw and wool lay scattered in between.

The sight was unnerving. The stench overpowering.

Stepping further inside, Aaron lifted his camera and took pictures. The flash went off like lightning strikes, illuminating the bloodstained floor and the arterial splashes on the support beams, rafters, and walls. Aaron stared in grim awe. A hundred sheep, the news story had said. All butchered.

A noise pulled him from his thoughts. A low growl that made his blood run cold.

Turning slowly, he saw a black and white sheepdog, its head lowered and its lips peeled back, revealing glistening fangs. Next to the animal, was a middle-aged man who looked like he hadn't slept in days, his unshaven face pulled into an angry glare. In the man's arms was a shotgun. It was pointed at Aaron's chest.

"What do you think you're doing?" the man said. "This is private property."

He raised the gun a little. By his side, the dog's growl grew louder. Aaron lifted his hands.

"I'm sorry," he said, taking a step back. "I tried the house but no one was there."

"And that made it okay for you to sneak around my farm, did it? To take pictures of things that ain't none of your business."

Ross Quick stepped forward, tightening his grip on the shotgun. The dog barked once, then whimpered as the farmer yelled at it to be silent.

"I have a mind to ask you to hand over that camera," he said.

Aaron glanced into the yard beyond, calculating his chances of escape. Even with just a few metres between them, he could smell the reek of alcohol. A sober man with a shotgun was dangerous enough, but a drunk man was deadly.

"I'm sorry," he repeated, taking another step back. "I tried calling. When I couldn't get hold of you I thought I'd take a chance and come out here to talk face to face."

Ross Quick glared at him, his eyes glinting dangerously.

"This don't look much like talk to me," he said. "This looks like snooping where you don't belong. I thought you newspapers were done with me. I gave you your interviews. Didn't get a penny for my time, either."

For a second, the farmer's shoulders sagged and the gun lowered an inch. Then he tightened his grip on the weapon and pointed the barrel at Aaron's chest once more.

Aaron's mind raced. He didn't want to die today, especially not in this blood-soaked barn.

"I'm not with the newspapers," he said, keeping his hands raised.

"Then who are you? What do you want?"

"My name is Aaron Black. I wanted to ask you about the attack on your livestock."

Ross wrinkled his brow. The tip of the shotgun lowered, now pointing at Aaron's stomach.

"You from the police? Because I already spoke to them, too."

Aaron shook his head.

"Well you ain't from the insurance company. Those bastards

won't give me a penny, all because I missed a couple of payments. I begged them. They didn't give two shits."

Aaron's eyes were fixed on the barrel of the gun, watching it sway from left to right, in time with the man's inebriated movements. He suddenly understood the man's frustration. Ross Quick hadn't just lost the sheep; he'd lost the farm, his livelihood. Everything. And right now, that made him even more dangerous.

Especially when he learned that Aaron was just another writer trying to make a living from other people's misery.

"Look, I'm sorry. I know I shouldn't have come here. But what happened to you is terrible. And not just to you. Someone is going around killing animals and destroying people's livelihoods. I want to find out who. I want to stop them from doing it again."

It wasn't exactly the truth. It wasn't exactly a lie, either.

"You didn't see anyone that night? Didn't hear anything?" Aaron asked.

The farmer shook his head. He lowered the gun a few inches. Beside him, the dog sat on its haunches, its eyes fixed on Aaron.

"I was sleeping," Ross said. "I'd had a bit to drink. Meg's barking woke me up. By the time I got to the barn, the sheep were already dead. Not just dead. Whoever killed them tore them apart. Lined parts of them up like dominoes."

"They killed all of them?"

"Every last one. I never seen such violence in all my days."

There it was again. Violence. Rage.

"You think it was Satanists like the papers say?"

Ross nodded. "Who else could it be? Perverted bastards. If I ever find them, I'll kill them with my bare hands."

He lowered the gun, letting it swing limply at his side. Relief surged through Aaron's body like a tranquilliser.

"It ain't right, destroying a man's livelihood like that." The farmer's voice trembled. "I got nothing now. The bank's taking the farm back. I won't even have a roof over my head." Beside him, the dog looked up and whined. Ross smiled sadly. "You're right, girl. I suppose I still got you."

"I'm sorry," Aaron said. He genuinely was. Across from him, Ross stood like a marionette with its strings cut. "I should go. I've wasted enough of your time."

The farmer didn't look up. "Plenty of time to waste now."

Daylight was already fading as Aaron drove away from Glebe Farm and along the road that would take him back to Porth an Jowl.

He was now more convinced than ever that Cal was responsible for the deaths of both Aunt Bessie the goat and Ross Quick's flock of sheep. Not only had the attacks occurred just a couple of miles outside of Porth an Jowl, but the similarities between the attacks were undeniable. In both cases, the animals had been subjected to horrible torture and mutilation. In both cases, parts of the animals had been laid out in deliberate fashion, for no other discernible reason than to taunt their owners.

Just like Margaret Telford's dog.

What kind of horrors had Cal Anderson been subjected to that he was now so poisoned by hate? Aaron could only imagine.

He was certain of one thing, though: wherever this path of investigation led him, he would need to look over his shoulder at every turn.

Because if Cal Anderson was capable of ripping apart an entire flock of sheep, what could he do to a lone, unarmed man?

18

ROSE'S KITCHEN was warm and welcoming. Aaron had arrived just a few minutes ago, and after a brief introduction, Rose had announced that dinner—or 'tea' as she had called it—was ready. Now, he and Nat sat at the table, while Rose served up beef stew and dumplings. Aaron thanked her for the invitation, then proceeded to attack the stew like a man rescued from starving in the wilderness.

"Tell me about yourself, Mr Black," Rose said, as they dined. Aaron had liked her immediately. Her eyes were honest and friendly, and she had a smile that could melt Winter's frozen heart. "It's not every day I have a famous author sitting at my table."

Aaron dabbed the corners of his mouth with a napkin. "Please, call me Aaron. And I wouldn't call myself famous."

"It's true," Nat shrugged. "I'd never heard of him."

"Don't be so rude." Rose waved a dismissive hand before returning her attention to Aaron. "It must be an exciting life."

Aaron shifted on his chair.

"Honestly? The most exciting things to happen in my life happen in here." He tapped his left temple, making Rose laugh.

"Still, you must love what you do? It's not many people who can say they're happy with their lot." She smiled warmly at Nat. "Guess we must be the lucky ones, Aaron."

Aaron smiled. *Lucky* wasn't a word he would have used to describe recent life events.

Rose continued with her polite interrogation. Where was he from? Where had he gone to university? How many books had he written? Was he married? Any children? Aaron answered as evasively as he could, occasionally glancing in Nat's direction, who watched him with amusement. Eventually, Rose's questions came to an end. Silence draped itself over the table as her jovial expression grew serious.

"Nat tells me she's helping you research a book about Grady Spencer," Rose said, interrupting the quiet.

Aaron nodded, noting her accusatory tone. "That's right."

Suddenly, he knew why he'd been invited to dinner.

Rose locked eyes with him. "Tell me, Aaron, I'm curious—why ever would you want to write a book like that?"

"Well," Aaron said, pausing to clear his throat. "I suppose because such a horrifying story needs to be told. It's this type of story that makes us feel safe in our beds at night, thankful that it hasn't happened to us but to someone else."

Rose leaned back, crossing her arms over her belly. "I see. The problem with that, though, is that it didn't happen to someone else, did it? It happened to us, right here in Porth an Jowl. And I can't see how writing a book about it will make any of us feel safe in our beds ever again."

Aaron glanced at Nat, who was busy staring at the table. Rose waved a hand. "Just my opinion, of course. But I'm concerned, like others in the cove, that this book of yours might do more harm than good."

"It's not my intention to cause harm," Aaron said, attempting to smooth out the irritation from his voice. "I'm simply trying to understand why Grady Spencer did what he did. Granted, it's not the most pleasant of subjects, but if we can understand the motives behind his actions, perhaps we can prevent something like this from happening again."

More silence. Aaron speared a chunk of beef with his fork and stared at it, his appetite rapidly fading.

"Tell me, Aaron," Rose said, after a long, awkward silence, "have you noticed that great archway of rock down at the beach, the one protruding from the left cliff?"

Aaron nodded. "I believe it's called the Devil's Gate."

"That's right. Do you know why it's called the Devil's Gate?"

"I can't say I do."

Rose shifted her weight, getting more comfortable. Aaron leaned forward, wondering where the conversation was heading. He had expected a pleasant dinner and an opportunity to interview his host, not to be the subject of a hostile interrogation. And why wasn't Nat coming to his rescue?

"It's from an old legend," Rose continued. "Hundreds of years old, it is. As you may know, Porth an Jowl translates from the Cornish language as *Devil's Cove*, but it can also be interpreted to mean the *Devil's Gate*. Legend has it that the archway of rock was a gateway to hell. One night, long ago, when Porth an Jowl was just a handful of fisherfolk, the gate opened and the devil came out. He rose up from the water to cross the beach and snatch the fisherfolk's children. Not because the people of the cove had done him any wrong, but because he was the devil. And the devil is evil incarnate. They say, to this day, that if you go down to the gate at night when the tide is low and you're standing in the right place, you can still hear those kiddies' screams coming all the way up from the fiery pits of hell."

A smile spread across Aaron's lips. "That's quite a story."

"It's more than a story," Rose said.

"How's that?"

"Because the devil came back again to take our children."

Laughter fell from Aaron's mouth, surprising even himself. "You don't believe Grady Spencer was the devil in disguise, do you?"

He was shocked to find no trace of amusement on Rose's face.

"Why not? Evil takes many forms. And what Grady Spencer did to those poor children was truly devilish."

"Grady Spencer was mentally unstable." The smile faded from Aaron's lips. "He was sick. A psychopath and a sadist. But he wasn't the devil."

He glanced across again at Nat, but she only shook her head.

"So, you're saying Grady Spencer did all those terrible things because he was unwell?" Rose said.

"That's exactly what I'm saying."

"Not because he had evil in him? Not because he was born bad?"

"I don't believe anyone's born bad," Aaron retorted. "I'm not excusing what he did, far from it. But I do think something terrible had to have happened to him to make him that way."

"And that's what you're hoping to do with your book, is it? Prove that Grady Spencer wasn't a monster but damaged goods? You want people to feel sorry for him?"

Tonight was going from bad to worse. "Not at all. Spencer

was a monster in every sense of the word. I'm just trying to understand why."

"Evil can't be understood, Mr Black." Rose's angry face stared at the space between them. "Bad people do bad things."

"Then how do you explain Cal Anderson?"

Aaron had the sudden urge to confess he had seen Cal, that he had witnessed the aftermath of his anguish and rage. How would Rose react, he wondered, if he were to tell her that the devil really was alive and well, here in Porth an Jowl?

He drew in a breath and shook his head. "Bad people do bad things because of illness or chemistry. Not because of ridiculous, superstitious nonsense like the devil made them do it."

Nat was staring at him, her mouth hanging open. At the end of the table, Rose grew silent and still.

"Let me tell you something, Mr Black. Some food for thought, if you like," she said at last, fixing him with a hawk-like stare. "You see, I know what outsiders like you think about a place like this. You come down here on your holidays, or your little research trips, and you think, 'what a funny little place with their silly superstitions and nonsense stories.' You say to yourself, 'Oh, aren't they so sweet and so naive?' But what you all fail to understand, Mr Black, is just how much we need those silly superstitions and nonsense stories.

"You see, Cornwall is a hard place to live. It's isolated. There's no jobs, no money. Winters are long and cruel. We're the ass end of the country, Mr Black, and nine months of the year, it feels like the rest of you forget we exist.

"Then summer hits and down you come for your ice creams and your pasties and your pretty cliffs and beaches. And as long as we have our superstitions and our stories, you'll keep coming. And as long as you keep coming, we'll have money in our pockets and food on our tables for another year."

She paused. When she next spoke, her voice was sad and pleading. "The thing is, Aaron, this town's been hit hard enough this year. A missing boy meant families stayed away in droves. And now, after all this horror next door, it's only going to get worse. You think your book will make families want to come back to our town again? You think it will make all our troubles go away?"

Aaron tried to speak but the words wouldn't come.

Rose shook her head, disappointment filling her eyes. "No, I didn't think so."

Dinner continued in subdued silence. Once the table had been cleared, Nat sent Rose off to the living room for a calming glass of port. Now, Aaron stood at the kitchen sink, sulking as he washed the dishes.

"You know, if that's how you try and get people on your side," Nat said, drying the clean plates and putting them away, "it's no wonder no one in this town wants to help you."

"I was defending myself," Aaron protested. "And by the way, thanks for coming to my rescue. Now Rose thinks I'm a know-it-all asshole from the city who's here for my own gain."

"Aren't you?"

Aaron flinched. "Is that what you really think?"

Nat leaned against the counter, watching him. "I think that's what the people of this town think. I think they'd tell you that the police are still identifying bodies, and that Cal's still on the run somewhere. People are hurting, Aaron. They've not had a chance to process it all."

"And you think I'm rubbing salt into their wounds?"

"I can guarantee that's what Rose is thinking right now.

What *I* want to know is why you're writing this book in the first place. You write trashy mysteries. It's a far cry from the real horror of what happened in this town. Why don't you just write another Sulky Winters?"

"It's *Silky* Winters," Aaron corrected her. "And I don't want to."

Nat flashed him a wry look. "Nothing to do with your last book sinking like the Titanic, then?"

Aaron's jaw swung open. "You've been checking up on me!"

"I was interested in your books, that's all. It's pretty easy to stumble across things on the Internet."

"Well, how about you mind your own business and stumble across the research I'm paying you to do?"

He could feel his mood turning to panic. Today had revealed a lot about Cal's psyche, but it hadn't brought Aaron any closer to finding him. And what about the book?

Nat was right. No one in this godforsaken town wanted to help him, especially not Carrie. Which was why it was imperative he found Cal, sooner rather than later, because if he didn't, he'd be filing for bankruptcy before spring.

"You find anything new about Spencer?" he asked.

"Only that he's had that limp for years."

"Anything else?"

"Not yet. I haven't had time."

"Well, find the time."

He thought back to his afternoon at Penwartha and at Glebe Farm. *Get it together, Black! Use that damn brain of yours.* There were three more attack sites on his list to visit. Perhaps they would reveal something, a clue to Cal's whereabouts. But before he could investigate them, he had an appointment with the

Baker family. At least they'd agreed to talk to him, unlike everyone else.

Nat was staring at him, eyebrow raised. "You've gone mute."

"Sorry. There's a lot on my mind."

The dishes done, he drained the sink of water. Nat dumped the towel to one side and pulled her tobacco pouch from her pocket.

"To do with your so-called 'development'?"

She stared at him, her eyes shifting from side to side. Aaron could almost feel her trying to penetrate his skull and read his thoughts.

"Those things will kill you," Aaron said, nodding at the cigarette she had almost finished rolling.

"So will the suspense if you don't tell me what you're up to."

"I don't know what you're talking about."

Tucking the cigarette behind her ear, Nat scowled.

"You're hiding something," she said. "This 'development'—is it to do with Cal Anderson?"

Aaron glanced away. She was sharp, this girl. Perhaps too sharp. He wondered if he should tell her. Two people searching for Cal Anderson would mean twice the chance of finding him.

But could Nat be trusted? Aaron shrugged. "Get that research done and *maybe* I'll think about telling you."

"I've got study time tomorrow afternoon. I'll work on it then."

"Good. Call me when you're done." Aaron smiled. The more he thought about telling Nat, the more it felt like the right thing to do. "I'm glad at least someone around here can stand the sight of me."

Nat wrinkled her face. "I wouldn't go that far."

19

A SHRILL BEEPING PULLED Nat from a dream in which she and
Jago were fighting bitterly. She shot out a hand towards her
mobile phone on the bedside table and silenced the alarm. All
those residual negative feelings leaked into the waking world as
she sat up amid a sea of black painted walls and posters of punk
bands, and immediately began rolling a cigarette. As she worked,
her gaze found its way back to her mobile phone.

Screw you, Jago, she thought. *You don't deserve my call.*

Dragging herself out of bed, she opened the window and let
in the grey, bitter morning. She smoked her cigarette and stared
into the empty street below. Even though it was Friday, the
thought of heading to college and spending her time with the
rest of the losers tainted her morning smoke. What was the
point when it all felt so . . . pointless? Her only chance now was
to save as much money as she could and head for London. What
she would do when she got there was another question entirely.
One for which she still had no answer.

Rose's voice rang up from downstairs, announcing breakfast
was ready. The muscles in Nat's neck tightened. Last night, Rose

had decided that Aaron Black was a despicable, unsavoury character, and had forbidden Nat from engaging in any further work for him. Nat had responded with a few choice words of her own and had stormed off to her room.

Rose had no right to tell her who she could or couldn't work for. And sure, Aaron Black was not the most likeable person she'd encountered, and his arrogance seemed limitless, but at least he didn't treat her like a damn child.

A thought struck her—if she could impress Aaron with her research skills, maybe he'd be open to letting her sleep on his sofa when she eventually made it to London, just until she could afford a place of her own.

Nat flicked the cigarette butt and watched the wind whisk it away. Closing the window, she moved to her desk and opened her laptop. If she was going to build an accurate profile of Grady Spencer's life, she would need to start at the beginning.

She spent the next five minutes seeking out birth and death registrars in Cornwall and ignoring Rose's repeated calls to the breakfast table. The good news was that the county's central registrar was walking distance from her college campus in Truro. The bad news was that the registrar was not open to the public. Instead, information had to be requested—and paid for—online, and even then, you could not undertake the research yourself but had to wait several days while it was collated for you.

"Damn it," Nat grumbled.

Making a mental note to ask Aaron for a research budget, she continued her search. A few minutes later, she found an alternative.

The Family Historical Research Society was a non-profit service, whose research library was contained within a grand

Georgian-era terraced building on Lemon Street. A quick search of their site revealed that library access was for society members only, but Nat was undeterred.

After breakfasting in near silence with Rose, she made her usual bus journey to college, then slipped away to the nearest cafe, where she drank black coffee and waited until the research library was open.

Upon arrival, Nat was greeted by the librarian, an ancient and bespectacled, white-haired man, whose name was Terence and who smelled faintly of boiled sweets. He listened earnestly as she spun a creative web of lies concerning a college project she'd been tasked with—which required tracing her family history—and while this was a relatively easy chore for the rest of her peers, for Nat, who had only recently discovered that she'd been adopted, it was proving an impossible task because she didn't have access to the right resources.

Terence nodded and sighed, and his eyes became glassy with pity. Finally, he agreed to let her enter for one hour only, on the condition that she paid for any photocopying and that she kept her visit a secret from her peers.

Nat's excitement quickly sagged as Terence showed her into the main library area. She'd expected a grand, musty hall filled with tall, cherry wood shelves. Instead, she was presented with a long and cramped room with yellowed ceiling tiles and harsh fluorescent strip lighting. Rows of cheap metal shelves containing boxes of files filled the space. The librarian's desk sat at the end of the room. An ancient computer sat on top. Next to the desk, a rickety photocopier looked as if it might collapse with one press of a button.

Terence explained how the shelving system worked then pointed out a floor map pinned to a noticeboard.

"Births are over there," he said, pointing to the left side of the room. "Marriage is in the middle. Death is on the right. Just like life, I suppose."

Nat nodded. Where did she start? She knew the date Grady Spencer died but that was about it.

Terence hovered beside her.

"Looks daunting, doesn't it?" he said, tipping his head towards the shelves. "Especially for you children today when all you need to do is look on the Internet. I'd be happy to assist if you need it."

Nat stared at the shelves, feeling them bear down on her.

"I'm not like other kids," she said. "And I'll be fine on my own, thank you."

Taking the hint, Terence raised his eyebrows. "Very well, if you think so. You have one hour."

She watched the librarian shuffle over to his desk and sit down. Then Nat pulled a notebook from her bag and stepped towards the shelves. She spent the next ten minutes stomping up and down the aisles and repeatedly referring to the shelving map in a frustrated bid to understand the library's ridiculous filing system. Twice, she looked up and was annoyed to see Terence watching her, an amused smile on his lips.

Fine, don't help me, she thought. But hadn't she just told him she could manage? Pushing the irritation down, she narrowed her eyes and continued her search for Grady Spencer's death certificate.

Another ten minutes passed by. Bubbling with exasperation, Nat eyed the wall clock. She was no closer to finding the certificate even though she was certain she'd finally worked out the system.

Perhaps it wasn't here.

Exiting the maze of shelves, she marched up to the desk, where Terence sat in front of the computer. He looked up, one expectant eyebrow arched.

"Can't find what you're looking for?" the old man said with a hint of a smile.

Nat bit her lip and shook her head.

"You're looking for a death certificate, I presume? When did the person in question pass away?"

"Three months ago," Nat said, her words clipped.

"Ah, that explains it. A copy of the certificate won't have been shelved yet, you see. We're just a skeleton crew of volunteers, we can only go as fast as we can. Which isn't all that fast, these days."

Disappointment pulled at Nat's shoulders.

Some research assistant you are, she thought. *You can kiss staying on Aaron's couch goodbye.*

Terence leaned forward, pushing his thick-lensed glasses back up his nose.

"We could try the database. It won't have the death certificate, but we can cross-reference the county parish registers. If the person you're looking for was ever baptised, married or buried within church grounds, there should be a record."

Nat stared at the dinosaur of a computer weighing down the librarian's desk. It had to be older than she was. And what would happen when she told Terence who she was searching for? As kind and helpful as the old man was, she had a feeling his benevolence would be immediately revoked. But the alternative was to walk away with nothing.

Screw it.

Nat sucked in a breath and pushed it back out.

"Okay, fine," she said. "I'm looking for Grady Spencer."

A veil of recognition, then confusion fell over Terence's features. "You mean that . . . you think you could be related to *him*?"

"I'd rather not discuss it," Nat said, a little too forcefully. She took another breath, forcing the tension from her features. "Please. Could we just look?"

Something had changed in the way the librarian was looking at her. Before, there had been sympathy. Now, there was fear.

Nat nodded at the computer. Let him believe it, she thought. After all, Grady Spencer was only marginally worse than her own parents, and she'd already conned her way into the library; what did it matter?

Terence cleared his throat. His skin had paled to the colour of skimmed milk. "Grady Spencer . . ."

He turned to the monitor and tapped on the keyboard with his index fingers. They waited in silence, avoiding each other's gaze, as the computer processed information.

"Here we are," Terence said at last, working the scroll wheel on the mouse with a shaky hand. "Grady Spencer."

Nat leaned over his shoulder, desperate to see what had been found. Her eyes grew wide and round. "You're sure it's the right Grady Spencer?"

"Ain't too many folk around here with that name."

Nat stared at the marriage certificate on the computer screen.

"Grady Spencer had a wife," she breathed.

20

ZENNOR WAS a tiny coastal village with a population of approximately two hundred people, most of whom lived in old cottages over a scattering of quiet streets. At the centre, the small and ancient St Senara's church stood directly opposite the Tinner's Arms—a pub that had been serving ale for over seven hundred years.

Aaron pulled into the car park at the edge of the village; a gravel stretch of potholed ground surrounded by tall hedgerows. The drive had been short but perilous, along narrow and winding single lane roads that predated the modern vehicle. Anxious to get his feet back on the ground, Aaron climbed out of the car, then swore under his breath as he realised he'd left his umbrella back at the hotel. The rain had started up again during the night and now it fell in a depressing drizzle with no sign of stopping soon.

Pulling up the collar of his jacket, he headed for the road. He could hear the low roar of the ocean somewhere behind him as he entered the village. Passing the church, he peeked through the open door. The interior was small and archaic.

Early this morning, he'd read about how one of the pews had an ornate carving of a mermaid etched into the wood; something to do with a local legend. His thoughts turned to last night's conversation with Rose Trewartha, and his cheeks started to burn.

Clearing the village without seeing a single person, Aaron found the private lane that led to the Bakers' home. A hundred metres along, the lane opened on to a gravel drive

A large granite house with a slate roof stood in the centre of a sodden lawn. Beyond it, cliffs the colour of rust rose like giants from the swell of a steel-grey ocean. Aaron was momentarily transfixed, his breath snatched away.

And then he remembered why he was here.

Charles and Anthea Baker were both in their early fifties. He was a retired Naval officer, while she had once made a living as a seamstress. For the past eight years, they'd run their sizeable home as the Clifftop Guest House, serving bed and breakfast to tourists during spring and summer. Like other small businesses dependent on the tourist trade, the guest house was closed for winter.

Charles Baker was short and stout. There was strength there but it had turned soft. Anthea was taller, slimmer, with a furtiveness about her that reminded Aaron of a hare.

Charles made a pot of coffee and the three sat down in a small living room with moss-green carpet and patterned flock wallpaper. Introductions and small talk were quickly exhausted.

"If you're ready, could you tell me about your son?" Aaron said after a prolonged silence. His digital voice recorder sat on the coffee table between them. All he'd gleaned so far was that Toby Baker had disappeared in 2007, and that his remains had been among those discovered at Grady Spencer's house.

Charles and Anthea stared at each other, both waiting for the other to speak. Anthea began.

"Toby was a happy boy," she said, her hands clasped neatly over her knees. "Always smiling and laughing. A bit of a clown, really. Everything was a delight to him."

Aaron leaned back on the sofa, feeling years of grief sweep across the room like a wave.

"He was bright, too," Anthea continued. "Not quite top of the class, but certainly nowhere near the bottom. And he was curious, always wanting to know how things worked. Why things were the way they were." She paused for a moment, the smile on her face wavering. "Perhaps he was a little too curious."

Aaron picked up his cup. It was good to give his hands something to do. He cleared his throat. "Did Toby have friends?"

He directed this question at Charles, who so far had been sitting in a silent daze. The man blinked, as if waking from a dream. When he spoke, his voice was quiet and measured.

"Yes, of course. He was a popular boy. No one had a bad word to say about him."

Aaron nodded, distracted by the blinking red light of the digital recorder. He looked up again, catching Anthea's disquieting stare.

"And that day . . . the day Toby went missing?" he prompted.

Husband and wife stared at each other. Something passed between them, through them, out into the air. It was heavy and smothering. Aaron recognised it instantly. Guilt.

"It was the afternoon, the first Sunday of August," Anthea said. "We'd been to church that morning and after lunch we decided to go for a walk along the cliff path. It's something we did occasionally, as a family. Toby loved the ocean, didn't he, Charlie?"

Beside her, Charles had slipped into a kind of trance. He gave a slight, faraway nod.

"That day, we put on our boots and followed the coastal path westward," Anthea continued. "Do you know, Mr Black, you can walk all the way across to St Ives? If you're ever here on holiday and you enjoy walking, you should give it a try. You'll see some truly stunning views, but you'll need a good pair of walking shoes."

Aaron smiled politely.

"That Sunday was nice and warm." Anthea unclasped her hands and slipped them beneath her thighs. "There were people walking the path. Tourists mostly, but a few familiar faces as well. Toby was certainly an adventurous child, but he knew he needed to be safe on the path, that being reckless could end badly. Well, with all the people around, he was in an excitable mood. He loved the summer, you see. He loved all the noise and new faces. And so, he wouldn't wait for us. He kept running on ahead, weaving his way between the bodies, showing off to the tourists about how clever he was on those paths, I suppose.

"Charles and I, we both called after him, but he raced on. We came to a section in the path where it suddenly dips and disappears behind a large outcrop of rock. When we got to the other side a couple of minutes later . . . the path was empty."

Anthea reached out a trembling hand. His mind still elsewhere, Charles automatically slipped his hand over hers.

"Toby was gone," Anthea said. "Just like that. One minute, he was there in the distance, the next . . . it was like he vanished into thin air."

Aaron stared from husband to wife, their sadness soaking into him like rain.

"All this time we thought he'd fallen into the sea." Anthea stared at Aaron with red-rimmed eyes filled with horror. "I wish he had. It would have been a merciful death in comparison."

What air had been left in the room was gone. Aaron's chest heaved. Rose's words returned to him again. What was he doing here? Why was he writing this book, stirring up terrible memories?

"I'm so sorry for your loss," he said, wanting nothing more than to be far away from the Bakers and their unbearable grief.

Anthea nodded, her tired eyes telling him she'd heard that line a hundred times before. "Tell me, Mr Black, do you know much about the other children? Do you know why—why he took them?"

Aaron shook his head.

"I'd like to know why he chose our boy," Anthea said. "Why choose him over some other child? Is that something you can help us understand with your book?"

Aaron shifted in his chair. He opened his mouth and closed it again. Did he tell her it was unlikely? That she was better off accepting she would never know because Grady Spencer was dead, and the reasoning behind the selection of his victims had died with him? That she would ask herself the same question, over and over, until the moment of her own death?

He averted his gaze from the Bakers, who were both now looking at him with hope in their eyes. He needed to tell them something, anything.

"I hope so, Mrs Baker," he said, nodding. "I truly hope so."

"You know, they couldn't find the rest of his body. Only his skull," Anthea said. "How can we let go when the rest of him is still missing?"

———

Guilt weighed heavy on Aaron's shoulders as he said goodbye to the Bakers and began making his way back to the village. Halfway along the lane, he slid to a halt. Something else was pressing down on him. Something he couldn't quite figure out.

He turned back to the depressing gloom of the Clifftop Guest House and to the stark beauty of the cliffs beyond. Something about Anthea's story didn't feel right.

A few minutes later, after negotiating muddy fields, Aaron emerged onto a rocky, winding path that travelled along the cliff's edge and disappeared into the distance. Wind and rain whipped his hair and battered his clothes. Far below him, the ocean boiled and churned, crashing violently against the rocks.

Ignoring his mounting fear—he'd never been a fan of heights—Aaron began walking along the coastal path, retracing the steps that the Baker family had taken one devastating afternoon.

The path twisted and bucked beneath his feet, dropping towards the sea then rising up until Aaron became breathless and his legs ached. Soon, the path descended again, twisting around a large, rocky outcrop.

This was the spot where the Bakers had lost their boy forever. Aaron followed the path around. The wind howled as it blasted him, threatening to knock him into the depths below. He came to a standstill.

The path straightened out again. The feeling that something wasn't quite right intensified. As he turned his head to the left and stared up at the barren cliff face sloping above him, he suddenly understood what was wrong.

At the time of Toby Baker's disappearance, Grady Spencer had been seventy-two years old and had walked with a limp. How had he managed to negotiate the potentially dangerous cliff paths of Zennor and abduct a child seemingly into thin air?

Aaron discovered the answer to the second part of the question a moment later, when the path forked in two. Following the left path, he climbed upward, until the ground flattened out and the village came into view once more. To his surprise, the path led him back to the large stretch of gravel where he'd parked his car.

Had Grady Spencer lured the Baker boy away from the cliff top and into a waiting vehicle? But how? Perhaps he'd used his age as a decoy—an old man in need of assistance after exhausting himself on the cliff. Passing tourists would have seen a grandfather being helped by his caring grandson.

But hadn't Anthea just said that the path had been empty? How could an elderly man with a limp have the speed and agility to lure Toby from the cliff path and disappear before the boy's parents had turned the corner? Surely, it was impossible.

21

AARON PACED about his hotel room in a distracted haze. It was entirely possible his intuition was wrong, but the more he thought about it, the more he was convinced that he had stumbled upon something on that cliff path.

Grabbing a coke from the mini-bar, he swallowed a mouthful, then sat down at the writing desk. He opened his laptop and began sifting through the various research files he'd collated on Grady Spencer, until he came upon a folder titled: *Victims*. Inside were scans of newspaper articles, pulled from online databases and detailing the disappearances of each of Spencer's known victims.

Aaron pored over one article at a time, caffeine buzzing through his brain as he scribbled down names, dates, and places onto a clean page of his notebook.

Twenty minutes raced by. Aaron leaned back on the chair, perspiration beading his brow as his eyes flicked over the list he'd made.

Reece Pilkington, 8 years old. Disappeared August 2001 from harbour area, St Ives. Family holiday—Grady Spencer aged 66

Lee Mallon, 8 years old. Disappeared June 2004 from Market Jew St, Penzance. Mazey Day (local festival)—Grady Spencer aged 69

Toby Baker, 9 years old. Disappeared August 2007 from cliff path near family home, Zennor—Grady Spencer aged 72.

Neal Carr, 5 years old. Disappeared July 2009 from promenade, Penzance. Family holiday—Grady Spencer aged 74.

There was something here, but what?

The hotel room phone pierced the silence, startling him from his thoughts.

"Good afternoon, Mr Black," the young man at the front desk said. "There's a young lady here to see you. Nat Tremaine?"

"I'll be right down."

Making his way to the lobby, Aaron found Nat sprawled in one of the armchairs, hood pulled up over her head, right foot resting on top of her left knee, military boots on full display.

"What are you doing here?"

"Well, hello to you, too," she said, staring up at him with a wry smile. "I'm here because I found something."

"You're not the only one. Let's go up to my room."

At the front desk, the receptionist raised his eyebrows, then quickly looked away as Nat shot him a glare.

Upstairs, Aaron picked up clothes from the floor and pulled up a second chair to the desk. He offered Nat a coffee, which she refused, while standing by the door with her hands shoved inside her jacket pockets.

"What did you find?" Aaron nodded to the chair next to him.

Sitting down, Nat took a notebook from her bag and a folded bundle of printouts.

"Grady Spencer had a wife," she said, handing Aaron a copy of a marriage certificate, before reporting what she had uncovered.

Kathleen-Ann Nancarrow had been born 29th May, 1944, and had lived most of her short life in the village of St Just in Roseland, situated on the east coast of Cornwall. Although the details of how she met Grady Spencer were currently lost to the annals of time, what was known was that they were married at St Just's Church, 16th September, 1963. Kathleen had been 19 years old, Grady Spencer, 28.

"But I thought Rose confirmed Spencer moved to Porth an Jowl alone," Aaron said, studying the marriage certificate.

"He did." Nat handed him another printout. "Kathleen-Ann Nancarrow died 14th March, 1966. Less than three years after she married Grady Spencer. Check out the cause of death."

Aaron read through the details of the death certificate.

"Suffocation from drowning?"

"I pulled this from an online archive of local news." Nat said, handing him another printout—a scanned newspaper article dated, 17th March, 1966. Set within the news article was a photograph of Kathleen-Ann Nancarrow and Grady Spencer on their wedding day. She was small in stature and fragile looking in her simple white gown, while Spencer stood like a giant beside her, staring intensely at the camera.

"Kathleen-Ann was found on the bank of St Just Creek by

churchgoers. The story says that after marrying Spencer and moving out of the village, she became a recluse, cutting herself off from her family. Spencer claimed his wife had been suffering a long depression, ever since a miscarriage had left her unable to get pregnant again. He let her friends and family believe she killed herself."

"You don't think she did?"

"She was married to a serial killer. What do *you* think?"

"I think you've made a good start. But there's more to find out here." He handed her back the news article and the certificates. "Keep going."

The pride in Nat's eyes turned to disappointment as she stuffed the documents inside her bag.

Aaron glanced at his list of Spencer's victims:

Reece Pilkington, 8 years old. Disappeared August 2001 from harbour area, St Ives. Family holiday—Grady Spencer aged 66

Lee Mallon, 8 years old. Disappeared June 2004 from Market Jew St, Penzance. Mazey Day (local festival)—Grady Spencer aged 69

Toby Baker, 9 years old. Disappeared August 2007 from cliff path near family home, Zennor—Grady Spencer aged 72.

Neal Carr, 5 years old. Disappeared July 2009 from promenade, Penzance. Family holiday—Grady Spencer aged 74.

"You said Grady Spencer walked with a limp for as long as Rose could remember, right?" he said. "How long are we talking?"

Nat shrugged as she stared at the floor. "About forty years. Spencer moved next door when Rose was a teenager."

Aaron's eyes shot back to the victims' details, racing through each line of information. Something was connecting in his mind, but it wasn't making itself clear.

"Spencer's victims—the ones identified so far—were all male and under the age of ten," he said, thinking aloud. "All were taken during the summer months, which would have meant lots of tourists and big crowds. Which, in turn, would have made it easy to lure a kid away without the parents noticing until it was too late . . ." Aaron closed his eyes for a moment. "Which makes sense with every one of his victims, except Toby Baker."

"The boy whose parents you visited today? Is this to do with your development?" Nat said, peering at the list of victim details.

Aaron stood and began pacing the room. "How does an old man with a walking stick snatch a kid from a dangerous cliff path without, one, doing himself an injury, and two, getting caught? The Bakers told me there were walkers on the cliff that day but not hundreds. They said Toby ran on ahead and disappeared behind an outcrop of rock. When they turned the corner minutes later, he was gone. They've spent years thinking he'd fallen to his death, his body swept out to sea."

What was his subconscious trying to tell him?

What was he missing? Returning to the desk, he snatched his notebook from Nat's hands and quickly added another name to the list.

Cal Anderson, 9 years old. Disappeared August 2010 from beach, Porth an Jowl, presumed drowned—Grady Spencer aged 75.

"Cal was kept in captivity for seven years until he was found unconscious on the shore," Aaron said. "With the other victims, there are gaps of two to three years between each abduction. Why the difference? Why did he get to live? And what about Noah Pengelly?"

"Spencer didn't abduct Noah. Cal did."

"How do we know that?"

There was a long pause before Nat spoke again. "Because Noah told Jago. And Jago told me."

Snatching up the pen again, Aaron added yet another name to his list.

Noah Pengelly, 4 years old. Disappeared May 2017 from backyard of home, Porth an Jowl—Cal Anderson aged 15. Grady Spencer aged 82.

Synapses fired in his brain. A picture was forming. "There's another difference between Cal and the other victims," he said. "What do we know about the day Cal vanished?"

"The police reckon he wandered from the beach to explore one of the sea caves, found an old smugglers tunnel, and followed it right into Grady Spencer's basement."

"Which means Cal wasn't a planned abduction."

The picture was becoming clearer. He could almost see it. "We know the remains of at least eight victims were found in Spencer's house. According to the most recent press release, forensics established that the murders of the four remaining unidentified victims *precede* those of the identified. Which makes five-year-old Neal Carr the last child to die by Spencer's hand. Spencer was already seventy-four. Seventy-five when Cal walked into his basement a year later. And then there were no more victims. Not until nearly seven years later, when Noah Pengelly was snatched from his backyard—which is a very different and very risky *modus operandi.*"

Aaron stared at the list, the words jumping up at him from the page. *Damn it, what are we missing?*

Beside him, Nat shook her head. "You know what I don't get? How does someone as terrifying as Grady Spencer persuade any of those poor kids to go off with his ugly ass? Most of them were old enough to know about stranger danger, don't you think?"

And just like that, the picture snapped into focus.

Aaron looked up from the list of victims.

"You're right," he said, his voice trembling with excitement. "Most of those boys *were* old enough to know about stranger danger. But what if those strangers happened to be other kids?"

Realisation sank claws into their minds.

Nat looked up, eyes growing wide. "You mean—"

"He groomed them," Aaron said. "That sick psycho groomed each of his victims to lure the next. Those poor kids probably thought they were bringing in a new friend."

Nat's usual bravado was gone, replaced by quiet horror. "And Cal?"

"Perhaps Spencer had grown too old to carry on his life's work. Perhaps he saw an opportunity for his legacy to continue."

Silence descended over the room.

"That's quite a theory," Nat said, at last. "Pity you don't have any evidence to back it up."

"But what if it's true? What if I *found* evidence? This book could blow the whole case wide open."

"And make you a rich man. What about the victims' families?"

"If it was my child, I'd want to know the truth."

"You think you'd feel better knowing that not only was your child brutally murdered but they'd also been brainwashed into being an accomplice?"

"No, but—" Aaron felt a stab of irritation. Why was he having to justify himself to a seventeen-year-old? "Look, there's clearly a crucial part of the story missing from the police investigation. We could do something about it. And if by doing something about it, I get to write my book and you get to earn a little money to help you escape small town hell, then what's so wrong with that?"

Nat glared at him, her nostrils flaring. "If you can't see what's wrong with profiting off the murders of young children, then you're no better than the tabloids."

"You didn't seem to have a problem with profiting off their murders when you broke into Grady Spencer's house."

Nat's face grew a deep shade of scarlet. Her jaw fell open, then snapped shut. Aaron heaved his shoulders as he paced the room once more. This was no time for a moral debate. The damage had already been done to those families. Grady Spencer was responsible for their pain. All Aaron was trying to do was tell the story. And if by telling this story he saved his career, then there wasn't even a debate to be had. Which was why Nat needed to know the truth.

"I saw him," he said, coming to a halt. "I saw Cal."

"*Excuse* me?"

He quickly told her about following Carrie that night, about seeing her almost end her life, about seeing Cal, about the animal attacks and his visits to Penwartha and Glebe Farm.

Nat was silent as he spoke, her complexion growing pale.

"Don't you see?" Aaron said, spinning on his heels. "Cal is

alive and he's out there. If he really has been brainwashed by Grady Spencer, if he's capable of killing animals, of abducting children, it's only a matter of time before he goes one step further. Porth an Jowl still isn't safe. Carrie and her family still aren't safe. We could do something about it."

"So, this is why you've got me doing your research? So you can go on a bear hunt?" Nat laughed, but there was no humour in her voice. "You're insane."

"Possibly," Aaron told her. "It's like looking for a needle in a haystack, I know. But unless you have any better ideas, what else can I do?"

"Here's an idea. How about going to the police and telling them who you saw up at Desperation Point?" She shook her head. "Have you even told Carrie?"

"I tried. She wouldn't listen. And I can't go to the police, not yet. They'll want evidence. Without it I'm just another prank call."

Nat stood and slung her bag over her shoulder. "Yeah, well, good luck. I'll keep looking into Grady Spencer but I'm not traipsing around the countryside, hunting Cal Anderson. I'm too young to have that kind of a death wish."

She moved to the door.

Aaron held up a hand. "Wait. Does that mean Rose will be hearing about what I've told you?"

"Which part of *death wish* didn't you understand?"

"Fine, so for now let's keep everything between you and me."

Hovering at the door, Nat glared at him. Her shoulders sagged. "The way I see it, if you want to find Cal, you have two options. The first, you continue following Carrie until either he makes another appearance, or she has you arrested."

"And the second?"

"Try using a map, dumb-ass."

Aaron followed Nat's gaze until he was staring at a framed print hanging on the wall, depicting an aerial view of Cornwall.

"I'm not sure what—"

Nat threw her hands in the air. "Plot out the attacks!"

Muttering under her breath, she pulled the door open and let it slam behind her as she left.

Aaron stared after her, blinking.

"She's right," he said. "You *are* a dumb-ass."

He had an ordnance survey map somewhere, purchased from a service station when he'd first entered the county. Jumping up, Aaron hurried over to the desk and began rifling through the mess of notepads and printouts stacked on top. He found the map a second later and unfolded it, spreading it out on the floor.

Grabbing his laptop, he started going through his notes on the five animal attacks he believed Cal was responsible for, including Aunt Bessie the Goat and Ross Quick's dismembered flock of sheep, then marked their locations on the map with a black marker pen. Next, he located Porth an Jowl. He quickly discerned that all five attacks had occurred between one and three miles from the town.

Trembling with excitement, Aaron drew a circle around the town and animal attack sites. If Cal really was responsible for the attacks—and Aaron was convinced that he was—then the circle represented his hunting ground.

It was within that circle that Aaron would find him.

But how?

Even though the circle covered an area of just a few miles, it was nearly all farmland. There were a few villages but he doubted Cal would be found in any of them. He would either be on the move or hiding where he'd be difficult to find—in woodland or abandoned structures, or outbuildings belonging to farms.

Even with the map, searching for Cal would be like searching for a grain of salt in a sandpit.

Aaron needed a plan.

22

Cal had been standing at the bedroom window for a long while, watching banks of rain clouds draw across the sky like stage curtains. Now dusk had fallen over the land, casting the fields in shadows. The oncoming darkness made his stomach twitch. For the briefest of seconds, he was back in Grady Spencer's basement, cold steel bars pressed against his skin. Then, like the day, the image was gone, replaced by his mother's face.

It had been three days since he'd last seen her. Three days in which he'd been forced to remain at the farm, the pressure that was always present in his chest growing stronger, until his bones ached and his lungs gasped and his heart threatened to rupture. He should have slipped away, waited until everyone was asleep, but Cynthia had made it clear what would happen. She would tell Jacob.

You should cut out her tongue, then she won't say a word. That would be fun, wouldn't it, boy? Tasty, too.

The problem was Jacob had already returned.

Exhaling plumes of frosted breath, Cal turned from the

window and stalked through the shadows, passing bare walls and empty bunk beds.

Throwing open the door, he stepped into the darkness of the landing. A deep, commanding voice floated up from downstairs. The others were gathered in the meeting room, listening to Jacob's nightly lesson. Cal knew he should be there, that to be elsewhere was a sin. But tonight, he didn't feel like it.

Besides, time had slipped away from him again, his thoughts repeatedly returning to Desperation Point, to his mother leaning precariously on the cliff edge, to the stranger who had been watching her. The man was a threat, Cal could see that now.

You should have taken care of him when you had the chance, boy.

The house had fallen silent. Tonight's lesson had come to an end. Somewhere below, the meeting room door opened. Cal shrank back as lanterns balled light onto the walls and feet raced up the stairs. The children filed into the bedroom, unaware of the figure cloaked in the shadows of the landing.

Cal listened to the rise and fall of their excited chatters. It was a sound that could often fill him with happiness. Other times, it was a sound that triggered frightening, violent urges.

Look at all those little hands and toes and chubby red cheeks. Ripe as juicy apples waiting to be peeled.

Another figure ascended the stairs, her features sharp and angry in the lantern light. Morwenna. Cal watched as she ground to a halt outside the bedroom door, her body tensing. Lifting the lantern, she turned her head in his direction.

"Jacob wants to see," she said, her words short and sharp.

A young voice called out from the bedroom. "Morwenna! Jack took my blanket!"

The young woman swore under her breath, shot Cal another

glare, then stalked into the bedroom. Cal tuned out her raised voice as he made his way downstairs and along the hall, stealing past the open meeting room door, where bodies still gathered, lingering in the warmth of an open fire. As he passed the kitchen, he saw Cynthia standing next to the coal oven, watching over a pan of heating milk.

Startled, she looked up, catching his gaze. A veil of guilt fell across her face. Then she was gone from view. Cal reached the end of the hall, stopping before a door, its painted surface cracked and peeling like everything else in the house. The pressure in his chest was becoming unbearable.

He knocked and stared at the soft glow of electric light seeping beneath the door. The feeling in his stomach turned into a swarm of bees as a voice told him to enter.

The study was cramped, with a low ceiling and cluttered bookshelves lining the walls. Jacob sat at an old oak desk, soft lamp light illuminating his features. He was a small, middle-aged man, with a lean, wiry frame and cropped, dark hair; the kind of nondescript man that would be passed by unnoticed in the street—unless you caught his attention.

It was his eyes that gave him his power, Cal had quickly come to understand. They were furtive and intelligent, darting about the room, absorbing every minute detail. And yet, underneath, there was something dark and predatory lurking, a savageness that belied their outward benevolence.

Jacob looked up as Cal entered, fixing him with a stare that penetrated skin and bone, that left him feeling as small and weak as the little ones upstairs.

"The children were whispering tonight," Jacob said, his deep voice calm yet instantly commanding. "They were wondering why you'd missed another lesson." Cal kept his eyes on the floor, his lips pressed together. "Look at me, boy. A downcast gaze is a sign of weakness. And you're anything but weak. You're strong. A survivor. You have the scars to prove it."

Cal shut his eyes. For a moment, he was back in Grady Spencer's basement, a scalpel in his hand as he advanced towards his terrified mother. *Do it, boy. Show your father how well he's taught you.*

He opened his eyes again.

"That's better. A sign of a true leader." Jacob's smile wavered as he leaned forward. "But those signs are fading lately."

He wanted to look away again, to stare at the floor or the books on the shelves, but Cal held Jacob's stare. That was how you survived as prey—by keeping your eyes on the hunter.

"You've been going out at night again," Jacob continued, the frown burrowing deeper.

Cal pressed his lips together so tightly they throbbed. Cynthia had betrayed him after all.

"After the incident with the sheep, you agreed to stay here on the farm, so that we could work on containing all that rage. So that we could hone it for its rightful purpose. Yet, the moment my back's turned, off you run. Where do you go, Cal?"

Cal's jaw was beginning to ache with tension. He stared at Jacob, at the space between his eyes.

"Do you go to see your mother?"

Anger flashed in Jacob's eyes, only there for the briefest moment, but as powerful as lightning.

"I'm becoming concerned," he said, leaning back and resting veiny forearms across his stomach. "Leaving the farm without consent not only endangers you, it puts us all at risk. I'm beginning to wonder about your loyalty, Cal. About whether I was right to allow you back into the fold. To trust you after you deserted us."

Cal felt his heart race a little faster as Jacob probed him with his eyes. It was as if he were trying to read the very fabric of his mind. Then the man's expression softened, and his shoulders heaved as he let out a heavy sigh.

"Don't you realise how important you are to me, Cal? To all of us. The other children look up to you, for guidance and inspiration. They look to follow your lead. And that's my worry." Another sigh escaped Jacob's lips as he rested his hands on the desk. "If the other children see you leaving the farm, if they see you coming and going as you please, with no care for the rules, it won't be long before they begin to question and doubt. If that happens, everything I'm trying to achieve—for you, for society—it will all be lost. I've worked too hard to lose everything."

Blood rushed in Cal's ears as Jacob stood, his glittering, black eyes reflecting the lamp light. He watched as the man moved around the desk and reached out a hand.

Cal flinched, but instead of feeling fingers clamping around his windpipe, he felt them gently wrap around the back of his neck. And Jacob did not squeeze or snap, but stroked Cal's skin with fatherly tenderness.

"I'm relying on you, Cal. We all are," he said. "When the time comes *you* will be the one to lead the Dawn Children into glory. To show the world it cannot continue its slow sink into depravity."

Cal looked away, frightened and embarrassed. Ashamed that he had shown fear. Slowly, Jacob moved his hand to Cal's chin and gripped it between finger and thumb.

"Tell me I'm right about you," he said. "Tell me I was right to take you back."

Cal nodded stiffly as images of his mother flooded his mind. Jacob leaned closer, staring into his soul. Slowly, he released his grip. A frown returned to his brow as he took his seat at the desk.

"Sometimes I wonder if your silence is an act of defiance," he said, leaning back on the chair. He was quiet, contemplating. Slowly, he shook his head. "Perhaps it's my fault. I've let you run wild for too long and without purpose. I thought you weren't ready for the next stage, but perhaps you've been ready for a long time."

Cal nodded, half listening. His eyes wandered to the window, where darkness waited on the other side, calling to him. Jacob's voice pulled him back to the room.

"I will not keep you locked in a cage like an animal, but if you leave the farm again of your own accord there will be consequences. Tonight, you'll sleep in with Morwenna and the others. Tomorrow, I have something planned for you. A test of your loyalty. One that will prove your allegiance to the Dawn Children. One that will turn you from a boy into a man."

Cal stared at Jacob, the pressure in his chest making his body tremble. If he couldn't see his mother, she would forget him. She would let Dylan and Melissa come home. And that would be the end of it. The door closed on him for good.

I should leave here, he thought. *I should just go home and walk right in.*

And then what, boy? You think you'll escape me? You think I'll just disappear? I'm part of you just like you're part of me. And I'll use your hands to tear her open.

No. Don't say that. I'll never do it.

Oh, but you will, boy. You will. I promise you—it's just a matter of time.

"Was there something else, Cal?"

Jacob peered at him, searching out treacherous thoughts.

Cal shook his head, pushed his mother from his mind, and filled the emptiness with darkness.

23

It was late. Carrie sat in the living room, with the curtains closed and the lights down low, slowly getting drunk on whiskey. Sally had already gone to bed. Ever since visiting Dylan and Melissa, her mother had been pressuring her into allowing them to come home. She knew Sally meant well, that she wanted to see Carrie happy and reunited, but all the constant prodding and poking had made Carrie lose her temper.

She'd shouted at Sally over dinner, making sure to remind her of all the terrible things she'd done, like abandoning Carrie for the last five years, like leaving her alone to deal with the grief of losing Cal.

Sally had paled and grown deathly silent. It had been enough for Carrie to know she'd made her point.

Now, she felt angry and confused, and the whiskey was doing nothing to drown her guilt. Why couldn't her mother just leave her alone? But wasn't the reason she'd exploded *because* her mother had done exactly that?

Amid this emotional tug-of-war, Carrie still hadn't told anyone about her encounter with Aaron Black—she'd even lied to Dylan about it. More importantly, she still hadn't told anyone about what had happened up at Desperation Point.

Silence. It could be so dangerous.

Carrie glanced at the half empty whiskey bottle on the table. Perhaps everyone was right. Perhaps it was time to put Cal to rest, to take back her husband and child, and get on with the rest of her life. She wasn't sure how it would be possible, not with a piece of her missing.

But that's how people overcame loss, wasn't it? They got up from the floor, brushed themselves down, and got on with living. Maybe not for themselves, but for the people who loved them and needed them.

Like Melissa and Dylan. Perhaps even like Sally.

Getting up, Carrie replaced the whiskey bottle in the drinks cabinet, then made her way upstairs. She paused on the landing, staring at the soft light filtering from beneath Melissa's bedroom door. She thought about apologising to her mother, but she was drunk now and apologies would only lead to more tears and more grief. More guilt.

She hovered, her gaze moving along the corridor until it came to the last door. She moved towards it, pulled by a magnetic force.

Cal's name plaque was still there. She should take it down, she thought. But that would be like erasing him or pretending he never existed.

She opened the door. His room was still the same, the walls bare, the furniture minimal, a handful of his favourite childhood toys lined up on the windowsill.

There hadn't been time to make the room his—he'd only returned from the dead for just a few weeks before disappearing once again. Perhaps that would make it easier to paint over the walls, to turn the room back into an office.

Carrie moved up to the sill and stared at the small battalion of plastic figures. Her eyes fell upon a green dinosaur. A Tyrannosaurus Rex. His absolute favourite.

Do you remember, Cal? You used to carry him around everywhere. He used to sleep under your pillow at night.

Picking up the toy, she held it between her forefinger and thumb. Her heart splintered, sending ripples of pain deep down to her core. This was all she had left of him. This was all she had to hold onto.

Carrie looked out the window, into the darkness of the yard.

"Come home," she whispered. "I can't bear this anymore, so please, come home."

She stood, silent and still, searching the shadows for a sign of him, until she heard her mother stirring on the other side of the wall.

An idea came to her.

Taking the dinosaur, Carrie tiptoed downstairs and into the kitchen, then opened the back door. The cold rushed in, but she barely noticed.

Carefully, she set the dinosaur down on the doorstep.

If it was still there tomorrow, she would drive to the hardware store in Truro to buy brushes and paint. If it was gone, she would do everything in her power to find her son.

She already knew what the outcome would be, but at least now the decision would be left in the hands of fate.

24

AARON SWORE under his breath as the narrow country lane he was driving along snaked sharply to the right. He hit the brakes a little too forcefully and the car skidded as it rounded the bend, the screech of rubber on asphalt startling a murder of crows. The birds flew up from the hedgerow, a black ribbon coiling into the sky.

Heart beating in his chest, Aaron slowed the car to a safer speed and continued through the countryside. If he was going to die, and he supposed he had to eventually, he would do it at a respectable age and surrounded by riches, certainly not alone in the middle of nowhere.

He was tired, which wasn't helping his concentration, and he was now regretting not stopping at the petrol station he'd passed a mile back and grabbing another coffee. Yesterday's revelations had kept him awake most of the night, wondering if today was the day he'd find Cal Anderson. It was a crazy notion, he knew. One that was stupid, not to mention dangerous. But now, as he glanced at the map sitting next to him on the passenger seat, excitement overrode anxiety.

The circle he'd made on the map contained a handful of farms. He would begin there. If the farms came to nothing, he'd scour the woodland. It was a terrible plan, he thought now, as he turned off the road and onto a tree-lined dirt track.

But it was the only plan he had.

Apple Acres didn't look much like a farm. Rows of barren trees stood in fields on either side of the track, their gnarled branches snatching at the ash-coloured sky. The yard was clean and the farmhouse was in good shape, with gingham curtains hanging in sparkling windows.

Aaron had pictured all farmer's wives to be ruddy-faced and full of smiles, like the ones found in children's stories, but the woman who answered the door regarded him through wary eyes.

"Yes? What do you want?"

Employing his most charming smile, he quickly introduced himself—Aaron Black, author—and explained what he was doing—researching a book about the Porth an Jowl murders.

"This ain't Porth an Jowl. And it ain't got nothing to do with us," the woman said, folding her arms across her chest.

"You haven't seen anything suspicious lately? No one sneaking around at night, bothering your animals?"

"Don't have any animals. We grow fruit. And the only thing suspicious I've seen around here is you."

Aaron's smile widened as the woman's eyes narrowed. He thanked her, decided against asking for a tour of the farm's outbuildings, and returned to his car.

"Thanks for nothing," he grumbled.

The woman remained on the doorstep, clearly not going anywhere until he did. Irritated, Aaron took a pen from his bag and drew a cross through Apple Acres on the map. He pulled his camera from his bag, snapped a picture of the house and the woman's now angry face, then reversed the car out of the yard.

Not a great start, he thought.

Why was everyone in this damn place so suspicious anyway?

He headed back to the road, disappointment threatening the already weak foundations of his so-called plan.

Holden Farm was his next stop.

Climbing out of the car, he made his way across the filthy yard and knocked on the front door of a granite farmhouse. When no answer came, he glanced over his shoulder, then circled the house, looking for signs of life.

The smell of livestock burned his nostrils as he came upon another yard and a collection of outbuildings. Scrawny looking chickens roamed freely, clucking and scratching at the ground.

Aaron called out a hello and was answered by a loud grunt. Following the sound, he entered one of the small buildings to find a family of rotund pigs staring up at him from the confines of their pen. Wrinkling his nose, Aaron returned to the yard and made his way past the buildings. A field lay beyond, and a tractor was moving across it, back towards the house. He could just make out the farmer at the wheel, his burly frame filling the cabin.

Deciding it was best to be gone before the farmer returned, Aaron returned to the car. He would not find Cal here—all the animals were still very much alive.

His hope dwindling, he pressed on.

By the time mid-afternoon came around, he'd cleared another two farms, both welcoming him with suspicion and borderline hostility. Now, he was hungry and cold, his mood darkening with the day. Staring at the map, he was suddenly tempted to toss it out the window. He needed a better plan. One that didn't involve traipsing around the countryside in the freezing cold and pissing off the locals.

I should drive back to London. Give Taylor back the money. Then drive off the nearest cliff.

It was a grim thought. One he quickly shook from his mind. A hot bath and a warm dinner was an appealing alternative. But there was one more farm not far from here, and there was just enough daylight to take a look.

He slowed down, looking for the turn off. It crept up on him a few seconds later and he almost missed it, spinning the wheel sharply to the left.

The dirt road before him was winding and narrow, filled with potholes. Hedgerows, wild and overgrown, flanked both sides. Thirty metres along, he came to a large field gate blocking his path.

A battered and faded sign was tied to the gate with twine, which he could just about read: BURNT HOUSE FARM. PRIVATE PROPERTY. KEEP OUT.

With the engine still running, Aaron stepped out of the car. The gate was unlocked. He moved up to it, peering over the bars. He could see silhouettes of buildings in the distance. Darkness was descending quickly now, sweeping across the land in a malevolent wave.

His gaze returned to the sign. Recalling Ross Quick's shotgun, he wondered if it was a wise idea to ignore the warning to keep out. But the only way to find Cal was to leave no stone left unturned.

"Screw it."

Sliding back the bolt, Aaron pushed the gate open, then ran back to the car. He drove on.

Soon, the dirt road came to an end, opening on to a

cracked and filthy yard. The farmhouse faced him. Most of the windows were boarded up or shuttered. Broken slates lay on the ground, fallen from a roof that was in much need of repair.

In fact, Aaron thought, as he killed the engine, the house was in such disrepair that it could easily be abandoned; making it the perfect hiding place for someone who didn't want to be found.

Anxiety fluttering in his stomach, he grabbed his camera and climbed out of the car. The cold was bitter now, biting at his exposed skin as he looked around. He turned, so that the house was now on his left. In the failing daylight, he saw a few outbuildings bordering the yard, including a large barn at the end.

He turned back to the house, lifted the camera, and took pictures, the flash lighting up the yard. He turned another ninety degrees to his left and stared at an empty field.

Aaron froze. Blood rushed in his ears.

Someone was watching him.

His first thought was that it was Cal. Then, as his eyes focused on the shadowy figure, he realised his mistake.

It was a scarecrow, staked to a roughly fashioned cross that had begun to rot, making the scarecrow lean drunkenly to the left. Relief flowing through his veins, Aaron pointed the camera at the eerie straw figure.

"Say cheese."

Quickly, the humour left him. What would he do if Cal really was hiding here somewhere?

His plan hadn't reached that far.

He could try and talk to him. Or grab a wrench from the car and knock him out cold.

Yeah, sure. Says the man who just almost pissed himself at the sight of a scarecrow.

Aaron's gaze returned to the house and the yard. There was only one way to find out if this place was truly abandoned. He would investigate the outbuildings first, then the house. If he found signs that Cal was staying here, he would take photographic evidence, then return during daylight. Perhaps he'd even convince Carrie to come along. But only if she agreed to be interviewed for the book.

His pulse quickening, Aaron stole across the yard and headed for the barn.

"You shouldn't be here."

The voice startled him.

Spinning on his heels, he turned to see a small figure standing in a rectangle of soft light in the farmhouse doorway.

It was a child.

Slowly, Aaron stepped forward.

"I'm sorry," he said, still surprised that people lived here.

Now he was closer, he could see the girl's pale skin and long, red hair. She was thin and slight, a little underweight perhaps. She held the door behind her, blocking his view of the inside.

"Is your mother home? Or your father?" Aaron kept his voice soft. "I'd like to talk to them."

The girl stared at him with strange, dark eyes.

Before she could reply, the door opened and a woman appeared. Aaron could just make out her features in the waning light. She was older than Aaron, perhaps in her fifties, with pallid skin and red hair like the girl, but cut short.

"This is private property," she said, pulling the girl into the house and the door behind her. "You need to leave."

Aaron apologised and held out a hand to introduce himself.

The woman shrank away.

"I don't mean to trespass," he said, keeping his distance. The woman had pulled the door to, so only a strip of light illuminated her. "I'm looking for someone. A boy named Cal. He's about sixteen years old, but small for his age. He's missing and his mother's anxious to see him."

Draped in shadows, the woman's face was unreadable. "Ain't seen him. No one comes out here and that's the way we like it."

"You've had no trespassers? No food going missing?" Aaron paused. "No animals getting hurt?"

"Nothing like that. Now, please go. Before I call my husband."

Aaron nodded. "I'm sorry to have troubled you."

He turned and walked the short distance back to the car, bothered by the fear he'd heard in the woman's voice. He supposed if you lived an isolated life in the middle of nowhere, a stranger appearing on your property would arouse immediate suspicion, especially in the dark.

But it was more than that. There had been something in the way she'd mentioned her husband, as if they'd both have reason to be sorry if he came to the door.

Country people, he thought, sliding the key into the ignition. They were a strange bunch.

He glanced at the woman still standing in the doorway, her skin white as paper in the glare of the headlights. She waved a hand, shooing him away.

Turning the vehicle around, Aaron drove away from Burnt House Farm, an uneasy feeling churning his gut. He was no closer to finding Cal Anderson than he had been this morning. Heading back towards Truro, he became increasingly convinced that tomorrow would be no different.

25

CYNTHIA CLOSED the door and slid the lock into place with trembling fingers. Sensing movement, she turned, ready to give Lottie a scolding. The child had been told time and time again: never to open the door to anyone! It was the boy's fault. His defiance was causing ripples. Ripples that would soon turn into waves.

But it wasn't Lottie standing behind her.

It was Cal.

He stared at the door with round eyes, fists clenched at his sides. Before she could stop herself, Cynthia raised a hand and brought it down hard against his cheek. Cal staggered back as the slap echoed through the hall.

"This is your fault!" Cynthia cried, her body trembling. "This is what happens when you ignore the rules!"

Even in the dim light, she could see the print of her hand tattooed on his skin.

Cal straightened. He grew very still, his eyes burning into her.

"Do you know that man?" Cynthia demanded. She glanced

over his shoulder to see the younger children had gathered in the hall behind. "Well, do you?"

Slowly, Cal shook his head.

"He seemed to know who you are!"

Somewhere upstairs, a door opened. A figure appeared on the stairs, a young man in his early twenties, who was broad and muscular, his face handsome in a boyish way. But there was nothing youthful about his eyes. Or kind.

"What's happened?" he asked.

Cynthia stabbed a finger at Cal. "Trouble, that's what. Don't let him out of your sight, Heath. I need to speak with Jacob."

Pushing past Cal, she marched along the hall, shooing the younger children out of her way. With each step, anger turned to deep-seated fear.

She couldn't remember the last time they'd had a visitor at the farm. No one was supposed to know they were here.

It was possible that the man was simply going door-to-door, hoping someone had spotted Cal, but what if it was more than that? What if he knew? What if his pretence was part of a larger plan to put an end to everything Jacob had built up?

She had tried to remain calm. To appear brusque, even. But now, she wondered if she'd been convincing enough.

Who was this man, anyway? He hadn't acted like a police officer. Perhaps he was a private investigator, hired by Cal's family, or perhaps some sort of bounty hunter, looking to hand him to the authorities in exchange for a cash reward.

Either way, Cynthia was convinced trouble was coming. She felt it, deep down in her gut like a tumour. It was the same feeling she'd had the first time she'd slept with Jacob. Of course, back then, she had been confused and scared, her feelings misguided.

She reached the office door. In her panic, she forgot to knock. He was sitting at his desk. Morwenna was leaning over him, one hand slung over his shoulder, the other reaching down his front. The desk masked what the girl was doing, but Cynthia was no fool.

She stood, frozen in the doorway, watching Morwenna's arm move up and down and Jacob's eyelids flutter. Jealousy and betrayal ignited her insides. But instead of flying into a rage, she pushed the emotions down and cleared her throat.

Jacob and Morwenna looked up.

There had been a time when Jacob's smiles had been reserved for Cynthia and he'd told her she was the only woman he needed. But now, he only smiled at the Dawn Children and at the other younger, prettier women he'd since brought into the fold.

Women like Morwenna.

Jacob glared at Cynthia, the look of a master regarding an intruding servant. Was that what she had become—nothing more than a scullery maid?

It didn't matter, though. None of it did. Because Cynthia loved Jacob. He was her everything.

She watched as he zipped himself up and gave a silent nod to Morwenna, who moved around the desk and swanned out of the room, smiling wryly at Cynthia.

Fighting the urge to lash out at the girl, Cynthia shut the door gently behind her.

"What is it?"

Jacob's voice resonated through Cynthia's body.

"There was a man," she said, glancing over her shoulder. "Lottie went outside. She spoke to him."

"What did he want?"

"He was looking for Cal."

Jacob stared at her with unblinking, remorseless eyes, his elbows resting on the desk, his fingers intertwined beneath his chin.

"And you intervened?"

"Yes."

"What did you say? Tell me your exact words."

Cynthia nodded. It was a test. She had to answer correctly to win his favour.

"I told him this was private property," she said, her mouth running dry. "That we didn't know anything about the boy, and that he ought to go before I call my husband."

"That's everything you said?"

"Yes. I mean, I think so."

"You *think* so or you *know* so?"

"I mean, yes. I mean, that's exactly what I told him."

"And why did you think it was best to intervene? To speak with this man?"

"Because of Lottie. Because she might have told him something she shouldn't."

She waited and watched, nervous as a dormouse, as Jacob continued to silently stare, his eyes giving nothing away.

"Then there's nothing to worry about," he said, at last.

"Do you really think so? What if he didn't believe me? What if he comes back? It's all Cal's fault—if he did as he was told then Lottie wouldn't follow his lead. He's a bad influence, Jacob. He'll be the downfall of us all!"

Jacob was silent and thinking.

"Who was that man, Jacob?" Cynthia continued, hysteria rising in her throat. "What if he tells the police? What if they already know Cal's here?"

"How could they know?"

"Maybe something was found at Grady's house."

"It's been three months. If they'd found something, they would have been here long ago."

"I don't know, then! Maybe Cal was spotted, someone saw him coming back this way. It's all this sneaking off! He doesn't care about us, Jacob. He doesn't respect you like the others do! Being kept in that basement all those years has made him unbalanced!"

Cynthia caught her breath. She glanced nervously at Jacob, whose eyes pierced her skin.

"I've spoken with Cal. He won't be going out again," he said.

"But you told him before and still he—"

"Are you doubting me?"

He leaned forward. The shadows in the room seemed to grow longer, the air thinner.

Cynthia trembled.

Before, she would have never dreamed of doubting Jacob. He had saved her from a worthless life all those years ago. He had given her purpose. He'd made her feel loved. And yet, lately, when he looked at her, all she could see reflected back was disappointment.

It was because of Cal.

Jacob had been bewitched by him. He believed Cal was the way forward, the torch bearer.

Not for the first time, Cynthia wished the boy had never returned to the farm. She wished Jacob had never tried to rescue him from Grady Spencer's basement.

Fixing her eyes on the floor, Cynthia shook her head. "Of course not, Jacob. I would never doubt you."

Silence filled the room.

Cynthia glanced upward to find Jacob had already lost interest in her. She felt the panic again, slick and wet against her skin. This was Cal's fault. He was putting everyone at risk. He was making her doubt the man she loved.

Cal's behaviour had become so reckless that strangers were now showing up at the farm like bloodhounds chasing a fox. Why was Jacob so blind to it?

She stared at him, willing him to look at her, desperate to feel his gaze upon her skin.

But he would not.

"You should prepare dinner. Get Alison to help you."

The words were like fists pummelling Cynthia's gut, punching the air from her lungs.

"Yes, Jacob. Of course."

"And ask Cal to come and see me. I think it's time for his test."

Cynthia wanted to laugh. Then she wanted to scream. Had Jacob lost his mind? How could it possibly be the right time after what had just happened?

But Cynthia nodded, pushing all her feelings down into nothingness.

At long last, Jacob looked up.

"You mustn't fear him," he said, gazing upon her as if she were a dumb animal. A sheep. "Cal is our way forward. The deliverer of our message. He will lead the Dawn Children into greatness."

Cynthia left the room, feeling Jacob's eyes on her back. It wasn't a pleasurable sensation, not like it had once been in those early days. Now, it felt like she was being appraised and judged. As if every movement she made was being tested for signs of betrayal.

And it was all because of that boy.

As she walked away, it was suddenly clear that she was growing to hate Cal. Not because he was dangerous or unbalanced, or because on more than one occasion he'd glared at her as if she were something to be erased. It was because he had Jacob's love. Cal had stolen it from her.

As she made her way along the corridor in search of the boy, Cynthia wondered if she would ever be able to steal it back.

26

THE BLACK TRANSIT van rumbled along the tree-lined lane, its dimmed headlights pushing back against the darkness. The three passengers were silent. Heath was at the wheel, his cold, furtive eyes fixed ahead. Beside him, Morwenna was hunched over, a sheath of foil balanced on her knees.

"Christ, learn to fucking drive," she growled as the vehicle lurched in and out of a pothole. "You're spilling the gear!"

Wedged beside the passenger door, Cal watched as Morwenna lifted a plastic straw to her nose and lowered the end towards the foil. She snorted some of the powder, then pinched her nostrils between forefinger and thumb.

"Jacob always brings back the good stuff," she said. "Heath? You want some?"

"I'm driving," he replied, his voice flat and emotionless. The lane turned and Heath steered into the corner. The girl waited until the lane had straightened out once more, then licked her finger, dabbed it into the powder, and brought it to Heath's lips.

"Open up, buttercup."

Heath did as he was told, taking Morwenna's finger into his

mouth, allowing her to rub the cocaine into his gums. She tried to remove her finger, but Heath gripped it between his teeth.

He glanced at her, life returning to his eyes. Morwenna grinned. Heath relaxed his grip on her finger and shifted his gaze to the lane.

"What about you, loser?" Morwenna looked at Cal, who sat watching her from the shadows. She held up the foil. "Are you going to be a good little doggy and make Jacob a proud master?"

Cal lowered his gaze to the mound of cocaine. He shook his head. The girl shrugged. "Suit yourself. But you know what Jacob would say. This is your power and your glory, forever and ever, Amen."

She giggled as she lifted the straw to her nose once more.

"Go easy," Heath said, elbowing her in the arm. White powder spilled into the air.

"What the fuck?"

"It's not all for you, Morwenna. Besides, we're almost there."

The car hit another pothole, throwing its passengers from side to side, spilling more of the drug.

Grumbling under her breath, Morwenna carefully folded the foil, sealing the cocaine inside, and rested it on top of the dashboard.

"So, who is this guy?" she asked. "Why's Jacob chosen him?"

"We don't ask questions. Questions are for doubters," Heath replied. He switched off the headlights, plunging them into absolute darkness. The van slowed to a halt and Heath killed the engine.

Cal peered through the windscreen, his eyes quickly adjusting to the nothingness. Shapes and shadows began to form: the winding, narrow lane; the trees on either side, their skeletal branches reaching towards the van. Cal let out a breath.

Usually, this was where he felt safest. Invisible, in the dark. A creature of the night.

But not tonight. That man—the one who'd been watching his mother—he was looking for Cal. He'd showed up at the farm, asking questions. Cal had heard the man say his mother was worried about him. He'd acted like he knew Cal's mother, like they were friends. But that didn't make sense, because just a few nights ago the man had stood and watched Cal's mother almost kill herself, and he'd done nothing to intervene.

From the corner of his eye, he saw Heath reach for the foil on the dashboard and snap his fingers at Morwenna, who reached up and flicked the interior light switch.

No, something was very wrong where that man was concerned. But he couldn't tell Jacob, or anyone else. He would have to find out for himself.

Heath snorted cocaine into his left nostril, then his right. Morwenna took another turn, as did Heath, switching back and forth until there was nothing left.

"The house is just around the corner. Everyone ready?" Heath said, crumpling the foil. Cal could already hear the change in his voice. The excitement and the anticipation. The pent-up anger preparing to be unleashed.

Morwenna let out a trembling breath. "Let's do this."

Cal heard the change in her voice, too.

Opening the driver door, Heath hopped out of the van, quickly followed by Morwenna, who slammed the door shut.

Cal's insides tightened as he listened to the clump of their boots on the ground. Jacob hadn't told him what the test would be. "You'll know it when the time comes," was all he'd said. "Be ready. Make the right choice. Prove you're the leader I believe you to be."

Now, sitting in the darkness of the van, Cal wondered how he could possibly know what the right choice would be when he didn't even know what they were about to do.

He was going to let Jacob down.

The side door of the van slid open. He heard the dull clang of metal on metal, followed by Heath's taunting voice.

"What are you waiting for, golden boy? Jacob's not here to hold your hand now. Get out of the fucking van."

His palms slick, Cal fumbled with the door handle then climbed out into the night.

Heath and Morwenna moved up to him.

"This is for you," Heath said.

Cal took the claw hammer, feeling the weight of it in his hand. His insides grew even tighter as he saw the serrated blades of the hunting knives that Heath and Morwenna carried.

A coil of thin rope was hooked over Heath's shoulder. In his other hand, he carried a torch, the beam pointing at the ground.

"Let's go."

Heath led the way, the torch pointed in front of him, giving them just enough light to complete the journey.

As they rounded the corner, the house came into view. A single porch light illuminated the front of the building, the rest of it was cloaked in shadows. It was an old house. The only house around. The exterior was granite, the windows latticed. Cal counted several of them.

Morwenna let out a breath. "That's a big fucking house for one person. I guess whoever he is, he doesn't need to worry about money."

"A king in his castle," Heath said. "I'm going to check around back. Wait here."

They watched as he shot forward, his shoulders hunched as

he cut through the yard and around the corner of the house, leaving the other two hidden in darkness.

Cal glanced at Morwenna, who stood silently beside him as they waited for Heath to return. He could smell perspiration beading her skin, could hear her breaths, quick and thin.

When Heath reappeared a minute later, he had undergone a transformation. His pupils were large and black in the torch-light. His nostrils flared. His chest heaved up and down. His whole body crackled with energy. Cal thought he looked like a dragon.

"Looks clear," Heath said, the words fast and sharp. "He must be asleep, so knock loud."

He took the torch from Morwenna and pointed the beam in her direction. Cal saw that her eyes were also round and black, her breaths shooting out in smoky, frosted plumes.

She nodded. Tightening her grip on the hunting knife, she opened her free hand and exposed the palm. Sucking in a breath, she drew the blade across the skin. Blood beaded in the wound. She raised her hand to her temple and smeared the blood across her forehead. She did it all without a flicker of emotion.

Slipping the knife into her back pocket, she watched as Heath wrapped a handkerchief around her wounded hand.

Morwenna stood.

"Be ready," she whispered to Heath, before turning to Cal. "Remember, this is your test. Jacob is counting on you. Don't fuck it up." Then she was on the move, faking a limp as she headed across the yard and towards the house.

Cal felt a jab of pain as Heath dug fingers into his ribs.

"Follow me, golden boy."

They stuck close to the woodland, Cal crouching down behind Heath, until they were just metres away from the house.

Morwenna glanced over at them and Cal thought he saw fear shining in her eyes under the porchlight.

Heath flashed the torch on and off. A signal that they were in position. With a trembling hand, Morwenna rapped her knuckles on the door.

They waited.

Morwenna tried again, this time curling her hand into a fist and hammering loudly. Cal held his breath as he saw an upstairs light come on. Beside him, Heath's body tensed.

"As soon as she steps through the door, we go in," he breathed. "Then it's down to you. Don't kill him. Just hit him hard enough to knock him out cold. We'll take care of the rest."

Heart pounding in his ears, Cal's gaze darted from Morwenna to the claw hammer clenched in his fist. A second later, the front door opened a crack. The man inside had kept the chain on.

"Please, can you help me?" Morwenna said, her voice filled with distress. "There's been an accident. My car came off the road and hit a tree. I've lost my phone. My sister—she's still out there."

Hidden in the shadows, Cal watched Morwenna play out her role, the blood in her hair shimmering in the porch light. She was convincing, he thought, the fear and panic in her voice palpable. And she was young enough and pretty enough to open any door.

"Please!" she cried, sobbing now. "Let me call an ambulance."

There was a pause. Cal held his breath. He heard the rattle of the chain lock being removed.

"Of course," the man said, his voice filled with concern. "Come in, come in. The phone's just over here."

They watched as Morwenna thanked him, then stepped forward. She turned her head slightly, her eyes wandering off to the tree line.

Then she was stepping inside.

"Go!" Heath hissed.

He sprang from their hiding place like a jaguar.

Blood rushing in his ears, Cal ploughed forward.

Their feet pounded across the yard. They reached the house, just as the man was turning to close the door.

In a flash of movement, Heath rammed his shoulder into the wood. The door flew inward, knocking the man from his feet with a startled cry. He landed heavily on his back, the air knocked from his lungs.

His heart hammering like a hummingbird's, Cal entered the house. He saw pairs of muddy Wellington boots lined up against the wall and a coat rack full of jackets. Beyond was a wide foyer with oak panelled walls and a grandfather clock in the corner. Large potted plants with thick, green leaves lined the edges. Normal things in a normal house.

Except for the man, who was scrabbling back on his elbows, his face contorted with terror.

"Don't move a fucking muscle!" Heath bellowed, brandishing the hunting knife.

The man froze, raised a trembling hand.

"Please!" he cried. "Please, don't hurt me."

Behind him, Morwenna stood with her feet apart and her eyes black as midnight, an unnerving grin fixed on her face.

Heath twisted around, staring wildly at Cal.

"What are you waiting for? Hit him!" he screamed.

Cal stared at the man, who was now hyperventilating in between braying sobs. He was older, Cal noted, around the same age as Grandpa Gary. But unlike Grandpa Gary, who had maintained a trim physique after years of physical labour working on boats, this man was flabby and unfit. Cal wondered who he was, and why Jacob had sent the Dawn Children to his house.

"Cal!"

He pulled his gaze away from the man and saw Heath's wide-eyed, pallid face. His teeth were clenched, his lips pulled back. A thick vein throbbed at the centre of his forehead.

"Do it!" he yelled.

Cal stepped forward, hammer gripped in his fist.

The man began to cry like a child with a grazed knee.

"Do it!" Morwenna cried, her unnerving smile growing wider.

Cal towered over the man. He raised the hammer high above his head.

"Please!" the man begged, hands flapping in front of his face.

"Last chance," Heath hissed. "Or you fail."

Cal hesitated. The hammered wavered.

Go on, boy! Do it! Make your father proud!

Cal brought the hammer down. The man shrieked and twisted away. The hammer slammed into his shoulder with a dull thud.

Cal pounced on top of him, straddling his chest. He raised the hammer and brought it down again, striking the man's temple.

Beneath him, the man stopped struggling. His eyes rolled back in their sockets.

Do it again! Smash his head like a pumpkin!

Cal raised the hammer.

A large hand wrapped around his wrist. He snapped his head up, lips curled back, staring at Heath.

"Jacob was right about you, after all," Heath said quietly. "Now get up. You've done your part."

Panting and wheezing, Cal glanced down at the unconscious man. He dropped the hammer with a clatter on the floor. In front of him, Morwenna started to laugh.

"Well done, Cal!" she said, nodding frantically. "You did it!"

Cal got to his feet. He stepped back, noting the thick blood leaking from the man's temple. Morwenna crouched over the man and pressed two fingers against his neck.

"Still alive," she said. "Unlucky for him."

Retrieving the coil of rope that had fallen from his shoulder, Heath set to work, binding the man's wrists.

Behind Cal, something moved. He spun around. A silver tabby cat sat half in the shadows, its green eyes fixed on its unconscious master. Cal approached it and crouched down. The animal turned to face him, making no move to attack or escape. Carefully, Cal ran his fingers along the length of the cat's spine. The cat arched its back and started to purr.

"What are you doing?" Heath stared at him as he tied the man's ankles. "Go outside and open the van door."

Cal stroked the animal's flanks, extracting loud, excited purrs.

"Cal!" Heath threw a key chain at him. Cal caught it with one hand. He stood up. And saw the child.

A young boy dressed in striped pyjamas stood on the staircase. He was no more than five years old, with a shock of blond hair and deep blue eyes that were round with fear. His face was pale and tear-stained as he stared at the strangers.

Morwenna looked at Heath. "Shit. I thought Jacob said he lived here alone."

Heath's black eyes were fixed on the boy. "He did."

No one moved.

Then the boy began to cry.

Something stirred in Cal's memory. The boy looked a lot like Noah Pengelly. Even the way he cried was similar.

"We'll have to take him with us," Morwenna said. "We can't leave him here. He's seen our faces."

She reached for the blood-spattered hammer.

On the stairs, the boy was slowly retreating, blindly searching for the next step with his foot.

"We have to take him," Morwenna said again, her voice taut with panic. "Jacob will know what to do."

Slowly, Heath got to his feet. "Or we get rid of him along the way. We can take the coastal road, past the cliffs."

"Heath, you can't—" Morwenna's voice was cut off by a loud groaning. On the floor, the man stirred. He grew still again.

Cal watched the scene with curious eyes. He glanced down at the cat, who was still purring and rubbing its flanks against his shins.

Heath darted forward towards the stairs.

The boy squealed.

Heath was upon him, sweeping him up in his arms, clamping a hand over his mouth. The boy kicked and squirmed.

Heath brought him down to the floor, pulling off one of the child's socks and stuffing it into his mouth. He removed his shirt and used it to tie the boy's hands behind his back.

"Get over here!" he barked, glaring at Cal.

Cal crossed the hall. Morwenna was no longer smiling. Both she and Heath were pale and trembling. Cal bent down and scooped his hands under the man's arms. Together, he and Morwenna lifted him into the air and began carrying him out of the house. Behind them, Heath slung the boy over his shoulder.

Reaching the van, they threw the unconscious man into the back. Heath threw the boy in after him.

"We don't hurt children," Morwenna said, her voice shaking. "Children are sacred. Children are the New Dawn."

Heath stared at the boy, who was weeping in the shadows, his sobs muffled by the makeshift gag.

He nodded to Cal. "Get in there and watch him."

Cal climbed in beside the boy. Heath slammed the door shut, plunging them into darkness. A minute later, they were back on the road and hurtling through the countryside. No one spoke. The air was heavy and cloying.

In the shadows, Cal watched the boy. He made no move to comfort him. The boy continued to sob quietly as they drove on through the darkness.

27

"HOW ARE WE DOING?"

It was ten a.m. on Sunday morning. Rose and Carrie sat at the kitchen table, waiting for the tea to finish steeping in the pot.

Carrie was exhausted. Her body ached. Cal's toy dinosaur had been sitting on the back step for two days. She hadn't visited the hardware store. Cal's room remained the same.

She was supposed to be moving on. She'd promised herself.

Instead, she'd retreated to her bedroom, refusing meals, refusing to speak. Instead, she'd been watching endless hours of mindless television and drinking enough booze to impress the swarthiest of sailors.

When she'd slept, it had been in fits and starts, in part due to the alcohol, but mostly because of the nightmares; terrible dreams in which Cal murdered her family, over and over, or Grady Spencer tied her down to the table in his basement of horrors and tortured her in unspeakable ways.

And now Rose was here.

Sally had let her in, then headed out for the day to visit

friends in Falmouth, desperate to get away from the misery. Carrie glanced across the table at her friend, who was staring at her with worried eyes, and slowly shook her head.

"I'm not doing so good," she said.

Rose smiled. She reached out a hand and Carrie took it in her own. "I'm not surprised. You've been to hell and back."

"I don't think I'm back yet."

"But you will be soon."

Carrie snorted. "Sally's about ready to call the men in white coats and have me carted away."

"She's your mother. She's worried, that's all. It ain't nice for her to see you this way."

"No one asked her to come here."

"But here she is, anyway. That has to count for something."

Shrugging a shoulder, Carrie reached for the tea pot.

As she poured the tea into cups, she was aware of a trembling in her hands. Rose saw it, too.

"How's that girl of yours?" she asked, accepting a cup. "She all right over there with Gary and Joy?"

Carrie spooned sugar into her tea, watching the grains sink beneath the surface. "She's fine." She pushed the sugar bowl across the table. "Dylan is taking good care of her."

"Well, of course. He's her father, after all."

Rose was staring at her intently, her brow creased, her lips pressed together. Oh great, Carrie thought. *Here we go.*

It was the same look that came over Rose whenever she was about to offer advice—advice that Carrie wasn't sure she wanted to hear. She leaned back in her chair and threw her hands in the air. "Go on, Rose. Say whatever it is you want to say."

Rose stared at her. She sipped some tea then heaved her shoulders. "How long are you going to keep this up?" she said.

"Keep what up?"

Now it was Rose's turn to throw up her hands. "All this! This house of despair! None of us can possibly know what you're going through. But what I do know is that Cal may be gone, but Melissa is still here. She's your daughter, Carrie. You're her mother. She needs you. She needs to come home with you."

Carrie winced at the words. She felt a headache coming on. "You sound just like Sally," she said, crossing her arms over her stomach.

"Well maybe you should listen to one of us. The quicker you let your daughter back in your life, the quicker you'll start to heal. You need to let the people that love you, *love* you. And Melissa has so much love for you." She paused, glancing away for a second. "Dylan, too."

"I know that." Carrie felt a stab of irritation in her chest. It was rare that her friend could cause such a feeling. "But it's not that simple. I can't just forget what's happened. I can't pretend everything is fine."

Rose picked up her cup and took a sip. "No one is saying it's easy. In fact, I'm telling you it will be bloody hard. But what's the alternative? You don't get to stop being Melissa's mother just because you feel bad. God knows, there are plenty of children in this world whose parents don't care about them. Look at my Nat. You know what she's been through at the hands of her so-called parents. How damaged she is because of it. Do you want that to happen to Melissa? Do you want her to grow up thinking you sent her away because you didn't want her?"

Carrie was quiet for a moment, irritation turning to anger. "This isn't about rejection, Rose," she said. "It's not about sending Melissa away because I don't want to be her mother."

"But that's the message you're sending, anyway. You really

think a four-year-old's going to understand why her mother would rather stay home and drink herself to death?"

Carrie flinched. She felt her face heating up.

Rose lowered her gaze to the table. "You reek of it, Carrie. I could smell it on you before you even came downstairs."

Both women were silent, their heads bowed.

"It's been nearly three months," Rose said at long last, her voice soft and gentle. "Are you really going to keep Melissa away on the off chance he might come back? She could grow old and die before that happens. We all could."

A single tear sailed down Carrie's cheek. She wanted nothing more than to run upstairs and drink herself into unconsciousness. But shame and guilt kept her pinned to the chair.

"I'm scared you're going to sink down into a hole and never come back up," Rose whispered. "After everything you've been through, you deserve more than that."

Carrie wiped the tear away, wondering if she really did deserve more. She glanced at her friend, silently debating whether to tell her about Aaron Black, about what he'd told her.

But it was as if Rose had read her mind.

"Anyway, no reason to keep on about it," she said, before arching an eyebrow. "Have you heard about the author who's in town? Aaron 'holier than thou' Black."

Carrie looked up. "Sounds like you've met him."

"I can do better than that. I've had him around for dinner."

Shocked, Carrie listened as Rose told her about her encounter with the writer and Nat's involvement with him. "I tell you," she said, "that girl is going to be the death of me. She'll send me to an early grave! I've warned her to stay away from him. I've told her that he's trouble. But you know what she's like. The girl's as stubborn as an ox. Has he been to see you yet?"

For a reason that she couldn't quite fathom, Carrie shook her head. "Nat's working for him?"

"Helping with research or some such." Rose sighed. "She says she needs the money, thinks she'll be cast out on the streets at the stroke of midnight on her eighteenth birthday, like she's Cinderella with a crew cut, or something. Daft bird! I've told her she has a roof over her head for as long as she needs it. I don't care about the money. But will she listen?"

Carrie nodded, not really listening either.

"Is it true what they say about him?" she asked. "That he's writing a book about, well, about all this?"

"A true crime account is what he's calling it." Rose waved a dismissive hand. "He's not a bad person, not really, not like some of those journalists you've had around. He's passionate, I'll give him that, and he seems to think he knows his stuff about all that psychobabble-whatnot. But honestly, I wouldn't worry. From the sound of things, he's not getting very far. No one's talking to him. No one except Dottie Penpol, of course. Give it a day or two, he'll probably give up and go home."

Carrie leaned back in the chair. Anxiety fluttered in her chest.

"So, you think he's genuine?" she asked, looking directly at Rose. "He's not a hack?"

Rose narrowed her eyes. "You're not thinking about talking to him, are you?"

"No. Of course not. I was just wondering, that's all."

But she had heard the hesitation in her own voice.

And so had Rose. She sipped more tea, her gaze fixed on Carrie.

"Probably just as well," she said. "There are more important things at stake."

Carrie nodded. She attempted a smile.

"You're right," she said.

But now, she couldn't think of anything more important than finding out if Aaron Black had been telling the truth after all.

28

AARON WAS PREPARING to leave the hotel room, ready for another day of driving in the cold and rain, of roaming from farm to farm in the vain hope that someone, somewhere could provide him with any kind of clue to Cal Anderson's whereabouts, when his mobile phone rang. The muscles in his shoulders immediately tensed. If it was Taylor calling again, he would need to seriously consider changing his number, or at least think about buying a disposable phone to use, so that he could switch this one off.

The guilt was starting to get to him, weighing him down. He supposed he should be thankful that Taylor hadn't involved the police. Not that there would soon be any money left for them to recoup.

Steeling himself, he glanced at the phone screen. The caller ID displayed a mobile number he didn't recognise. Perhaps Taylor was getting sly, trying to trick him into picking up. Try all you want, he thought. *Aaron Black is smarter than that.*

Hooking his bag over his shoulder, he waited for the mystery caller to hang up, then slipped the phone inside his pocket. As he rode the lift down to the lobby, the phone started to ring again.

The usual receptionist sat at the front desk, his eyes glazed with boredom. As Aaron entered, he sprang to life, like a marionette having its strings pulled.

"Don't you ever go home?" Aaron asked him, a wry smile on his lips.

The receptionist scowled.

Leaving the hotel, Aaron pulled his jacket collar around his neck and hurried to his car. He let the engine run for a minute and rubbed his hands together as he waited for the heaters to kick in. Then, laying the map out on the passenger seat, he glanced over the circled area and the number of places still left to investigate. He winced, attempted to push back the taunting despair.

His phone rang for a third time.

"Son of a . . ."

Pulling the phone from his pocket, he checked the screen with one eye shut. It was that same number again.

Switching on the radio, he turned to a local station and cranked up the volume, drowning out the ring tone. A news reader was in mid-flow.

". . . police were alerted to the scene early this morning, after Beaumont's cleaner found the front door open and scenes of a struggle inside. The former councillor's four-year-old son is also believed to be missing. Beaumont stepped down from his councillor position a year ago following allegations of child abuse. All charges were eventually dropped. Mr Beaumont had recently acquired weekend visitation rights for his son after a lengthy custody battle with his ex-wife. Detective Inspector Angela Wells has stated that Devon and Cornwall police are still establishing the crime scene. We'll have more on the story as it comes in."

Aaron turned down the volume, until the news reader's voice was just a whisper. He stared at his phone screen. Whoever had called had left a message. His thumb hovered over the voicemail icon. He didn't want to hear Taylor's angry and accusatory words. But curiosity got the better of him.

He tapped the icon and pressed the phone to his ear.

His heart missed a beat as he listened. Slowly, his face lit up with a toothy smile. Aaron hung up the phone, punched the air in excitement, and reached for his seatbelt. Moments later, he was racing out of Truro towards Devil's Cove.

29

TWENTY MINUTES LATER, Aaron found himself sitting on the edge of a leather couch, nervously tapping his foot on the carpet and staring at the display of framed family photographs on the mantelpiece. The living room curtains were open, but the dull day allowed in little light, and so he sat in the gloom, anxiously waiting for Carrie to return.

When she entered the room a few moments later, he felt his pulse race with excitement. She ignored his stare as she handed him a mug of coffee then positioned herself in the opposite armchair. She looked exhausted, he thought. The knitted pullover she wore swamped her thin frame.

For a moment, the two sat in silence, Aaron nervously waiting while Carrie pressed her hands together on her lap.

Aaron cleared his throat. "Thank you for agreeing to see me," he said. "I know it must have been a difficult decision but I want you to know I'm extremely grateful. Your cooperation will help to present a much stronger, unbiased presentation of the facts."

Carrie watched him as he produced his digital voice recorder and placed it on the coffee table. She shook her head. "You seem to have misunderstood. I didn't ask you here because I want to be interviewed for your book. In fact, quite the opposite. I don't want anything to do with your book. I don't understand what you're doing here or why you want to write about something you have absolutely nothing to do with."

The sinking feeling in Aaron's stomach was immediate and despairing, like hearing about the sudden death of a friend who had always been a picture of health. His eyes moved from the recorder, which he had yet to switch on, to Carrie's steely gaze.

"Oh? But I thought on the phone, you said—"

"The only thing I agreed to do was meet with you." Carrie paused, her gaze wandering over to the drinks cabinet. When she looked back at him, her face was taut with anger.

"Did you lie to me?" she said, looking him square in the eyes. "Did you lie to me about seeing my son?"

Aaron shook his head. "Everything I told you was true. I followed you that night, hoping to get an interview, I saw you walk up to that cliff, and then I saw your son. Why would I lie?"

"To get a reaction. To get me to agree to help you."

"Don't you think I could have come up with a better story that doesn't involve me looking like a crazed stalker? Besides, I'm not some headline-thirsty reporter. I have a reputation to protect."

"Except it's not much of a reputation from what Nat told me."

Aaron swallowed. His face flushed scarlet. Nat was so fired.

"So now I know why you're really writing this book," Carrie said. "It's not about telling the truth, or because of a passion for the subject. It's about trying to save your failing career. So how can I be expected to trust anything you say?"

Aaron clenched his jaw.

Leaning back in the armchair, Carrie regarded him coolly.

"Did you really see him?" she said.

Aaron nodded. "I told you. He was there."

For the briefest of moments, a deep longing swept over Carrie's face. It fell away into desolation. "I want to believe you. But I can't. I've seen nothing, not a sign of him. I think you're playing a sick game with me."

"I'm not playing any kind of game. I'm trying to—" Aaron caught his breath. He leaned forward, his eyes pleading with her.

"Trying to what?" Carrie demanded.

They were both quiet, staring at each other like poker players trying to guess their opponent's next move.

Aaron picked up his mug of coffee. He put it down again.

Fuck it.

"I'm trying to find him," he said. "I'm trying to find your son."

Carrie's mouth hung open. She stared at him for a long time, her dark, haunted eyes boring into him.

"What makes you think you can achieve what the police can't?" she said.

Aaron sucked in a breath.

He told her everything—the animal attacks, the map, his fruitless scouring of what he believed to be Cal's hunting ground. He told her about his theory that Grady Spencer had groomed each of his victims to abduct the next, and about how he believed Spencer had been grooming Cal to continue his horrific legacy of murder.

As Carrie listened, her complexion paled to a sickly grey, her body grew more and more still, until she resembled a lifeless statue. Then, when Aaron was finished, she slowly rose from the chair and shuffled over to the drinks cabinet. Taking out two glasses, she filled them with whiskey, and handed one to Aaron. Returning to the chair, she sank down and drained half of her glass in two large gulps.

Aaron stared at the drink in front of him, his mouth running dry. *Push it away. Don't even look at it.*

"You think Cal is responsible for all of those animal attacks?" Carrie's voice was heavy and lifeless, but it forced Aaron's attention away from the whiskey.

He looked up and saw pain spreading across her face like splinters across glass. What a terrible thing, he thought, to be reunited with your child after years of believing he was dead, only to lose him again, only to watch him change into . . . into . . . Aaron didn't know what. A psychopath? A monster?

Whatever he was, he was no longer Cal Anderson. Cal had died seven years ago. He was never coming back.

Slowly, Aaron nodded. He told Carrie about the similarities between the attacks, about the malice in the way the corpses had been displayed, just like Margaret Telford's dog.

Carrie emptied her glass. Before she could refill it, Aaron pushed his full glass towards her. She took it. For a long time, she was quiet, staring at the floor, the glass of whiskey tipping dangerously in her hand.

When she looked up again, her eyes were red and raw.

"You think my Cal could do that to a living creature? Could tear it apart until there was nothing left? You think he could slaughter an entire flock of sheep?"

"If he's filled with enough rage, yes. Grady Spencer spent years poisoning his mind, shaping it into something else. God knows what kind of psychological damage has been done."

Carrie flinched at the words. Tears splashed down her face. She made no move to wipe them away.

"But he's just a boy. *My* boy."

Aaron heaved his shoulders. "Carrie, it's not my intention to cause you more pain. I don't want to hurt anyone. But what if I'm right about your son? What if it's only a matter of time before he tires of killing animals and moves onto—"

"Stop! I don't want to hear it!" Carrie slammed the glass onto the table, whiskey spilling over the sides. "He's my son. He would never— He's not like that."

"Carrie, I think—"

"Why haven't you gone to the police?" She glared at Aaron. "If you're so convinced that Cal is dangerous, why haven't you told them?"

"How do you know I haven't?"

"Because if you had we wouldn't be sitting here right now." Her face twisted with despair. Her shoulders sagged. "I shouldn't have asked you to come here."

Aaron leaned forward. "Then why did you? If you're not going to help me with the book, why am I here?"

"Because I need to know if my son really is alive!" Carrie cried, her hands clenched into fists. "And if he is, I need to know why he won't come home to me!"

She stared at him, eyes round and wild, her body trembling.

"He's alive, I promise you," Aaron said. "And I haven't told the police because I was hoping I could find him first."

"Why?"

"So I could use him as a bargaining chip."

"To blackmail me?"

"Something like that, yes. I thought if I showed you proof, I could get you to agree to an exclusive interview for the book. In exchange, I could lead you to Cal, give you a chance to try and reach out to him before the police moved in. You save your son, I save my career. Two birds, one stone."

Aaron leaned back, shocked at the words spilling from his mouth. But it was obvious now that Carrie would never help him, so why bother hiding the truth?

He drew in a breath as he waited for Carrie to explode, to scream at him to get out of her house.

But Carrie was motionless, her face blank, her gaze unfocused.

"How close are you to finding him?" she asked.

Aaron sat up. This was unexpected.

Clearing his throat, he reached for his bag, pulled out the map, and unfolded it on the coffee table. "Wherever he's hiding out, it has to be nearby. I can't imagine he's hitching rides to Devil's Cove, can you?" He pointed to the black circle on the map. "He's in there somewhere, I'm sure of it. I mean, he must sleep somewhere, right? An abandoned building or a shed. There are plenty of places to hide away on farms. So, in answer to your question, I'm close. I just need to keep looking."

Carrie was quiet as she studied the map. Slowly, she shook her head. "If it was this easy, he would have been found by now," she said. "I mean, there was a search party, for Christ's sake. They found nothing. People think he's dead."

"But I know for a fact that Cal is alive," Aaron argued. "And I'm pretty sure he doesn't have an invisibility cloak, so unless someone's hiding him, he *has* to be out there."

Her mouth hanging open, Carrie suddenly sat up.

Aaron waited for her to speak. He quickly grew impatient.

"What is it?" Their eyes met across the table. Electricity crackled between them.

"They tried to take him away from me. But he came back."

"Who? What are you talking about?"

Carrie's eyes grew larger. "That's what he said to me. He said, 'They tried to take him away from me. But he came back.'"

"Who said that to you? What are you talking about?"

"Grady Spencer!" Carrie cried. "When he had me tied up in his basement, when he had my son leaning over me with a scalpel in his hand, he said, 'They tried to take him away from me. They tried to take him to the *farm*.'"

Something connected in Aaron's mind. He knew *something*. But what?

"The farm," he repeated. "What farm?"

Carrie was on her feet now, pacing the room. "It stuck in my head, but I thought it was just the ravings of a mad man. 'They tried to take him to the farm, but he came back.'"

Aaron looked up, a smile spreading across his face. *Of course.*

"That's why no one can find Cal," he said. "Because someone really is hiding him."

Carrie stopped pacing. She came back to the coffee table and, dropping to her knees, stabbed a finger at the map.

"Who's hiding him?"

"And at which farm?" Aaron said.

The feeling that he already knew the answer surged through him. He stared at Carrie, and for the first time since they'd met, she looked truly alive. It was an opportunity he couldn't afford to miss.

"If I can find him, if I can bring you proof, will you agree to an exclusive interview?" he said.

Carrie glared at him. "I could take this map and go to the police myself."

"And then they'll find him and arrest him. They'll take him

away from you. They'll send him to a mental institution, a detention centre, somewhere you'll never get a chance to reach out to him. To save him."

Carrie opened her mouth. She drew in a breath.

"I'm trying to give you that chance, Carrie. And I know it's for selfish reasons, but it's the only chance you have."

They were both silent, staring at each other with desperate gazes. And then voices filled the quiet. Aaron and Carrie turned in unison towards the living room door. The door opened and Sally appeared.

"There you are," she said to Carrie. "See who I bumped into on my way home. We thought we'd surprise you . . ." Her voice trailed off as she noticed Aaron sitting on the couch.

Aaron raised a hand, then shot a glance at Carrie, who had grown deathly pale. And then Melissa came rushing into the room in a whirlwind of excitement.

"Mummy!" she cried, barrelling forward with outstretched arms. She slammed into Carrie, almost knocking her to the floor.

Dylan's powerful frame appeared moments later. His smile quickly faded as his eyes found Aaron.

"What's this?" he said. "What the bloody hell's going on here?"

Aaron glanced at Carrie. She stared back.

Then she nodded.

30

NAT HAD BEEN BUSY. Ever since Aaron's painfully underwhelming reaction to her discovery of Grady Spencer's marriage, a black cloud of frustration had been hanging over her head. On Friday night, after returning from his hotel, she'd headed straight for Porth an Jowl Wine Shop with the purpose of buying tobacco but had left with a half bottle of vodka stashed inside her jacket pocket.

Yesterday morning, she'd woken with a hangover and had barely spoken a word to Rose over breakfast. The rest of the day she'd spent in her bedroom, swinging back and forth between self-pity and self-loathing.

Nat had honestly believed her discovery about Grady Spencer had been revelatory. After all, there had been no mention in the media about a wife. But Aaron had barely batted an eyelid.

Okay, so her research hadn't revealed anything new about the case like his had done, but that wasn't what Aaron had hired her to do. Her job was to create a profile of Grady Spencer; a man no one knew anything about except that he was

a cold-blooded killer of children, and that he was now thank-
fully dead.

But now Nat knew he'd had a wife. And ever since she'd
found out, she'd been unable to stop thinking about what had
happened to the woman. Add to that her growing desire to
prove she was, in fact, an excellent researcher, come Saturday
evening she'd decided to get over herself, get over her hangover,
and get back to work.

Using her own money, she'd signed up online for a member-
ship to the Family Historical Research Society. Then she'd spent
the rest of the night hunched over her laptop, accessing their
database and a whole cluster of subsequent websites, putting
together an admittedly patchy framework of Grady Spencer's
life.

Spencer had been born on 5th January 1935 to Mrs Eleanor
Spencer (maiden name Pethick), a local seamstress, and Mr
Anton Spencer, a tin miner, who resided in St Just in Roseland,
six miles south of Truro on the Roseland Peninsula. It was the
same village where Grady would marry Kathleen-Ann Nancarrow, and where her body would be found less than three years
later, on the shore of St Just Creek.

Nat had found nothing about Grady Spencer's childhood,
which was understandable due to it being decades before the
invent-ion of the world's greatest archive, the Internet.

What she did find were the death certificates of both his
parents. Both had died on the same night in June 1954. A search
of a local history news archive had revealed why.

The fire that had burned the Spencer household to the
ground had started in the basement in the early hours. Mr and
Mrs Spencer had been asleep upstairs. Suffering from insomnia,
nineteen-year-old Grady Spencer had allegedly been out for a

late-night walk. By the time he'd returned home, the upper floors were already ablaze. At the time the article had been published, the cause of the fire had yet to be determined.

Nat had found nothing more about the fire, and nothing more about Grady Spencer until the day of his marriage, which had brought her circling back to Kathleen-Ann Nancarrow.

What had attracted her to an unspeakable monster? Had Grady once been kind? Had he made a young woman laugh? Had he made her feel respected and cared for?

It was highly unlikely.

Perhaps it was the naivety of youth that had blinded Kathleen-Ann to what she was marrying. But she'd only been two years older than Nat was now, and sometimes Nat felt as old as the hills.

Kathleen-Ann Nancarrow had died at the age of twenty-one, when her life should have been blossoming. It didn't matter whether she had thrown herself into that creek and allowed the water to flood her lungs; Grady Spencer was responsible for her death. Of that, Nat was certain, and she was determined to find out more.

Kathleen-Ann had been forgotten, and people needed to know her name. Just like the rest of Grady Spencer's victims.

That was why now, on a bitter cold Sunday afternoon, Nat was stepping off a bus and entering the village of St Just in Roseland.

Much like Porth an Jowl, the place was deserted. The quiet was unnerving as she walked past rows of white houses with slate roofs and low garden walls. She felt conspicuous, like she shouldn't be here. But she didn't know why.

Perhaps it was guilt. This morning, before Rose had left to visit Carrie, Nat had lied to her, telling her she was going out to visit a friend. It was an obvious lie—Nat didn't have any friends —but Rose had nodded and told her to be home in time for supper. There had been hurt in her eyes when she'd said it.

Now, as Nat turned right, heading out of the village and along a single lane road lined with trees, she wondered if Rose knew she was still working for Aaron. She hung her head. She was such a liar.

But she was not the only one who'd been lying to Rose.

Twenty minutes ago, while riding the bus, Nat had been surprised by a phone call from Carrie. She'd asked for Aaron Black's phone number, which Nat gave her, then she'd begged Nat not to tell Rose that she'd called.

What was going on there? She'd thought it best not to ask, but when Carrie had started questioning her about Aaron, she'd answered honestly. Which she now regretted.

Even more reason to hope that further revelations were waiting to be discovered at St Just in Roseland.

The road was descending, leading her down a hill. A minute later, she found her destination on the right.

Set into the hillside, the churchyard was a maze of stone paths and steps leading through copses of evergreens and palms trees, thickets of bamboo, rhododendron, and winter blooms of bright camellias.

The air was thin and icy, the breeze laced with sea salt.

Nat descended through the churchyard, staring in awe at its natural beauty, until she reached the bottom of the hill.

St. Just's Church stood before her, a beautiful, 13th century stone construct framed by the backdrop of St Just Creek. A few boats bobbed up and down on the tidal waters, gently tugging at their moorings.

On the opposite bank, pine trees grew tall and proud. A few

white houses sat nestled in between. Beyond them were rolling, hilly fields. Even in winter it was a breathtaking sight.

Nat felt the peace around her like a comforting blanket. It was a shame she had come here under such morbid circumstances. Circling the church, she peered curiously through its ornate windows. If there had been a Sunday service, it had already come to an end; no one was inside. In fact, she hadn't seen a single person since she'd arrived. Which was eerie and comforting at the same time.

Where did she start looking?

On her way down, she'd spied hundreds of headstones, some peeking through the trees and undergrowth, others lining the paths or climbing the hill in tiers. It could take her hours to find what she was searching for. And she had maybe two left of daylight at most.

Chewing her lower lip, she glanced around at the nearest headstones. They were old and moss-covered, their engravings worn down by sea salt and years of weather. Most of the death dates were from the 1800s.

She glanced up the hill, trying to see beyond the trees and shrubberies. Then she started climbing the stone steps, retracing her route. At the top, near the gated entrance, the headstones were newer, shinier. A lot of the death dates were from the 1980s.

Nat pulled out her phone and unlocked the screen. Opening the photographs folder, she flipped through pictures until she found the one she was looking for—a screenshot of Kathleen-Ann Nancarrow's death certificate, taken from the Family Historical Research Society database.

"14th March, 1966," she read aloud.

She turned and looked downhill. If the older graves were

closest to the church and the newest near the churchyard entrance, then Kathleen-Ann's grave couldn't be too far from where she was standing. The only way she was going to find it was to start looking.

So, Nat began, moving from headstone to headstone, reading names, dates, and epitaphs, walking up and down rows, ducking in between trees, and stepping along paths. And as the minutes ticked by and the sky grew dim, she didn't once stop to think *why* she was looking for the grave of Grady Spencer's wife, whose body had washed up on the shore below fifty years earlier. Perhaps it was because she felt a strange connection to Kathleen-Ann Nancarrow; a connection which she didn't truly understand.

Or perhaps it was because she couldn't quite believe that Grady Spencer had not been birthed from a nightmare. Perhaps she had needed to see that monsters were born just like anyone else.

Grady Spencer's birthplace was beautiful and filled with peace, and even though she didn't believe in a higher power, she could feel it all around her. But the greatest horror could be born out of the greatest beauty, she knew that only too well. And she saw it for herself again, almost two hours later.

As the day grew dark and bruised the sky, Kathleen-Ann's headstone revealed itself, partially hidden in foliage beneath the fronds of a Trachycarpus palm. Dropping to her knees, Nat swept back the leaves and read the neatly etched epitaph.

"Kathleen-Ann Nancarrow, born 29th May, 1944, died 14th March, 1966. Taken from this world far too soon. Loving wife. Loving daughter."

Then she stared with terrified eyes at the crudely chiselled words below: AND USELESS BITCH MOTHER.

31

WHAT DID HE KNOW? Aaron was back at the hotel, his research notes scattered across the bed and the desk, his mind a mess of colliding thoughts. As soon as Dylan Killigrew had appeared in Carrie's living room with a face full of thunder, Aaron had quickly made his excuses and left. The tension in the air had been palpable, and the way that Dylan had reacted to Aaron's presence had suggested it was best to leave before bones were broken. Besides, he'd got what he'd come for.

Carrie had agreed to an exclusive interview.

Yes, there was the small issue of finding Cal in exchange, but now Aaron had knowledge that the police didn't: someone was deliberately keeping Cal hidden.

He'd spent the last hour poring over his notes and printouts, scouring every word and sentence, searching for the key that would unlock a door in his mind and reveal what it was that he knew.

Because Aaron was certain he knew something about Cal's whereabouts. He had known it as soon as Carrie had recalled

Grady Spencer's words: *They tried to take him away from me. They tried to take him to the farm. But he came back.*

There was something here, hidden among all the information he'd gathered. But where? What had he missed?

He cast his eyes around the room. Like a flash of lightning, the answer came to him.

"My camera."

Grabbing his bag from the floor, he removed the camera, switched it on, then sat down heavily on the edge of the bed. Setting the camera to 'review' mode, he began sifting through all the images he'd taken since arriving in Cornwall. He moved backward in time, past photographs of all the places he'd visited, the people he'd interviewed, the rooms of Grady Spencer's house, until he was back at the beginning, staring at those first images he'd snapped of the beach at Devil's Cove on a windswept Sunday morning,

"What am I looking for?" he breathed.

He flipped forward again, returning to the photographs of Grady Spencer's house of horrors, until he came to the pictures of the basement. Whatever it was, suddenly he knew he would find it here among the bloodstains and bricked up doors and ghosts of murdered children.

He slowed down, zooming in on each picture.

His breaths grew fast and shallow. His intuition tightened its grip on his gut.

And there it was. The connection he'd been missing.

He stared at the photograph. He pinched the screen, zooming in. The image was of the etchings he'd found scraped into the basement wall; childlike scratchings of figures and animals and buildings.

There, in the middle, was a crude etching of a house with

broken windows. Next to the house was a Christ-like figure with claws for hands; hands that were nailed to a cross. Except it wasn't Jesus Christ like Aaron had first presumed.

It was a scarecrow.

And yesterday, he had seen one just like it.

With trembling fingers, he raced forward in time, flicking through the thumbnail images until he found the photograph he was looking for.

It had been taken at dusk. The house was visible on the right side of the picture, its boarded-up windows like eyes watching from shadows.

The scarecrow was on the left; a chilling silhouette that Aaron had first seen from the corner of his eye.

It had frightened him. He'd thought it was Cal.

What was the name of the farm?

He scanned back a few images, until he came upon the rusting field gate and its faded, ominous sign.

BURNT HOUSE FARM.

This was it.

This was where Cal was hiding.

There had been a little girl. A little girl and a red-haired woman, who'd threatened to fetch her husband if Aaron didn't leave.

Who were these people? Why were they keeping Cal hidden like a terrible secret?

Aaron turned back to the photograph of the scarecrow and the house with broken windows.

They tried to take him from me. They tried to take him to the farm. But he came back.

These people knew Grady Spencer. They were connected to him somehow. And if they'd known about Cal, if they'd tried to rescue him, had they also known about all the children Spencer had murdered?

His head swelling with confusion, Aaron dropped the camera on the bed and moved over to the window. Outside, the street was quiet and empty.

"What's going on here?" he thought aloud.

Why had these people tried to rescue Cal but not reported Spencer to the police?

It didn't make sense.

Unless . . .

"Unless they're somehow involved, too."

A shrill ringing pierced the air, startling him. It was the hotel room phone.

"Mr Black, you have a visitor," the receptionist said, sounding harassed. "The young woman from the other day."

Nat? What was she doing here?

"Tell her I'm busy," Aaron said.

"I'm afraid she's already on her way up."

Aaron hung up. *Shit.*

He quickly gathered up his notes from the bed and tidied them into a rough pile on the desk. Switching off the camera, he slipped it back inside his bag.

He was so close now that he could almost sense Cal moving in the shadows. He could tell no one, not even Nat. Especially not Nat. She couldn't wait to tell Carrie all about his failing career and she'd almost wrecked his chances of getting Carrie on board in the process.

What would Nat do if she knew how close Aaron was to finding Cal? Who would she tell? One phone call to the police and they'd be crawling all over Burnt House Farm before Aaron could stop them.

No one was going to take this opportunity away from him. Not when he was this close to success.

A loud hammering on the door pulled him from his thoughts. He crossed the room and let Nat in.

"I've been trying to call," she said, barging past and throwing her bag onto the bed. "Why haven't you been picking up?"

"I've had my phone switched off. I've been busy," he said.

"Busy doing what?" Nat glanced at the pile of papers on the desk. Aaron moved into the room, blocking her path.

"What are you doing here?" he asked.

Nat's face twitched as she reached into her pocket and pulled out her phone. "I found something. Like, something major! This afternoon I went down to St Just in Roseland, to the churchyard where Kathleen-Ann Nancarrow is buried."

Aaron frowned. "Why?"

Sucking in a deep breath, Nat proceeded to tell him what she'd learned about Grady Spencer's origins—his parents, the fire, how she believed it was no accident—and then she showed him the photograph she'd taken of Kathleen-Ann's final resting place.

Aaron took the phone and stared at the awful words someone had hacked into the headstone

"Don't you see?" Nat gasped. "Grady Spencer had a child!"

Aaron was quiet, staring at the picture. This was a good find; a development he hadn't expected. But his own, very recent revelation had him distracted.

"How do you know for sure?" he said, handing the phone back.

The excitement in Nat's eyes died. "What the hell are you talking about?" she said. "Why else would someone come along and carve those words into her headstone?"

"You tell me."

Nat was quiet for a moment, gathering her thoughts. "Well, you remember that old news article I found? It said that Kathleen-Ann had been estranged from her family for over a year. That she'd hidden herself away. No one had seen her. Grady Spencer told everyone that she'd had a miscarriage and become depressed because she'd been left sterile. But what if she hadn't miscarried? What if she'd had that kid?"

"So, you think she killed herself not because she'd miscarried but because Grady Spencer had what? Murdered their own child?"

"At first that's what I thought. That Spencer had killed their child, then murdered Kathleen-Ann, or had driven her to suicide. But that theory left me with a question."

"Who carved these words into the headstone?"

"Exactly. The actual epitaph mentions nothing about Kathleen-Ann being a mother. But someone knew the truth. Someone came to her grave and carved those awful words. And I think it could have only been one of two people. Either Grady Spencer thought he'd add his own epitaph."

Aaron looked up. A missing piece of the puzzle snapped into place. "Or Grady Spencer didn't murder his child after all. Jesus Christ . . ."

"There are two things I don't understand, though," Nat said. "Why did he keep the child alive? And where was that child when Grady moved to Devil's Cove? Rose said it herself, Grady Spencer moved there alone."

"Yes, but Grady Spencer also murdered at least eight children inside his house without anyone ever knowing. He'd kept Cal locked up for seven years while everyone else thought he was dead. Sneaking his own child in would have been a breeze."

"Okay, fine, but it still doesn't answer the question why Grady kept him or her alive."

Aaron's mind raced. Why was he suddenly thinking of Toby Baker and the cliff path at Zennor?

And then it was obvious. How had he gotten it so wrong?

He stared at Nat. The room closed in on him.

Grady Spencer hadn't groomed those kids to help abduct their replacement. Grady Spencer had groomed his own child to abduct them all.

But what about Cal?

He hadn't been abducted, had he? He'd walked right into Grady Spencer's basement, a gift wrapped in a bow. What had happened next? Where was Grady Spencer's child now?

At that moment, he knew the answers were waiting for him at Burnt House Farm.

He had to leave. To go there right now. Even if going there meant risking his life—because Aaron was convinced that whatever he found there was about to change his fortune for good.

Nat was staring at the image on her phone screen, her face pulled into a frown.

"Those words are so angry," she said. "*Useless bitch mother.* But if Spencer's child wrote them, doesn't that mean they're free? So, where are they? *Who* are they?"

Aaron had to get rid of her.

In the next minute, maybe two, Nat was going to work it all out for herself. He couldn't let that happen. Because Nat would do something sensible, like tell Rose. Or worse, tell the police.

"You did good," he said.

He moved over to his jacket, which was hanging on the back of the chair, and pulled out his wallet. "In fact, you did great. Thanks for your help."

He handed her a large wad of notes without counting how much was there. Her eyes wide, Nat took the money. Confusion rippled across her features.

"Wait, that's it? But we've only just found out that—"

"You've done your job, Nat. I asked you to build a profile of Grady Spencer, and you found out as much as you could."

"But I haven't finished. There's still a ten, fifteen-year gap between Spencer leaving St Just in Roseland and arriving in the cove. I haven't found out what he did for a living. And what about this kid?"

"Don't worry about it. I can take it from here."

Aaron picked up Nat's bag from the bed with one hand and grasped her gently by the arm with the other. In one fluid movement, he was moving her towards the door.

Nat pulled away from him, wrenching her arm from his hand.

Her mouth fell open. A vein began to pulse in the centre of her forehead.

"Wait a minute, what the hell's going on?" she demanded. "Is this because I told Carrie about your flagging career? I'm sorry, I didn't mean to—it just kind of slipped out."

Aaron opened the door, and kept it held open.

"It's nothing to do with that. I'm busy, that's all. And like I said, you've done your job."

"So, what? That's it?"

"I'm not sure what else you want me to tell you." He stared at her, watching her eyes grow glassy and wet and her shoulders sag.

But what else was he supposed to do? He couldn't let her know where he was about to go. Not only because it was dangerous, but because this moment was his—and he hadn't lost everything to share it with someone else.

Nat looked up at him, her eyes hardening and her lips pressing together in a pale white line.

"Fine," she growled. "Like I give a shit, anyway."

She barged past him, her shoulder slamming into his arm as she stormed through the door and out into the hallway. For a second, Aaron thought she was going to keep on walking. But then she turned, spinning angrily on her heels.

"Fuck you, Aaron Black!" she cried. "You're an asshole and you're a loser. And I hope your book fucking fails!"

She spun around again, then stomped away.

Silently, Aaron shut the door. He rested his back against it, staring at the emptiness of the hotel room, feeling the walls close in on him. He couldn't breathe. It was as if Nat had stolen the air. She was right, of course. He was an asshole. And he was a loser. And she deserved much better treatment than he'd given her.

When he was dripping in success and riches, he would make it up to her. But right now, he needed to keep a clear head. Right now, he needed to prepare himself.

Because he was going to Burnt House Farm, where he would find Cal Anderson and get the proof he needed.

Where he would find Grady Spencer's now adult offspring.

32

CAL WAS RESTLESS, pacing through the rooms of the house. He was beginning to feel like he was back in the cage down in Grady Spencer's basement. It had been two days since the passing of his test. They'd returned to the farm with the man still unconscious and the young child still sobbing and afraid.

The man had been taken down to the basement, where he remained. Jacob had given the boy to Alison. She'd been taking care of him ever since. Cynthia had grown increasingly agitated since his arrival. And with good reason.

The atmosphere in the house had changed because the new boy wouldn't stop crying. Even now, his relentless wails were grating Cal's ears.

Heath and Morwenna had already had enough of the noise. They'd been taking turns watching over the man in the basement, but now they shared the duty together.

Even the younger children, who were always filled with energy and delight, had changed. Now, they spoke in tiny whispers and all of them had stopped smiling. But it wasn't just the boy making Cal grow increasingly restless, or the boy's father tied up in the basement.

It had been days since he'd last seen his mother. Days that felt like years. The longer he spent away from her, the more he was convinced she was forgetting him.

And what about that man? Had he been busy whispering in his mother's ear while Cal had been kept away?

Cal couldn't bear not knowing. He couldn't bear being kept inside this house like a prisoner. With every second that passed by, he could feel the cord that connected them gradually wearing thin. If he didn't see her soon, he knew the cord would snap.

Pacing the hall, Cal tried to shut out the boy's sobs. Somewhere, deep down inside, he understood his desperation. All the boy wanted was to be reunited with his father. All he wanted was to go back to his toys and his home and his safe little world.

But that was all gone now. And the quicker the boy got used to the idea, the better it would be for him.

For everyone.

Cal stopped in the doorway of the meeting room. Alison was sat cross-legged in the centre of the threadbare carpet, a lantern flickering next to her. Two of the younger children, Judith and Ben, sat beside her, taking turns to roll a ball. The boy sat on the other side, his tear-stained face shining in the lantern light. They all looked up as Cal stood in the doorway. The boy's cries grew louder.

"You're scaring him, Cal!" Alison said, her voice tired and exasperated. She was two, maybe three years older than Cal, yet behind her eyes she looked as if she'd lived a lifetime. "Why don't you go and see if Celia needs help with the dishes?"

Cal ignored her, his gaze moving from Judith and Ben to the crying boy. *Shut up,* he thought. *Shut up or I'll make you shut up.*

He didn't know the boy's name. No one did. Jacob would give him a new one, anyway. He'd given everyone new names. Everyone except Cal. Jacob had said his name was already strong and powerful.

Fists clenching and unclenching, Cal backed away from the room and glanced along the hall. He could hear Celia moving around in the kitchen, cleaning up after the evening meal. Screwing up his face, he turned in the opposite direction and wandered through the shadows, until he came to the basement door.

Curiosity pulled at him. Opening the door, he stared into the darkness. Cold crept up the steps like a fog. The sharp smell of mildew hung in the air. Cal cocked his head and listened. The boy's cries rang in his ears.

I'll slit your throat. That will keep you quiet.

No! He's scared, that's all. He'll calm down soon.

You're weak, boy! Nothing but a disappointment.

Cal descended into the darkness.

Reaching the bottom of the steps, the boy's sobs faded away. A little of the tension left Cal's shoulders. He moved forward, running his hands along the corridor walls. He didn't need a lantern. Having spent years in Grady Spencer's basement, he was quite accustomed to moving around in the dark.

A faint light flickered in the near distance. It was coming from beneath a door. He knew the man was in there somewhere. Heath and Morwenna, too. He'd never been into that room. He was forbidden. He wasn't even supposed to be down here.

Pressing his ear against the wood, Cal listened. He heard movement, someone walking around. He heard low whispers. Then he heard a dull thud, followed by a short, sharp gasp. They were hurting the man. That's what they were doing. He pressed his ear to the wood again. He caught his breath. Someone was leaving the room. Stepping back, Cal turned and hurried back down the corridor. Behind him, the door opened and a voice stopped him in his tracks.

"I know you're there, Cal," Jacob said. "Come into the light where I can see you."

Cal hovered for a moment, trying to make himself small.

"Don't be afraid. Fear is weakness," Jacob said.

Slowly, Cal made his way back to the door. He appeared from the shadows like a ghost.

Jacob stood in the doorway, his face glowing in the lantern light. "You're not supposed to be here. How long have you been standing outside?"

Cal shrugged.

He kept his eyes on the ground, then remembering it was also a sign of weakness, looked up into Jacob's eyes.

"You're curious," Jacob said. "I understand that. But curiosity leads to questions. And when we question, we doubt. I know you would never doubt me, would you?"

Cal's eyes wandered to the side and over Jacob's shoulder.

"Would you, Cal?"

He snapped his gaze back. Slowly, he shook his head.

In the lantern light, Jacob smiled. "Good, that's very good. All you need to know right now is that this is all part of your journey to enlightenment. Tomorrow, will be the second part of your test. Then you'll truly be awakened." He shifted in the doorway, peering over his shoulder for a second, then back at Cal. "This evening's lesson will begin shortly. Tell Alison to take the boy upstairs. Is he still upset?"

Cal nodded.

"It won't be forever. Soon he'll join the Dawn Children with open arms, and you'll lead him along the path to glory. Now, off you go." Jacob shut the door, plunging Cal back into darkness.

He stood for a moment, listening to Jacob walk away. Then he turned and made his way along the corridor. He reached the top of the steps. The boy's sobbing attacked his ears once more.

Suddenly there was no air in the house. Suddenly all Cal could think about was to be running free outside. Keeping his feet light, he moved along the hall until he reached the meeting room. He pointed to the boy then pointed at the ceiling. Alison nodded and clapped her hands.

"Come on little ones, let's take our friend here upstairs."

Cal moved on. His chest grew tighter. His lungs burned. He felt the darkness call to him. He hurried past the kitchen. Then slid to a halt. The kitchen had been empty.

Backing up, he peered through the doorway. Pots were neatly stacked and drying on the drainer. A kettle of water was heating on the stove. But Cynthia was nowhere to be seen.

He could go outside.

Just for a moment. Just to breathe in some fresh air. Besides, he'd been good, hadn't he? He'd stayed at the farm for days. He'd passed his test. He'd done as he'd been told. Didn't he deserve a reward for that? Didn't he deserve to step out, even for a minute?

He glanced over his shoulder and checked the hallway. Then he was moving through the kitchen and unbolting the locks of the back door.

What do you think you're doing?

He opened the door a crack.

Are you listening to me, boy?

The evening chill rushed over him. Before he realised it, he was standing in the yard, sucking in lungful of air.

Do not defy me, you worthless runt! You know what will happen if you go there!

Before he could stop himself, Cal was moving through the darkness, crouched down like an animal. And then he was racing towards Devil's Cove.

If he cut through the fields, he could be there in twenty minutes, eighteen if he pushed himself.

He'd take a quick look. That was all he needed. A quick look to see if his mother had forgotten him. He would be back before the evening lesson had even begun.

33

THE LIVING ROOM WAS QUIET. Carrie sat on one end of the couch, while Dylan sat on the other. Neither of them had spoken in several minutes. Carrie's eyes kept moving towards the drinks cabinet. But she knew this was not the time. She knew that things were hanging by a thread.

Melissa and Sally were upstairs. They had all had an awkward dinner together. Sally had kept glaring across the table at Carrie, her eyes full of contempt. Dylan had avoided looking at her and had barely said a word the entire meal. Even Melissa had stayed quiet.

They were all blaming her. But this was not Carrie's fault. They weren't even supposed to be here. This is what happened when her mother tried to interfere.

Carrie risked a glance at Dylan.

Who was she trying to kid? This was all her fault. And now she had made it worse. Because she had lied to Dylan, to her mother, to her daughter. She had told them that yes, she'd invited the writer over, but not to help him with his book, not to be interviewed, but because she'd wanted to know why he was here. Why he thought it was a good idea to be writing a book about all the terrible things that had happened to her family. And although that wasn't a lie exactly, she had omitted everything else.

Now she was worried. More than worried.

If Dylan found out what she'd agreed to, if he knew what she now knew, things would suddenly be a lot worse. Melissa wouldn't be upstairs, sleeping in her room. The police would probably be here, or on their way to Aaron's hotel wanting to question him. And maybe that was the right thing to happen. Maybe this really all should come to an end.

But she couldn't let that happen. She had to try one last time. And if it paid off, if she was able to save her son, then it would all be worth it.

She felt Dylan's eyes upon her.

"What were you thinking?" he said. There wasn't anger in his voice, just disappointment and confusion. "We'd already discussed this, Carrie."

"It hadn't really been a discussion though, had it?" she replied. "You *told* me not to see him."

"I suppose I did. Now I feel like it's my fault. If I hadn't told you about him, you wouldn't have asked him here."

"This is a small town. I would have found out about him sooner or later."

"So, you would have seen him anyway? You wouldn't even care about the effect it would have on our family?"

Carrie shook her head. "Dylan . . ."

She didn't want to have this conversation. She just wanted them to leave. To stay. For their lives to return to normal. To get her son back. She could see the hurt in Dylan's eyes. The betrayal. It made her heart ache.

"Honestly, I don't know why I asked him here." Another lie. What was she doing? "I guess, maybe I just wanted to know what he knew. I guess maybe I thought—"

Dylan looked at her. His shoulders heaved. "You thought maybe he knew where to find Cal?"

Carrie turned away. She was making things worse. She should just tell him what they had really discussed. Then it would all be out in the open. She glanced back at him, forcing her eyes to stay on his face. But all she saw was sadness now. Sadness and a broken heart.

Then Dylan knocked the air from her lungs.

"I don't know if I can do this anymore," he said. "I just—I mean, I can't—"

Carrie's mouth fell open. Her heart thumped in her chest. But she stayed silent, waiting for him to finish his sentence.

Dylan remained quiet. He wouldn't even look at her.

"Dylan . . ." How did she stop this? How did she make him change his mind? "I just—I just need a little more time."

It was the wrong thing to say.

"Jesus, Carrie!" Dylan threw his hands in the air. "I know, all right? It's all you ever tell me—you need more time. But you've had more and more time, and nothing's changed. Not a single thing! Actually, that's not true. Melissa's changed. This is killing her. And I can't let that happen."

The room wavered. Carrie shook her head. Fear crept up her throat. "What are you saying?"

"I'm saying that I have to put Melissa's best interests first. I have to bring some stability back to her life."

"Don't you mean *we*? *We* have to bring stability back to her life?"

Dylan finally looked up, meeting her gaze. "But you're not

even trying, are you? If you were, then you wouldn't have had that writer here today. You wouldn't be drinking your damn life away!"

Carrie's heart stopped. How did he know?

But it was obvious. *Sally.*

Carrie opened her mouth to protest. To claim her innocence. But it would just be another lie. And she had told so many lies to Dylan lately that she couldn't remember the last time she'd told him the truth.

Worse still, now she was angry with him.

"So, what is this?" she hissed. "Some sort of ultimatum? Get over it or get out?"

She wanted him to lose his temper. To shout at her. Then *he* could be the villain. The awful husband that didn't understand, that demanded she snap out of it, press the reset button like she was nothing more than a Stepford wife.

But Dylan didn't get angry. He just grew sadder.

"I want my wife back. I want my family back. I want us to be happy again. But I want Melissa to stop having nightmares. I want her to stop wondering if she's ever going to come back home. And it's you, Carrie. It's you that's making me choose between our daughter and my wife."

He hung his head and turned away. It was hard to tell in the low light, but Carrie was sure that she saw a tear slip from his eye.

Guilt knocked the wind from her stomach. She was tearing her family apart. She was spreading her misery like a disease, poisoning everyone in her path. But what was she supposed to do?

Whether he knew it or not, Dylan was asking her to choose between her children. And she knew that she may have already lost one, she knew that she may never get him back, but that didn't mean that she couldn't still save him. And she had to save him. Because no one else would; not even Aaron Black—because as well-intentioned as he seemed, his motivation to reunite mother and son was driven only by fame and success.

Carrie's head swelled with confusion. She looked up. Reached out a hand. "Dylan," she whispered. "I'm sorry. I'm so sorry." She didn't know what to think anymore. She didn't *want* to think any more.

Dylan turned towards her, his sad eyes glistening. She had never seen him look so lost. So afraid.

"I miss you," she said.

"I miss you, too," he said. "This is tearing me apart."

Carrie got up and moved beside him. She took his hand in hers. Kissed the back of it. Turned it over and kissed his palm.

"Please," she whispered. "Can't we just forget about it for one evening? Can't we just pretend everything is fine just for an hour?"

She reached up and kissed him. It had been so long since she'd felt her lips on his without feeling only numbness. Now, she felt electricity crackle between them.

Dylan pulled away, his eyes piercing hers.

"Forgetting doesn't fix anything," he said. "Forgetting just puts everything off."

Carrie leaned forward and kissed him again. This time he kissed her back. She reached up a hand and gripped the back of his neck. Then his arms were around her and it was as if none of the horror of the last few months had ever happened.

It was like they'd gone back in time, to when they'd first met. To when passion had been unbridled and the touch of Dylan's lips on hers had meant everything. But then, as they lay down together on the sofa, their bodies pressing against each other, their hands grasping, Carrie felt her body run cold. And she realised that she didn't know if she was allowing this to happen because she wanted to save their marriage, or if it was because she wanted to save her son.

34

HE'D MADE it in sixteen minutes. He'd counted the seconds in his head. Now, he was crouched behind a parked car, sweat making his clothes stick, frosty plumes billowing from his mouth as he tried to catch his breath.

It felt dangerous to be here so early; there were lights still on in people's homes all over town. But here, hidden in the shadows outside his former home, Cal felt safe. But that protection could be torn away at any moment.

Still sitting on his haunches, Cal spun around. His breathing was a little steadier now, but his heart was racing. Pushing himself up, he peered over the car, hoping to catch a glimpse of his mother.

His blood ran cold.

She was in the living room, sitting on the couch. And she was not alone.

He was in there. Dylan. His arm draped over her shoulder. And she was leaning into him. She was happy he was there.

Dylan Killigrew, who had never wanted Cal. Who had done everything in his power to turn Cal's mother against him.

He wasn't the only one here, either. A light was on upstairs. In Melissa's bedroom. They were here. They had come back.

And they were going to stay.

For a second, Cal felt shut out, abandoned like an unwanted animal. Then his hands balled into fists and he pressed them to his temples. Hate boiled his insides.

I told you, boy. Didn't I warn you? Didn't I tell you she doesn't care?

Grady Spencer had been right all along. His mother had never wanted him. Not from the day he was born. And she'd been glad when he'd disappeared because it meant she could have another child, one that she loved. Because she had never loved him the way that she loved Melissa.

Trembling uncontrollably, Cal checked the street, then like a cat, stole across the road and through the garden gate.

He was moving on autopilot, barely aware of his actions as he made his way along the path, until he was beside the living room window, pressed against the wall. He leaned out a little and stole a glance inside.

The hate inside him burst into fire.

They were kissing. Carrie and Dylan. Kissing with their hands all over each other.

She doesn't love me. She doesn't want me. All this time I thought she cared. All this time I thought she was waiting for me to come home.

Dylan and Melissa were going nowhere. How long would it be before Cal's room was turned back into a home office?

You should tear her heart out and feed it to her.

How long would it be before they decided to have another baby and the office was turned into a nursery?

Spit on her grave and piss on her bones.

How long would it be before Cal was forgotten forever?

I can't. I love her. And she loves me!

Cal stole another glance through the window. He saw Dylan pull his mother into a tight embrace. He saw his mother bring her lips to Dylan's, saw her look lovingly into his eyes.

If she loves you why is she in there acting like a dirty whore? Why is her runt daughter upstairs while you're locked outside?

Cal squeezed his eyes together, pushed his fists into his temples again. He wanted to call out to her. To run inside and throw his arms around her.

She's never loved you, boy. She doesn't care if you live or die. She has her family with her now and you're not part of it. You're nothing to her. She wishes you were never born.

His fists struck the wall. He felt the skin break, the sting of cold air on open wounds.

We'll punish them. We'll make them suffer together. And when we're done, she'll know exactly how it feels to be left all alone in this stinking world.

Shaking with rage, Cal sprang to his feet. Hot tears stung his eyes as he turned the corner and followed the path along the side of the house. He entered the backyard, almost tripping over Melissa's little blue bike with its plastic stabilisers and front basket. He caught it before it hit the ground and a memory shot into his mind.

He wished he'd been around to see the looks of horror on those little girls' faces. To hear their terrified screams when they'd found what he'd put inside the basket.

That's what you get for being such a happy stinking family.

He hoped those girls had cried for days.

Cal cut through the shadows, heading for the back door. He

didn't know what he was going to do once he got inside. All he knew was that they needed to feel his pain.

He stepped up to the door and tried the handle. The door was unlocked. It swung open a few centimetres.

Cal slipped a hand inside his pocket and pulled out a blade. It was the one Grady Spencer had given him. The one he carried with him always. The one that cut through animal flesh like it was cutting through water.

He pushed the door open further. He lifted his foot to cross the threshold and kicked something over.

Cal looked down. A familiar shape was lying on the doorstep. He crouched down for a closer look. It was his dinosaur. Rex. The one he'd had since he was a child. What was it doing out here?

In an instant he knew.

It was my favourite.

She had brought it to him at the hospital in those early days following his return. She had brought it to remind him of the child he had once been: a happy child, who was always smiling, who loved ice cream and pirates, and who wanted nothing more than to go sailing the seven seas in search of buried treasure.

Had she left the toy out here for him? A sign to tell him that she was still here waiting for her happy little pirate to come home?

No, it's a lie! If it were true she wouldn't be in the living room right now, letting that man put his dirty hands all over her.

Picking up the dinosaur, Cal drew back his hand and threw it as hard as he could. The toy sailed off into the darkness.

Then he was crossing the threshold and entering the kitchen. The house was quiet, his ragged breaths the only sound.

The downstairs hall light was off. Cal moved forward, the

blade pointed in front of him, until he stood outside the closed living room door. His heart hammered in his chest as he pressed his ear to the wood.

It was quiet in there. He heard soft rustles of skin and clothes that made him feel nauseous. Then he heard his mother's voice, so close that the hairs on the back of his neck sprang up.

"Dylan, maybe we should stop. Melissa's probably not even asleep. And my mother . . ."

Cal hovered in the dark, barely breathing.

Then *he* spoke. "Sure, of course. Whatever you want. Besides, we don't have to rush anything. There's still so much to talk about."

Bile climbed Cal's throat. He wanted nothing more than to throw open the door and plunge his blade deep into Dylan's eye.

Oh yes, boy—cut it out and swallow it whole! But not yet.

Cal turned his head until he was looking at the stairs.

First, we must take her most precious jewel. First, she must feel unimaginable pain.

Silently, he stole past the living room door and climbed the steps. Reaching the landing, he pressed himself up against the wall. Melissa's door was open a crack. He looked along to his old room. Light was spilling out from under the door.

At first, he was confused. Then he remembered Sally was here.

One big, happy family.

Gripping the knife, Cal darted forward until he was by Melissa's door.

Then he stepped inside.

She was asleep in her bed, blonde hair spilling over her angelic face. A projector sat in the corner, sending animal shapes and patterns of light dancing across the walls.

Cal stepped noiselessly into the centre of the room.

Why does she get to have such a happy life full of love? Why does she get to have everything she wants when I have nothing?

They could have been a family. He could have lived with that. But now he didn't even exist.

Yes, boy. Oh, yes! I'm the only one who cares about you now. The only one who can show you your true path. Do it, boy. Make Father proud.

Cal stepped closer. White hot tears spilled down his face. The blade trembled in his hand.

If he didn't exist, then what he was about to do didn't even matter. But it would make him feel better.

35

THE SCREAM SHATTERED THE AIR, making the hairs on Carrie's arms prickle. She and Dylan pulled away from each other, their eyes growing wide and dilated, their mouths hanging open in shock.

They both jumped to their feet, hearts hammering in their chests. With Carrie in front, they raced out of the room and towards the stairs.

The screams came again, terrified, high-pitched. Carrie and Dylan flew up the stairs. They reached the landing, slamming into each other as they turned the corner.

Melissa's bedroom door was open.

The screams were coming from inside.

Dylan pushed past, thundering into the room. Carrie dashed after him. The first thing she saw was Melissa sitting upright in bed, her eyes bulging from their sockets, her mouth hanging open in a terrible scream. Then she saw Dylan drop to his knees in the corner of the room.

Something was slumped there. With horror, Carrie realised it was her mother. Her back was against the wall, her legs splayed out. A deep, dark wet patch was blooming at the centre of her chest. Animals and patterns from the projector danced across her skin.

Carrie was paralysed, unable to comprehend what she was seeing. Her ears hurt with Melissa's high-pitched shrieks. The room spun, faster and faster. Then she was spinning too, her eyes cycling back, over and over, to her mother's crumpled shape.

Dylan was shouting something. Shouting and looking at her, pointing to the door. It was as if his voice was coming through the walls. Carrie turned and stared at her daughter, who'd never looked so terrified. And then Melissa was pointing to a space behind Carrie. She was pointing and screaming hysterically.

Slowly, Carrie turned. And she saw him.

Her son. Cal.

He was standing behind the open door. Knife in his hand. Murder in his eyes. There was nothing human about him. It was like a wild animal had broken into their home.

The air fled her lungs. Her heart smashed against her chest. She looked her son in the eye and saw nothing there. She opened her mouth and screamed his name. "Cal! Cal, what have you done!"

Cal's lips curled back and he bore his teeth like a wild dog.

And then Dylan was on his feet, a look of pure rage on his face. Cal turned, his eyes meeting Dylan's. Like lightning, he shot out of the room. Before Carrie could stop him, Dylan leaped forward, chasing after him.

Melissa continued to scream. Sally gasped and reached out a hand. Carrie came to her senses. She darted forward, grabbing one of Melissa's T-shirts from the floor and falling to her knees in front of Sally. She pressed the T-shirt against the wound. But the blood was coming thick and fast, spreading across Sally's nightdress.

Sally tried to say something. Carrie leaned in closer. Tears splashed down her face. Her heart was going to smash right through her rib cage.

"I just came to check on Melissa," Sally croaked. "He was standing over her . . ."

Her eyelids fluttered. Her eyes rolled back in their sockets.

Carrie's head shot towards the door. She opened her mouth and screamed. "Dylan! Call an ambulance!"

Somewhere downstairs she heard a door slam. Then feet were hammering up the stairs. Dylan appeared in the doorway, his shoulders heaving up and down.

"He's gone!" he cried. "He got away!"

Carrie stared at him incredulously.

"Call a fucking ambulance!" she shrieked.

Behind her on the bed, Melissa's wails swelled to an unbearable crescendo. Dylan stared at Carrie. He flashed her a glare, one that was all too easy to read: *this is your fault*, it said. *If your mother dies, it's on you.*

Dylan ran from the room.

Carrie turned back to her mother.

"Stay with me!" she breathed, putting more pressure on the wound. "Please, Mum, stay with me!"

Blood spilled over her hands.

36

THE COUNTRYSIDE at night was pure darkness. In the city, light pollution painted the night a muddy green, sometimes a murky orange. But never black. Not like this. This was a primal darkness that manifested all kinds of horrors in Aaron's mind as he drove along the winding ribbon of road, the car's headlights struggling to light the way.

His grip on the wheel was too tight, his throat too dry, his nerves too shredded. He found himself longing to be back in London, amid the noxious smog and the millions of people and the never-ending cycle of light and noise. But it was too late for that.

The turning for Burnt House Farm was coming up on his left. Easing his foot off the accelerator, Aaron pulled over onto a grassy verge and killed the engine. He was immediately plunged into darkness.

Aware of the terror that was climbing his throat, he reached up and flicked the overhead light switch. Dull yellow light illuminated the car's interior. He stared out into the night.

Was he really going to do this?

People had died doing far less dangerous things than what he was about to do. But he was never going to get his proof during daylight; not without getting caught.

Grabbing a torch and his camera bag, he pushed open the car door. The cold attacked him. Shivering, he switched on the torch and breathed a sigh of relief as the beam sliced through the darkness. He swung the torch from side to side, checking the road, then the hedgerows.

He was alone out here. He couldn't even hear a distant hum of traffic, or the low of cattle.

Except he wasn't alone at all, was he? Somewhere not too far from here, Cal was hiding in the shadows. And so were the people who were keeping him safe.

Aaron walked forward until he came to the turning. He pointed the torch beam into the mouth of the dirt road. Suddenly, it seemed like a wise idea to switch the torch off. He wasn't here to draw attention to himself. He was here to take pictures, that was all. Not to confront. Not to act like an idiot and get himself killed.

With trembling fingers, Aaron flicked the torch button and was plunged into darkness again. Letting out an unsteady breath, he turned and headed in the direction of Burnt House Farm.

His boots sounded like thunder as he walked, his chattering teeth like machine gunfire. The dirt track coiled and twisted like a serpent, leading him further away from the road and the safety of his car. Shadows moved all around him. Somewhere in the near distance, an owl cried out into the night.

It wasn't long before he reached the gate. His hand found the bolt and tried to draw it back. It wouldn't budge. Feeling around in the dark, he found a padlock that hadn't been there before.

They knew about him. They were onto him.

A rush of fear twisted his stomach. What the hell was he doing out here? He was going to get himself killed.

He shut his eyes and pushed the thoughts from his mind because once he started down that road, it would turn him around and lead him straight back to the car, empty-handed. Aaron had come too far to let that happen.

Grabbing the top of the gate, he began to climb the rungs. The gate rattled and clanked underneath his weight. He reached the top and swung his leg over.

He froze. Someone was coming.

He heard footfalls, the swish of grass. Someone was running through the field on the other side of the hedgerow.

Panicking, Aaron swung his other leg over and started to climb down. Whoever was in the field was getting closer.

Somewhere behind him, just around the bend, the hedgerow exploded with noise. Then he heard something land on the track with a heavy thud.

Aaron launched himself to the side, leaping into a ditch. He landed heavily, knocking the breath from his lungs. The ditch was cold and wet, but Aaron barely noticed. He lay rigid on his back, hands clamped to his sides like a dead man in a coffin.

He heard the person running up the track, then the clang of metal as they vaulted over the gate in one fluid movement.

Feet landed heavily on the ground just centimetres from his face. Aaron caught his breath and squeezed his eyes shut, waiting to be caught. But whoever it was kept on moving, their footfalls growing quieter as they ran away.

Aaron waited another minute, until his lungs were about to burst. Then he sat bolt upright in the ditch, gasping for air.

Still reeling from the realisation that he had not been seen, Aaron searched the darkness for the runner.

He already knew who it was. He'd smelled the same animal-like odour that had choked his senses that night up at Desperation Point.

It was Cal.

He had come to the right place. He should have felt excitement, elation that he was so close to turning his life around. But all he felt now as he climbed to his feet and hoisted himself out of the ditch was blind terror.

Taking a series of deep, calming breaths, Aaron fought off the urge to turn around and run back to the car.

He was so close now. All he had to do was get to the end of the dirt track, keep to the shadows, and wait for the proof that he needed to come walking into shot. Then he would take pictures and video footage. Then he would go to Carrie with a contract and a ballpoint pen, and that would be it: his life back on track at last.

Except, he'd forgotten about Grady Spencer's child.

What did he do about that? The sensible thing to do would be to go to the police—once he'd taken his proof to Carrie, of course—but then what would happen to Cal?

Get Carrie's signature on that contract first then worry about the rest later.

Maybe they could work something out together. After all, despite some of his more recent behaviour, Aaron was no monster. Carrie deserved a chance to reach out to her son before the shit truly hit the fan. Besides, it would provide a powerful and emotional ending to his book.

Wet and shivering, Aaron checked the contents of his bag. The camera was still working, the phone still switched on;

although this far out in the countryside there was no signal. At least he now knew the extra money he'd shelled out for the waterproof bag had been worth it. But the torch, which had been tucked inside his jacket pocket, was lost.

Slinging the bag over his shoulder, Aaron brushed himself down. Then, fear making his heart skip and jump, he continued his journey towards Burnt House Farm.

37

By the time Cal reached the farm, his skin was slick with sweat. His muscles screamed, his blood roared in his ears. He'd run all the way from the house, through the streets of the town, not caring if he was seen, all the way past Grady Spencer's house, through Briar Wood, and into the fields beyond. He'd run as if the devil was chasing him, head down, arms pumping, feet tearing up the ground. Fire burned in his heart; white hot anger that spat out molten metal, burning him alive from the inside. It felt good and it felt terrible, like he was going to die.

The knife was still in his hand, his grip like iron, as if the blade was melded into his flesh and he could never let go. He had plunged it into his grandmother's chest, right up to the hilt. He hadn't meant to. She'd startled him, stopped him from hitting his true target. And then the world had turned to fire.

He'd come face-to-face with his mother. He'd wanted to throw himself at her, to take the knife and drive it through her heart, over and over. And yet he'd wanted to run into her arms and never let go.

He wondered if he should feel guilty for doing what he'd

done to his grandmother. But he felt nothing. Not a flicker of emotion.

Now, he was outside the farmhouse, willing his heart to slow down and his breaths to become calm and even. He didn't know how long he'd been gone. He'd lost track of time. It had slipped away when he'd seen his mother and Dylan on the couch. Now he would be in trouble with Jacob. But he wasn't sure he even cared.

Cal walked up to the kitchen door and tried the handle. As he'd expected, it was locked.

He circled the house, cutting through the yard, past the barn and the outbuildings, until he came to the laundry room window. He knew the board that covered the window could be loosened. He knew the window lock was broken.

His chest still heaving up and down, he made quick work of the board, then spent a minute fiddling with the handle of the window until it swung open.

The laundry room was dark. Everyone would be in the meeting room for Jacob's lesson. Cal hoisted himself up to the window ledge, then like water, poured into the room. Reaching back down he grabbed the board, slotted it back in as best he could, then shut the window.

Moving through the darkness, he slipped from the room and entered the hall. He stopped still. Jacob's voice should have been filling the house with his sermon. But Cal heard only silence.

Stealing along the hall, his furtive eyes searching through the dark, he stopped outside the meeting room. He looked over his shoulder at the closed door of Jacob's office.

Moving along, he came to the kitchen.

Voices floated down from upstairs. He could hear the children chatting in low whispers. The sound brought no relief.

Cal was alone in the world. He belonged nowhere. He thought he'd belonged here but he found it difficult to follow the rules. The rules were like the bars of his cage in Grady Spencer's basement.

The one place he longed to be, the place where he thought he could be again, had just been snatched from him.

He was nowhere. Nothing. An empty void. Perhaps that was why it had been so easy to drive the knife into his grandmother's chest. He wondered if she would live. He wondered what his mother thought of him now.

He waited in the darkness, wondering if he would feel anything ever again. But he did feel something. Thirst.

Tiptoeing into the kitchen, he moved to the sink and reached for a glass.

"You lied to me."

The voice made him spin on his heels, made him brandish the knife. Jacob was sitting in the corner of the room, knees pressed together, hands resting on top. He stared at Cal, his eyes glittering in the shadows.

"I asked if you would ever doubt me. You told me you wouldn't. And yet, here we are."

Cal stood by the sink, his breaths thin and shallow, watching Jacob's every move. He felt something else as he lowered the knife—shame. Maybe he did have feelings after all.

Jacob looked at Cal for a long time, saying nothing. Then he leaned back again, bringing his hands to his temples.

"It's my own fault. I said it before, I've let you run free for too long. Were you happier in our father's basement, Cal? Should I have left you there? Do you long to go back?"

Cal lowered his head but kept his eyes on Jacob.

"I should have stopped this behaviour. I shouldn't have

turned a blind eye. I know where you go, Cal. I've known all along. But I thought you'd realise your life with your mother no longer exists. I thought you'd see you weren't wanted there. Now I truly believe you don't think you belong anywhere. But you're wrong, Cal. Your place is here. You just need to open your eyes and see it for yourself."

Jacob stood. Shadows moved in the doorway. Cal turned to see Heath and Morwenna.

"But I can't let you betray us again," Jacob said.

Cynthia appeared behind Heath and Morwenna, her eyes staring wildly into the room until they found Cal. Her face filled with anger.

"Go and get the children," Jacob instructed without looking at her. "Leave Alison with the boy. Bring everyone else to the barn."

Cynthia hovered for a moment, her mouth opening and closing. Then she lowered her gaze and headed for the stairs.

At the door, Heath folded his arms across his chest, a smug smile rippling across his lips. Morwenna shifted her feet.

Jacob smiled. The shadows curved his lips into a demonic grin.

"Bring him up," he said.

Cal watched Heath and Morwenna leave. He glanced back at Jacob, his thirst becoming unbearable.

"I was going to wait until tomorrow, but I'm afraid by then it will be too late," Jacob said. "It's time for your final test, Cal. It's time to prove your commitment to the Dawn Children once and for all."

38

Silence permeated the hospital waiting room. Melissa was asleep, sprawled across Dylan's lap, her father's arms wrapped protectively around her. A uniformed police officer stood in the corner, her gaze fixed on the carpet.

Carrie paced the room, biting her nails. Her heart wouldn't stop racing. Sally was in the operating theatre. The blade had punctured her left lung. It had missed her heart by two centimetres.

She pictured her mother slumped against the bedroom wall, blood blossoming at the centre of her chest and pooling on the carpet. Melissa had seen it happen. She'd watched Cal stab her grandmother in full technicolour glory. But Sally hadn't been his intended victim, had she?

The knife had been meant for Melissa.

There were no words to describe how Carrie felt about it. Just numb horror. Her son had tried to kill her daughter. If Sally hadn't checked in on Melissa at that very moment . . .

She shook the thought from her head. She couldn't go there. If she did, she'd never come back. And she had to be here, present and focused, because her son had almost murdered her mother. There was a chance he still might. She glanced at Dylan, whose gaze was cast downward at Melissa's sleeping form. He looked exhausted. Deep worry lines taunted the corners of his eyes. They hadn't spoken a word to each other since they'd arrived at the hospital, but Carrie knew he was blaming her.

This was her fault because it was her son. This was her fault because she'd kept saying she needed more time. This was her fault because she'd kept Dylan and Melissa at arm's length.

Now, as Carrie pressed herself up against the wall, trying to make herself disappear, she wondered if Dylan was right. Would any of this have happened if she'd kept her family together?

Cal had been watching her, that was obvious now. He'd been following her on her nightly walks. He'd been watching the house. He'd seen that she was alone, that Melissa and Dylan had gone to live elsewhere. What had he thought? That he could come home again and it would be just the two of them like old times? Did he think Carrie would just forget about Melissa?

Had she unwittingly given him that impression? Now her mother could die. Now Melissa would be traumatised for the rest of her life. Now Dylan would want a divorce. Carrie felt sick. She was going to throw up.

A soft knock on the door disrupted her panic. She looked up and saw a familiar face enter the room; a handsome man in his early forties dressed in a charcoal suit.

Detective Constable Turner smiled politely.

"Hello again, Carrie," he said, then nodded at Dylan. "It's nice to see you both. I just wish it was under better circumstances. How are you both holding up?"

Carrie only stared at him

Dylan laughed and shook his head. On his lap, Melissa

stirred a little. "Oh, we're just fine, Detective Turner. Why wouldn't we be? I mean, if you lot had actually done your job three months ago, maybe we wouldn't be sitting here right now at the bloody hospital, waiting to see if Sally lives or dies."

His eyes flicked accusingly towards Carrie as he nervously stroked Melissa's hair.

"We're doing what we can, Dylan," Detective Turner said, that polite smile still on his lips. "Cal can't have gone very far. We're putting together a team right now and we've requested the dog crew. Plus, we're trying to get the helicopter."

"Trying?"

"It covers both counties of Devon and Cornwall, as well as the Isles of Scilly, so it may already have been deployed."

Dylan snorted. "Explains why you failed to find him three months ago."

The smile wavered on Turner's face. "It's the reality we're facing right now. We've had another police station close this month, resources are scarce. As I said, we're doing the best we can."

The detective turned away to speak to the uniformed officer in the corner. Carrie watched them, her paranoia growing. She glanced over at Dylan, who looked as if he might put his fist through the wall at any second. Everything was coming apart.

The uniformed officer was leaving the room. Turner was coming back over. Carrie couldn't breathe. Where had the air gone?

"I understand this must be a shock," he said, addressing Carrie directly. "But I need you to go over exactly what happened tonight."

"But I already told the—"

"Please, Carrie. I'd like to hear it from you."

Feeling exhausted and weak, Carrie slumped into a chair and pressed her face into her hands. Detective Turner sat down a few seats away. Dylan just shook his head.

Carrie went over it: her meeting with Aaron Black, the surprise visit from Dylan and Melissa, the horrible screams they'd heard coming from upstairs, finding Cal in Melissa's bedroom and her mother bleeding to death on the floor.

When she was done, she leaned back in the chair, exhausted and spent.

Detective Turner looked up from his notepad. "And tonight was the first time you saw Cal since he disappeared?"

Carrie hesitated, her mind racing back to that night at the cliff. "In the flesh, yes."

Turner frowned. Dylan looked up.

"What exactly does that mean?" he said, staring uncertainly at his wife. Avoiding his gaze, Carrie sucked in a breath. Her chest felt tight. It was too hot in here.

"Carrie?" Turner prompted.

She bit the inside of her cheek and tasted blood.

"Last week, I walked up to Desperation Point. I thought I heard someone following me through the wood. But they ran away before I could see who."

"What were you doing up at Desperation Point?" Dylan's mouth hung open. His eyes were wide. He looked afraid, Carrie thought. As if everything he loved was slipping away from him.

Her mouth was dry. She needed a drink. Whiskey. Water. Anything. And now she was going to have to tell the truth. Now Dylan was going to find out she'd been lying to him more than he knew.

"The next morning," she said, ignoring his question, "I had a visit from Aaron Black."

Detective Turner frowned. "The writer who came to see you today?"

"Yes." She could feel Dylan's eyes burning into her, could feel his anger and disappointment, their marriage falling apart. "He told me that he'd followed me on my walk because he'd wanted to talk to me, to ask me to be part of his book. He told me he saw Cal, and that Cal had been watching me but then he'd seen Aaron and had chased him through Briar Wood."

The detective scribbled into his notepad. "Did this Aaron Black tell you anything else?"

Carrie dug her nails into the side of her thighs. Her thirst was becoming unbearable. And where were the bloody doctors with news of her mother?

"Answer the damn question," Dylan said, spitting the words out.

"He told me that he wanted to find Cal. That if he found proof of where Cal was hiding, he'd bring it to me in exchange for helping him with his book." Tears ran down her face. Her voice trembled. "So that I could have a chance to reach out to my son before he was taken away from me for good."

The truth was out. She didn't have to lie anymore. She no longer had to pretend. And yet, there was no relief.

Carrie looked up, meeting Dylan's gaze. His face was scarlet. His eyes were wet with tears. In his arms, Melissa looked safe and comforted.

"This is your fault," he said. A tear escaped and ran down the contours of his face. "Your mother is in that operating room because of you. My daughter was almost murdered by your son because you knew he was out there but you didn't say anything. You didn't say *anything.*"

Dylan stood up, clutching Melissa's sleeping form to his chest.

"I don't know you anymore," he said as another tear escaped his eye. "I can't even be in the same room as you."

"Dylan . . ."

Carrie watched him move to the door. She watched him balance Melissa against his shoulder while he fumbled with the handle. She watched him leave the room. She watched the absent space left behind by her husband and her daughter.

Beside her, Detective Constable Turner cleared his throat.

She turned, unable to meet his gaze.

"He'll bring her back, won't he?" she asked him, her voice a numb whisper.

The detective placed a gentle hand on her shoulder.

"Do you know where Aaron Black is right now?" he asked.

But Carrie wasn't listening. A doctor in surgical scrubs was entering the room and staring at Carrie with eyes she could not read.

Slowly, Carrie got to her feet.

"How is she? How is my mother?"

39

AARON DREW CLOSER to Burnt House Farm, his heart beating faster with each step. He reached the yard. The farmhouse was directly in front of him, transformed by the moonlight into a haunted house filled with ghosts.

Except these ghosts were very much alive.

Staying in the shadows, he cocked his head and listened for signs of life. The only sound was the lonely howl of the wind.

Aaron pressed on, moving in a clockwise motion, checking each boarded up and shuttered window, then entering the field on the left. Above him, clouds shifted, hiding the moon. He passed the scarecrow, moving through the field in a circle, until he reached the back of the house.

He froze.

A single light shone from an upstairs window.

Ducking down, Aaron took a few steps back, trying to get a clearer view. Standing in the middle of the field, he felt suddenly exposed, not just to the elements but to whoever was inside that room. All they had to do was look down and they would see him.

He took more steps back, his boots sinking into mud, his gaze trained on the rectangle of light. The room inside was becoming more visible. He could see the ceiling, part of a wall.

The top of someone's head as they darted by.

His heart racing, Aaron continued to walk backward. He was at the wrong angle. He needed to get a better view. He spun around, staring into the vastness of the field, and saw a tree.

Letting the camera hang around his neck, he hurried towards it. It was an old sycamore with gnarled, leafless branches that were in easy reach. Casting a look over his shoulder, Aaron began to climb. It was a struggle—he hadn't climbed a tree since his childhood—but he persevered, hoisting himself up until he was almost level with the window of the house.

With his back pressed safely against the trunk and his legs wrapped around a sturdy branch, Aaron raised the camera to his eye and twisted the zoom ring, until the window filled his vision. His finger hovered over the shutter release.

He could see them. Figures moving about a large bedroom with peeling wallpaper. There were children mostly, and a few young women no older than their mid-twenties. One of them cradled a baby while the children ran about.

Aaron held the camera as still as possible and pressed the shutter release. The camera snapped away, taking grainy image after grainy image.

Switching the camera to video mode, Aaron began filming. He watched the scene through the viewfinder, growing increasingly confused. Who were these people? How were they connected to Cal? To Grady Spencer?

His mind racing, he continued to film.

Someone else was coming into the room. It was the red-haired woman he'd encountered yesterday. The children froze.

The women visibly tensed and exchanged looks. What was going on? Any frivolity he'd witnessed in that room had vanished.

And now they were leaving. The children first, exiting in a neat line, followed by the women. But the woman with the baby was staying behind. Aaron zoomed in closer. He could see now that she was no woman but a young girl, maybe sixteen, seventeen years old. There was someone else staying behind, too. He zoomed the camera in further. A young boy was huddled in the corner of the room. Although the image in the viewfinder was grainy at best, Aaron could tell the child was frightened.

Where were the others going? And where was Cal?

There was only one way to find out.

Aaron carefully made his way back down to the ground. He was suddenly aware of how cold it had become, of how much his body was shivering, but he pressed on, heading back across the field, then flanking the house.

Rounding the far corner, he passed a rusting water tank and a large shed. Machinery hummed inside. Wires ran from the shed to the house. A generator, perhaps?

He edged along the side of the house, passing a large transit van and a car, then slid to a halt. He was at the edge of the yard, standing between the house and the barn.

The doors were open. It was pitch black inside. But the cold was becoming unbearable.

Slipping between the doors, Aaron was enveloped by darkness. Trying not to panic, he cupped his hands together and blew air into them. Even though the barn was just a couple of degrees warmer, it felt good to be less exposed.

From here, he had a perfect view of the house. But what did he do now? Did he lie in wait, hoping to spot a glimpse of Cal and whoever else lived here? Or did he look for a loose window board, maybe try to get inside?

Not unless you want to get yourself killed.

The only option then was to wait.

But he didn't have to wait for long. From somewhere outside, he heard hushed voices and footsteps cross the yard. Aaron ducked down in the darkness, his heart leaping in his throat. Seconds later, he heard vehicle doors open and close, then an engine roar to life. He inched closer to the barn doors, trying to see outside.

Headlight beams splashed across the concrete. The van he'd spotted moments ago rolled through the yard, passing the barn and heading in the direction of the dirt track that led back to the road.

Who was inside? Where were they going? He thought about the women and children he'd seen leaving the bedroom. Were they being taken somewhere? And where the hell was Cal?

The questions plagued him as he listened to the rumble of the engine slowly fade. And then they were torn from his mind as a strange, strangled noise came from somewhere behind him.

Aaron stopped breathing. Goosebumps crawled over his flesh. Slowly, he turned.

Something was in here with him.

And now he could smell a terrible odour; a rancid concoction of piss and shit and blood and fear.

With a trembling hand, he slipped his bag from his shoulder. Slowly, he pulled on the zipper and reached inside for his phone.

He was going to touch the screen. To activate the torch. He was going to hold it up and shine it on whatever the hell was in here with him. And then he was probably going to scream.

Aaron took out the phone. He touched the screen.

He didn't get any further.

Outside, a shaft of light cut across the yard. Aaron spun back towards the barn doors. The front door of the house was open. People were filing out of the house, carrying lanterns, heading straight for him.

Aaron was frozen to the spot.

Behind him, the darkness made a terrible noise.

More people were coming out of the house; women and children. Soon the lanterns would be close enough to expose him.

Aaron bolted forward. Keeping his step as light as possible, he slipped through the doors and headed right, around the side of the barn. Pressing himself up against the wood, he willed his body to become still.

He heard the echoes of footfalls on the yard, could hear the swish of clothing as they silently entered the barn.

Aaron turned. There was a small window above his head. Light flickered out of it.

He looked around on the ground, found a wire crate. Carefully placing it beneath the window, he hoisted himself up.

Blood pounded in his ears. He stood on his toes and peered in. Lanterns had been hung on hooks around the barn, illuminating the interior in flickers of orange light. The women and children he'd seen through the window were gathered in a large circle. There were others joining them, too. Young men and teenage boys. The woman with red hair.

Aaron scanned the faces of the children. He counted six; four boys and two girls who all looked between five and twelve years of age. All shared nervous expressions, but there was something else in those wide eyes. Something dull and empty, like dried up puddles.

At the centre of the circle stood a man, who was small and wiry, yet whose presence commanded attention. Next to the man, tied to a stake on the floor, was a pig.

Aaron was too frightened to breathe. Instinct kicked in. Grabbing his phone, he switched to video mode and tapped the record button. Pushing himself back up on his toes, he pressed his free hand against the wall, then held the phone up to the window. He watched as the man slowly raised his hands, until his body resembled a cross.

Where was Cal?

The man's deep and hypnotic voice floated through the open barn doors. The children looked up, their eyes glittering with fear and awe. The young men and women stared at him, utterly in love.

"A new dawn is coming," the man said, turning in a circle, making eye contact with each one of them.

The young women, men, and children repeated the words as if they were part of a familiar ritual, one they'd all spoken many times.

"You are the children of that new dawn," the man continued, his face glowing with pride.

Aaron's ankles were beginning to ache. The cold bit into him, numbing his bones. But he ignored it all, holding his breath so he could hear every word.

"The world we live in is cold and cruel, filled with depravity," the man said. "Every minute of every day, children's minds are being poisoned by lies on the television and the internet, by toxic adults who think they know best, who only want to corrupt and to defile. Every minute of every day, children are robbed of their innocence. They are abused, assaulted, murdered . . . their curious eyes plucked out."

He drew in a breath, and slowly shook his head. "This world wants to take our children and force them down onto their knees. To keep you locked inside cages down in the dark, until all your power and all your freedom and all your desires are stripped away like flesh from bone. Until there's nothing left of you but submission. Until there's nothing left but weakness!" The man's voice grew loud and angry. Around the circle, eyes were wide and staring. "Well, I say no more! I say we stop this sink into depravity. I say this is the dawn of a new age, where our children rule the world!"

The circle erupted with cheers and cries. The man held out his hands triumphantly.

At the window, Aaron gasped.

"It's a cult," he whispered. "It's a crazy fucking cult!"

The man called for silence. He glanced down at the pig, which pulled at the rope and squealed as it tried to get free.

"Tonight is a test," the man said. "To be ready for the dawn, you must be strong and powerful. Ready to strike down those who try to suppress you without thought."

Aaron watched as one of the older boys broke the circle to bring the man a sharp looking butcher's knife. Gripping the hilt, the man looked around at the children. Aaron saw the same expression sweep from child to child like a wave; a mix of fear and anticipation. The man's eyes came to rest on someone Aaron couldn't see.

He pushed himself up on the crate, his toes complaining painfully. When the man next spoke, Aaron caught his breath.

"Cal, step forward."

Aaron watched as the sinewy, lithe young man he'd seen up at Desperation Point stepped into the circle. Even through the dirty glass, he saw the boy's empty, dark eyes.

The man held out the knife.

"Take it," he said. "Make the first cut. Show your brothers and sisters how powerful you are."

Cal moved in silence and took the knife. He stepped back, the blade swinging at his side. He turned to face the pig. Behind him, the circle broke apart and formed into a line.

Aaron was frozen, transfixed with horror. He wanted to turn away, to run from this place and never look back. But he had to see.

Cal stepped forward, the knife pointed at the animal. The pig thrashed and squealed. Cal made the first cut. The squealing grew high-pitched and unbearable as blood began to flow.

Cal silently handed the knife to the next in line, a boy no older than eight years old, who stepped forward, his eyes large and round. He glanced across at the man, who smiled and nodded like a proud father.

Aaron thought the boy would cry, that he would drop the knife and run. But he brought the knife up and did as he was told. Then he handed the knife to a girl behind him. It went on, each child taking the knife and plunging it into the poor, helpless beast, until they'd all taken a turn. Until the pig was still and the barn was silent and the floor was a dark, glistening pool.

Aaron had watched it all in breathless horror, reeling from the shock of what was unfolding inside. This was not what he'd come here in search of. Yet, this was what he'd found. And he would never unsee it. Never again, not until the day he died. The question now was what did he do about it?

Inside the barn, Cal and a handful of the older children were dragging the dead pig to one side. The Dawn Children formed a circle again. What Aaron saw next drove a stake of terror straight through his heart.

A man was brought in, his hands tied behind his back, a sack thrust over his head. His feet were bare and he was naked except for his underwear. He was brought into the centre of the circle and forced onto his knees, his hands tied to the stake in the ground. He knelt there, swaying from side to side, not struggling, not fighting back. Aaron wondered if the man had been drugged.

A murmur rippled through the circle. Looks of confusion followed looks of uncertainty. The man who was leading all this horror stepped inside the circle and placed his hand on the bound man's head.

"And now the true test begins," he said. "But this test is only for you, Cal." He held out the knife, which was still dripping with pig's blood, and beckoned to the boy. "This is where you show us the true nature of your leadership."

40

IMAGES of his grandmother's horrified face filled Cal's mind.

He was frozen, his eyes fixed on the bound man, who moaned and muttered inaudible words beneath the sackcloth.

"Take the knife," Jacob commanded. "Show the Dawn Children what they must become. Show them how you will lead them along the path of glory."

He held out the knife, waiting.

"Take it, Cal."

Slowly, Cal stepped forward and took the blade. He flinched as the sounds of Melissa's terrified screaming echoed all around him.

Jacob's eyes twitched. He reached over and pulled the sack from the man's head.

"This man," he said, "is a molester of children. A depraved pervert who abused his position of power, who the law saw fit to find not guilty and release back into the world, where he remains free to continue his deplorable acts."

The man was beginning to wake. Cal saw his eyelids flutter open then close again, his bruised and battered face wrinkle into a frown. The man opened his mouth and let out a deep groan.

Jacob jabbed a finger at the man's temple. "Left alone in a room with any one of you," he said, pointing his finger at the youngest in the circle, "this man would corrupt you and defile you. He would take away your power, make you weak. He would break you down until you obeyed his every command. This man is legion. This man is everywhere in this world. And he must be stamped out! He will be the first of many to be destroyed, so the Dawn Children may rise and take their rightful place of power!"

Cal watched as the man looked around, terror dawning on his face as he realised his predicament.

"Do it," Jacob commanded. "Deliver this man to the cause."

Around the circle, children stared at each other, shifting uncomfortably on their feet.

"Eyes forward!" Jacob bellowed.

Startled and afraid, the children obeyed his command, all turning their eyes on Cal and the man. One of the children began to cry. The young woman standing beside him reached out a hand, then drew it back as Jacob shot her a warning glare.

"Do it," he repeated, returning his gaze to Cal. "Show the children what must be done. Become the leader they need."

Cal stepped forward. The man began to beg for his life.

"Please. What is this? Please, let me go!"

Cal came closer. He raised the knife above the man's head.

You let me down earlier, boy. Don't do it again.

"Please," the man wailed, tears flowing from his eyes. "Let me go. I've never hurt anyone. It was a mistake. A misunderstanding!"

"Do it, Cal," Jacob whispered.

"I've done nothing to you. I won't say anything, just let me go," the man pleaded.

Cal took another step forward. Something moved at the corner of his eye. Something up at the window. He ignored it, bearing down on the man, waving the blade in his face.

Cal's eyes narrowed. His jaw clenched. His lips pressed tightly together. He thought of the blade slicing into his grandmother's chest. He thought of Melissa's tiny body asleep in the bed. He thought of the toy dinosaur his mother had left out on the back doorstep.

I can't.

You can. You must. Let me show you how.

"Do it!" Jacob bellowed. "Do it now!"

Cal raised the knife. He tightened his grip on the handle. And suddenly it wasn't the man before him, begging for his life, but Cal's mother. Inside his chest, a dull ache began. He tried to focus all his anger, all his rage, but the ache washed over it like a tidal wave.

He stared at the man's begging eyes. He stared at Jacob's face, which was contorted with gleeful bloodlust.

The knife wavered in his hand. His arm trembled.

I can't do it.

Slowly, Cal lowered the knife and hung his head.

Anger rolled over Jacob's face like storm clouds.

"As I expected," he hissed, his eyes burning into Cal's. "You've grown weak. You don't have it in you to lead these children. And I know why. Our father had been right about you all along. I tried to reason with him, to tell him he was wrong, that we could show you the ways here. That we could make you forget your family ties. But he knew. That's why he kept you in a cage. Because he knew that one day, you'd want to return to your family. But I thought *we* were your family, Cal. I thought the Dawn Children were your brothers and sisters. But you can't do it, can you? You can take the life of an animal. But you can't take the life of another human because you can't let go of your attachment."

He's right. You shame me. You're nothing but a disappointment.

Cal stared at the space between him and Jacob. The knife hung by his side, but his fingers began to tighten around the hilt.

"I was wrong about you, Cal," Jacob said, pity and defeat in his voice. "I should never have thought that you could lead us while you still cling to your mother. I should never have allowed these children to have faith in you to show them the way." He came closer, a strange expression on his face, until his lips brushed against Cal's ear. "Which is why you've forced me to take steps."

Cal looked up and met the man's gaze.

"I have to sever those attachments, Cal. Or you'll never be what you must become. As painful as it will be for you, the cord must be cut so that you may never look back, only forward into the dawn."

Realisation birthed in Cal's mind. He looked from face to face, noticing that Heath and Morwenna were missing.

"You have a choice," Jacob said. "You can kill this man and finally accept your place with the Dawn Children, or I can use the radio to send a message to Heath and Morwenna, who will have almost reached your mother's house by now."

Cal stared into Jacob's fathomless eyes. The world burst into fire.

"The clock is ticking," Jacob said.

On the ground, the man began to scream.

"Let my boy go," he bellowed. "Take me but let him go."

There was a long moment in which all that existed in the room melted away, leaving only Jacob and Cal, and the darkness that burned between them.

A single image played in Cal's mind: his mother lying in a pool of blood, her lifeless eyes staring up at him. Suddenly, he knew Jacob was right.

Despite everything, he could never let go of his mother.

Cal turned, raised the knife high above his head, and plunged it into the man's chest.

The man stopped screaming. He stared up at Cal in disbelief. Then he coughed, spraying blood from his mouth across Cal's stomach.

It was as if a trigger had been pressed somewhere deep in Cal's mind. He tore the knife from the man's chest and brought it down, again and again, in a fevered frenzy. Blood spurted and sprayed in arterial arcs. The man choked and gurgled, then collapsed over.

The children in the circle, watched with wide, horrified eyes. Cal was an animal: cutting, stabbing, hacking.

Jacob reached out and gripped Cal's arm. Cal turned on him, eyes black like a shark's, lips pulled back into a snarl. Jacob prised the knife from his grip.

Cal came back to the room. He staggered to the side, dripping with blood and sweat, his shoulders heaving up and down as he drew in ragged breaths.

The others were silent, frozen like statues.

Jacob smiled, slowly nodding.

"This is your leader," he said to the others. He held Cal's limp arm in the air. "This is the man who will lead us into a new dawn."

But the others did not look revered by Cal or overcome with awe. They looked terrified.

Cal stared from face to face, his chest heaving up and down, rage and anger burning inside him. He was all powerful, all mighty. He could tear this world to pieces and no one could stop him. And yet that emptiness still pervaded. The fire was still hollow.

He turned and looked at the dead man lying on the ground. He stared down at his own blood-drenched clothes. He waited for Grady Spencer to voice his congratulations, but his mind was strangely silent.

And then something caught Cal's eye again. Movement, at the window. He turned his head. And saw the man who'd been watching his mother that night up at Desperation Point.

41

THE BOTTLE HIT the ground hard and shattered into pieces. Nat swore under her breath as she watched a foaming trail of liquid run downhill. She'd stolen from the wine shop again, a couple of beers and a half bottle of vodka. One of these days she was going to get caught.

The vodka was long gone, downed as she froze to death sitting on the promenade railings, watching the white surf of the ocean illuminated in the darkness. Now, she was drunk. But not enough to drown the panic that was spreading inside her like an unstoppable forest fire.

Her fight with Aaron had pitched her into a place she spent most of her time trying to avoid. But he'd pushed all the wrong buttons and now here she was, in a pit of despair, hating the world, hating Aaron Black, but most of all hating herself.

Was she really that stupid, thinking a hack like Aaron would happily welcome her into his London home while she looked for a place of her own? How had she even entertained such a ridiculous thought? She was an idiot, a total loser, thinking for even a second that Aaron Black cared about her.

Aaron Black didn't give a shit. The only thing he cared about was saving his career. Maybe not even that.

But it was her own damn fault. Hadn't she learned by now that the world owed her nothing? That she could rely on no one? Not even Rose.

She turned, swaying on her feet, feeling stupid and reckless and humiliated. Below her, Devil's Cove sat quietly in darkness, a few twinkling lights pushing back against the shadows.

"Fuck this place," she whispered.

If she didn't do something about it soon, she would be stuck here forever. And she would rather die than let that happen.

Sucking in a deep breath, she bellowed at the top of her lungs: "FUCK THIS PLACE!"

The words soared over the town and into the night sky. Nearby, a dog started barking.

Nat stared down at the broken bottle. She drew back her foot and kicked the glass, sending sparkling shards tumbling downhill.

People like Aaron Black didn't deserve her help.

Single-handedly, she'd discovered that Grady Spencer had been married. Single-handedly, she'd discovered that Grady Spencer had fathered a child.

No one else had done that. Not even the police.

And how had Aaron Black rewarded her?

By throwing money at her like she was a cheap whore who'd served her purpose, and who he'd now grown tired of.

No. Aaron Black didn't deserve her help. Aaron Black deserved every piece of shitty luck that was flung at him.

In fact, she decided, as she turned and stomped towards her home, her one remaining beer nestled safely in her jacket pocket, if she saw Aaron Black lying battered and bloody in front of her right now, she would spit in his face and carry on walking.

As Nat turned onto her road, she stared up at Grady Spencer's house. Someone should knock it down, she thought. Its existence was like a cancer spreading through the whole damn town.

No one could escape its poison. No one.

She hurried past and pushed open her garden gate, barely aware of the black van that was moving down the hill like a shadow, its headlights switched off as it cruised into town.

AARON HAD WATCHED the man get dragged into the centre of the circle. He'd watched him get tied down. And then he'd watched Cal stab him to death in an animalistic frenzy. Now, he realised he'd done more than watched it; he'd done nothing to stop it. What's more, he'd filmed the entire horrific scene.

And now Cal was staring directly at him.

Aaron couldn't move. Worse still, a painful spasm had gripped his ankle and was travelling up his leg.

Now the leader of the Dawn Children was pointing at him and barking orders. Cal was brandishing the knife and turning in the direction of the barn doors.

Run, you idiot!

Aaron spun around and jumped down from the crate. He hit the ground running, dashing from the shadows, past the barn doors, and across the yard.

Behind him, he heard the smash of feet on concrete. He shot a glance over his shoulder. Cal was racing towards him, a look of murder in his eyes, the bloody knife gripped in his hand. Terrified, Aaron raced forward, plunging into the mouth of the dirt track. He could hear Cal closing the gap, his footfalls tearing up the ground.

As he raced through the dark, one thought screamed in his mind: get to the road and get to the car, start the engine, and get the hell out of here.

He pushed his body harder, faster. His chest was on fire. His lungs grew tighter and tighter as he pumped his arms like pistons.

Get to the road. Get to the car.

He chanted the words in his head like a mantra, over and over, timing the words with each swing of his arms, each slam of his racing feet. Cal's footfalls were louder in his ears. He didn't need to turn around to know what that meant.

Aaron ran on. Terror gripped him. Sweat beaded his brow. His blood was rushing so quickly he thought his heart might explode.

He felt Cal's fingers at the back of his neck.

Then they were gone again as Aaron hurled himself forward with a cry.

He was almost at the road, his car maybe thirty metres away.

Get to the road. Get to the car. Drive and keep on driving.

The road was closer now. Ten metres. Seven metres. Six. Five.

And then the unthinkable happened. Aaron stumbled in a pothole. His ankle twisted a hundred and eighty degrees. With a scream, he went down hard.

The impact knocked the breath from his lungs.

Gasping for air, Aaron flipped over onto his back. He swung his legs around and pushed himself up on his hands.

He was on the road. His car was just up ahead.

He got to his knees.

He glanced up and saw Cal leaping towards him.

Instinctively, Aaron lifted his hands. Cal landed on his chest, pinning him to the ground.

He raised the knife.

Aaron wrapped fingers around Cal's wrists, pushing the blade away from him with all his strength.

There was a frenzy in Cal's eyes, like a shark mid-attack. His teeth were exposed and clenched together. Spittle frothed at the edges of his mouth. The smell of blood—of man and pig—reeked from every pore.

Cal pushed down harder.

Aaron's arms buckled. The blade came down, dangerously close to his throat. Aaron pushed back again. The blade moved away.

Cal raised his free hand, bunched it into a fist, and drove it down. Pain splintered Aaron's temple. He saw a flash of white.

Cal raised the knife again, the blade glimmering in moonlight.

Aaron's vision cleared and he saw Cal's eyes. There was nothing human there. He was an animal. Primal. A predator in the throes of bloodlust.

Cal raised the knife higher.

Aaron's hand scrabbled furiously at his side. His fingers found a chunk of rock that had fallen from one of the stone hedges.

Cal drove the knife down.

Aaron smashed the rock into the side of his head.

Cal toppled forward. His body went limp.

Aaron lay still, gasping for air. Cal was a dead weight on his chest, and for a moment, he wondered if he'd killed him. Then he felt the boy's breath against his neck. Cal was unconscious.

But for how long?

Channelling his energy, Aaron pushed up with his hands. As he tipped Cal onto the tarmac, indescribable pain ripped through his gut. Aaron screamed. He heard the knife slip from Cal's hand and clatter on the ground. He placed a trembling hand against his abdomen. When he raised it again, it was wet with blood.

"Fuck!"

Panicking, he pressed his hand to his belly again, this time harder. He shrieked in agony. He felt blood seeping through his shirt and soaking into the legs of his jeans.

He'd been stabbed.

That little bastard had got him after all.

Shock began to take hold. But he couldn't allow it. If he did, he was going to bleed out and die right here on the road.

Adrenaline pulsing through Aaron's veins, he pulled himself onto his elbows then rolled on to his side. Burning agony blazed through his abdomen. He got to his knees, found the knife, and picked it up. Clenching his jaw, he staggered to his feet and over to the car.

By some miracle, his bag was still attached to his shoulders. He winced as he grabbed the car keys from inside, then he turned to see Cal's hand twitch on the ground.

Aaron unlocked the door and climbed inside.

He could feel his blood trickling down his skin as he slipped the key into the ignition. He got the engine going and switched on the headlights.

Cal's body was illuminated on the road. He was waking up, slowly shaking his head, touching his bloody temple.

Aaron's hands tightened on the wheel. The temptation to

slam his foot on the accelerator and drive over Cal overwhelmed his mind.

Horrified by the thought, he shook it from his head. He was no killer. This was not a horror film.

But he needed to go. Now. Because Cal was getting to his feet.

Aaron rolled the vehicle forward, swerved around Cal, then sped away from Burnt House Farm.

Suddenly the book meant nothing to him. He had watched a man get slaughtered like an animal in front of a circle of wide-eyed children, and he had done nothing to stop it.

And now he'd been stabbed and was losing blood.

Now, he was probably going to die unless he could get to the nearest hospital.

He needed to call an ambulance. He needed to call the police so they could put a stop to whatever the fuck was going on at that—

My phone! Where is it?

One hand on the wheel, Aaron slapped the pockets of his jacket. Relief overrode his pain as he pulled out the phone.

There was no signal.

Perhaps he'd still be able to get through to the emergency services and call for help. Or perhaps he should just keep driving and head straight for the hospital in Truro.

But now, something was screaming at him from inside his mind. Something about Cal, about the way he'd refused to kill that man at first.

The cult leader had whispered something in his ear. Something that had made Cal afraid and look around the barn, as if he was searching for someone. Something that had made him change his mind and drive the knife straight into that man's chest. What had the cult leader said? Why was it so damn important right now?

Aaron glanced in the rear-view mirror. To his horror, he saw a Land Rover pull up next to Cal. He watched as Cal climbed in. Then the vehicle was racing along the road, quickly closing the gap between them.

Aaron floored the accelerator, swerving around a bend in the road. Suddenly he knew. Suddenly it all made sense. He had seen that van leave the farm just before the ceremony had started. Now, it was obvious where it was going.

And he had to do something about it. Because if he didn't, more people would die.

The other vehicle was closing in. Whoever was behind the wheel was determined to catch up. And now that Aaron knew he'd been stabbed, now that his blood was pouring from his body like water from a tap, all he could feel was pain.

He tried to make the car go faster as it shot along the country road with the Land Rover close behind.

His phone slid about on the passenger seat. But there was no way he could make a phone call. Because right now, he was either going to bleed to death or die in a car crash. He would not save Carrie if either of those things happened.

Aaron spun the wheel. Pain ripped through his abdomen. He was coming up to a T-junction. One direction would take him to Truro and the hospital. The other would take him to Porth an Jowl.

He slowed the car. Behind him, the Land Rover was coming up fast. He had to decide.

Now.

43

CARRIE SAT in the shadows feeling dazed and exhausted. She had no idea what time it was. Just that it was late. Very late. It felt as if this day had gone on forever. But her mother was safe. She was going to live. And that was nearly all that mattered.

She hadn't seen her yet. The doctors had said it would be a while before she woke from the surgery. Carrie found herself relieved that she didn't have to face her mother for a few more hours. Their relationship was already strained, and now she was scared it was about to be tipped over the edge. Because her mother had almost died. Because Cal had almost killed her.

Because this was all Carrie's fault.

She should have gone to the police earlier, should have told them what she knew. Even if she hadn't even really believed it herself.

Now everything was a mess.

She still hadn't called her father to tell him what had happened to his wife. She still hadn't talked to Dylan, to try and explain things.

And now Dylan was gone.

Gary and Joy had turned up at the hospital and taken him and Melissa away. He'd called them himself. He'd told Carrie they were going to a hotel in Truro, and that they were going to stay there until they knew Cal had been caught.

He'd told Carrie to stay away until he was ready for a serious conversation about their future. Because right now, he told her, he wasn't even sure if it was safe for Melissa to be around her.

Carrie had sat silently as Dylan spoke, staring at the floor, nodding and agreeing, because she knew Melissa deserved so much more than she could give her. She deserved so much more than watching her grandmother bleed out on her bedroom floor.

And now, sitting in the back of the police car, her face pressed against the window as she focused on the soothing drone of the engine, Carrie couldn't stop thinking about her other child.

Everything was her fault. All because she'd taken her eyes off him just for those few seconds all those years ago. It's funny, she thought, how just a few lapsed moments could turn into a lifetime of hell.

She wondered where her son was right at this moment, if he was still in the cove, or if he'd run back to wherever he'd been hiding all this time.

Carrie had told the police everything she knew, everything that she and Aaron Black had worked out together. Now the police knew that someone had been helping Cal. Perhaps when they spoke to Aaron, he'd be able to fill in some of the missing pieces. Perhaps by now he'd worked out which farm Cal was hiding at.

She wondered what would happen to him when he was caught. She was no longer expecting a miracle. She was no longer expecting him to suddenly transform into a normal boy, to be her son once more. But Cal deserved safety. He deserved to be protected because none of what had happened to him was his fault.

Her only hope now was that somewhere, in the months and years to come, in the right facility and with the right treatment, Cal would eventually be able to lead a normal life. Become an integrated member of society. She wished for that more than anything, even if it meant he never wanted to see her again, because anything would be better than living his life as an animal in the wilderness, or as a fugitive on the run.

As the police car turned onto Clarence Row and pulled into a parking space just down from her home, Carrie suddenly realised that it didn't matter if Dylan left her, or if Melissa never wanted to speak to her again. All that mattered was that both her children were kept safe from harm.

Police Constable Evans got out of the driver's seat, then she opened the back door. Carrie climbed out, the cold waking her from her hypnotised state. As they walked through the gate, she looked up at the house. A chill numbed the back of her neck. She didn't want to go in there. Her house had been violated. It was now a crime scene, no longer a home.

Another uniformed officer was stationed outside the front door. He was young, Carrie thought. Perhaps recently graduated.

She waited as PC Evans spoke to him, explaining that Carrie had been permitted to come back and pick up some of Sally's things.

"You here on your own?" she asked the younger officer.

"CSI finished up a few minutes ago. They pulled everyone else." His eyes wandered over to Carrie, who looked down at the ground. "I guess we're having a busy night."

PC Evans turned to Carrie. "Ready?"

Carrie nodded. Together, they went inside.

The younger police officer closed the door behind them and returned his gaze to the road. It was cold, his police issue jacket not quite warm enough to keep off the chill. He stamped his feet then rubbed his hands together. Just as he thought about doing a quick sweep of the backyard, a young girl appeared under the streetlight.

The police officer watched her, his senses growing alert as she stumbled towards the house.

"Please," the girl called. She staggered through the garden gate, heading straight for him. "Please, can you help me?"

The officer stepped onto the path.

"This is a crime scene," he said. "You need to keep back."

But the girl came closer. She was young, maybe late teens, he noted. And she looked terrified.

"Please," she begged. "There's been an accident. My sister, she's still out there. Can you help me?"

She came closer still.

The officer saw the blood-matted hair at her temple. Then he saw the cold curve of her lips. She was no longer terrified. She was smiling. Somewhere to the side of him, the shadows moved.

44

HIS VISION WAS BLURRING. He was getting dizzy. Aaron squeezed his eyes shut then opened them again. The car drifted into the opposite lane. He turned the wheel, bringing it back.

For the first time since he'd sped away from Burnt House Farm, he realised he wasn't wearing a seatbelt. Slowly, carefully, he removed one hand from the wheel and reached for the strap.

He braced himself, waiting for the pain to tear through his body as he brought the seatbelt across and fastened the catch. But all he felt was a cold, tingling sensation. He shivered. He didn't know how much blood he'd lost but judging by the wetness of his clothes and the growing numbness in his extremities, he imagined it was a lot. He'd managed to put some distance between him and the Land Rover, but the way he was driving now, it wouldn't be long before they caught up to him.

The road turned around a bend. Aaron hit the brake pedal too hard. He spun the wheel, almost losing control. The road straightened out again. Aaron pressed down on the accelerator, grateful for the late hour. He hadn't seen a single car pass him since making his escape from Burnt House Farm. It was just as well.

He checked the rear-view mirror. There was still no sign of the Land Rover, but he knew they were not too far behind. He didn't know how much longer he could keep driving. His hands felt very far away. His leg muscles were turning to jelly.

But he'd just passed a sign for Porth an Jowl.

He was close.

He'd almost gone in the other direction, almost saved himself. But then he would have had to live his life knowing he'd let Carrie die. Maybe a week ago he would have let her. He would have saved himself and taken a chance on the police getting to her in time.

But there was no time.

That van had almost certainly arrived at the cove already. And ever since witnessing the murder of that man, Aaron couldn't help but feel in some way responsible.

He hadn't killed anyone. He hadn't brainwashed a child or blackmailed them into committing murder. But he had come swanning down here with self-serving intentions, without a thought for the feelings of the people of this town, without caring at all about the already troubled lives he was going to make so much worse.

And for what?

To save a flagging career. For money. To prove to himself he wasn't a failure. To redeem himself for being a liar, a drunk, and a thief.

But there was no redemption in hurting other people. And now that he had a hole in his gut, now that he was bleeding out slowly and painfully, now that he'd seen terrible things happen at Burnt House Farm, he had a new perspective.

If he'd gone to the hospital, if he'd let Carrie die so that he could live, then he would have been no better than Grady Spencer.

So maybe he was going to die. But at least now he would be remembered for doing something good. For being more than a miserable failure.

A flash of light pulled his focus back to the road. Aaron glanced at the rear-view mirror. The Land Rover was back. And now they were on a straight stretch of road, it was coming up fast.

Aaron slammed his foot on the accelerator pedal. Just a few more minutes and he'd be there.

Just a few more minutes and he'd be able to save Carrie and put an end to the horrors of Burnt House Farm.

A sign shot past him on his left: *Porth an Jowl Holiday Park, 100 Metres.* He passed the school. Briar Wood stood like a shadowy fortress up ahead on the right.

He was almost there. He was going to make it.

And then his vision blurred so badly he could no longer see the road. Aaron's fingers slipped from the wheel. The car skidded.

No! Not yet!

He shot his hands back up and regained his grip on the wheel. The car veered to the side, heading straight for Briar Wood. He was losing control. He was going to crash.

Aaron slammed on the brakes. The car screeched to a halt, filling the air with scorched rubber. He flew forward. His seat-belt caught, yanking hard against his chest. He was done. He couldn't drive any further. He had to find another way.

Wrenching open the car door, he freed himself of the seat-belt and climbed outside. He could hear the Land Rover coming up behind. Diving back into the car, he grabbed his camera bag and his phone from the seat, then stumbled forward, There was no time to get to Carrie. He'd have to try and call her instead.

Behind him on the road, the Land Rover was slowing down. Staggering forward, Aaron entered the darkness of Briar Wood. As he moved, he fumbled with the phone, squinting his eyes as he tried to locate Carrie's number. Behind him, he heard car doors open then slam shut. The line connected. He pressed it to his ear, waiting for her to pick up.

"Come on!" he hissed. The call rang off and connected to an automated voicemail message.

Now he heard voices and footsteps.

Aaron hung up. Perhaps he was already too late. Perhaps there was nothing he could do.

But someone else could.

Now the footsteps were coming up behind him through the trees. As his own steps became more faltering, as bright light splashed through the trees and the bitter taste of sea salt pricked his tongue, Aaron dialled another number.

45

NAT WAS AT HER DESK, hunched over her sketchpad, headphones on, *The Kills* screaming in her ears. She had finished her last beer a few minutes ago. Now, she smiled with wicked glee as her pencil moved up and down the page. She'd drawn a book cover. The title was: *The Case of the Big Fucking Loser—A Sulky Winters Mystery*. Below she'd sketched a perfectly rendered image of Aaron Black having his throat torn out by a feral-looking boy.

Her fingers aching, Nat dropped the pencil and spent a minute clenching and unclenching her hand. She wished she had more beer. Or something stronger. She had reached a frustrating line of inebriation where drunk wasn't enough. She needed obliteration. She needed her mind to go as blank as a sheet of her sketchpad. She was no longer angry, or at least, she was less angry, but now she was feeling desperately alone.

When she got to London—and she would get there if it killed her—she would reinvent herself. Maybe change her name, make up a past that didn't involve years of physical and mental abuse at the hands of her parents, or being shipped from foster home to foster home like a misdirected parcel.

When she got to London, she would morph into a different person. Maybe even dress differently, or more extreme. Whoever she decided to become, one thing was certain—she would be erasing all traces of Natalie Tremaine. Sometimes it was the only thing you could do to become who you really are.

Finished with stretching her fingers, she picked up the pencil again. She set back to work, graphite scratching onto paper, music blaring in her ears. Then a flash of light made her look up. Her phone was vibrating on the desk, its screen glowing.

Nat glanced at the caller ID. Immediately, her anger returned.

Aaron Black was calling her. She glared at his name on the screen. She clenched her jaw and flared her nostrils.

Pulling off the headphones, she picked up the phone. Her thumb hovered over the answer key.

She was tempted to give him a piece of her mind, to yell at him. Tell him to go to hell or jump off a cliff.

But what good would it do? Screaming at him as she'd stormed out of his hotel room hadn't made her feel better. Getting drunk hadn't made her feel better.

To answer the phone now and hurl more abuse would only open her up for more hurt. It would leave her feeling vulnerable and weak. Besides, it was stupidly late. Who the hell did Aaron Black think he was?

Nat dropped the phone on the desk and let it ring out as she picked up her pencil and returned to her drawing. She was done with people taking advantage of her. People like Aaron Black. People like Jago Pengelly who had once been her best friend.

No, from now on, Nat could only rely on herself. From now on, she was on her own; just like she always had been.

46

Darkness enveloped the hall. Flipping a light switch, Carrie blinked away black spots from her eyes. She hovered by the door, reluctant to enter her own home. Next to her, PC Evans put a gentle hand on her shoulder.

"There'll be some mess," she said. "The CSI team is thorough but they're not exactly tidy. You may see a lot of fingerprint powder. Has someone spoken to you about hiring a crime scene clean up team? Unfortunately, it's not something we're qualified to do."

Carrie wasn't listening as her eyes wandered up the stairs. It was almost surreal to think that just hours ago, Cal had been inside and had done terrible things.

"I just need to get some clothes for my mother," she said.

PC Evans nodded.

Carrie took the stairs, with the police officer close behind. They reached the landing. All the bedroom doors were open. Fine powder lay in drifts. Carrie stood still, drawn to Melissa's room by a magnetic pull. Through the gap, she saw her mother's blood still on the wall and floor.

Nausea climbed Carrie's throat. She wanted to leave this house and never come back. But she forced herself forward, entering Cal's old bedroom.

While PC Evans waited on the landing, Carrie grabbed Sally's nightwear and threw it into a duffel bag. Then she went into her own bedroom to fetch clean clothes for herself.

When she was done Carrie stepped back and stared at the bed she used to share with Dylan. A deep ache rose from the pit of her stomach. She forced it back down, scared that if she succumbed to it now, if she let all those hurt feelings in, then she would never climb out of the hole. And she had to, for her children's sake; even if she never saw them again.

Letting out a shuddering breath, Carrie picked up the duffel bag. Switching off the bedroom light, she headed back down the landing.

PC Evans was gone.

Carrie stopped outside Melissa's bedroom.

"PC Evans?" she called.

The house felt suddenly empty. Perhaps she'd gone downstairs. Carrie had been so lost in her thoughts that it was possible she hadn't heard the police officer leave. She called out the officer's name again. When no answer came, she gripped the stair rail and made her way down to the ground floor.

Carrie stood in the hallway, staring at the front door, wondering if the officer had gone outside. But she wouldn't have just left her here alone in the house.

Something moved behind her.

Carrie spun around, staring down the hall into the darkness of the kitchen.

"Hello? PC Evans?"

Something was wrong. She felt it in the air like electricity.

She suddenly wondered if Cal was here, if he'd come back. A memory of him flashed in her mind, from those few precious days when he'd first returned, and she'd found him lying on his bed and immersed in a comic book, looking even if for the briefest of moments like a regular teenage boy.

"Cal?" she whispered.

Her heart began to pound. A voice in her head told her to turn around. To walk right out the front door and keep going.

She stared into the kitchen. Someone moved in the shadows.

"Who's there?" she called.

The person in the kitchen grew very still.

Panicking, Carrie spun around to face the front door. She sucked in a sharp, shocked breath.

"Who are you?" she managed to say.

A girl was standing in front of her. She was young, with long dark hair and huge pupils that filled her eyes. There was blood in her hair. And she was smiling.

Carrie took a step back. She noticed the hunting knife in the girl's hand. It was slick with blood.

Slowly, Carrie backed away. Then she remembered the shape in the kitchen. She turned.

A boy, maybe a year or two older than the girl, blocked her way. He was grinning at her, those same dark pupils reflecting the hallway light, the same knife with the serrated teeth gripped in his hand.

"Who are you?" Carrie cried. "The police are right outside!"

The girl stepped forward. The boy, too.

"We are the Dawn Children," the girl said, a wicked smile on her lips. "We are your salvation."

Carrie swung her head from side to side. Her eyes found the

living room door. She could dive in there, try and get to the window, climb through or call for help.

There was a moment of pure stillness, as if the world had fallen silent, as if all life had been drained from it.

Carrie ran for the door.

The boy and girl were on her before she could even reach the handle.

47

"Damn you, Nat!" Aaron was out of options. And he was out
of land.

Stumbling from Briar Wood, he found himself at Desperation Point, the wind whipping his face and blowing hair into his
eyes. Above him, the lighthouse beam sliced through the clouds.
The roar of the ocean filled his ears. Far below, waves crashed
over razor sharp rocks.

His phone still clutched in his hand, Aaron stumbled
towards the lighthouse. A small house was attached to the base
of the main tower. The lights were on. A Range Rover was
parked outside.

Lurching forward, Aaron hammered on the lighthouse keeper's door. "Please!" he cried. "I need your help! You need to call
the police!"

He waited. No one came to the door. He hammered again,
smearing blood over the wood. Moving over to the window, he
peered through the net curtains. A cramped living area was
inside, containing a sofa and a TV, and a bed in the corner. The
room was empty.

Aaron staggered back, tripping over his feet. And then he saw Cal emerge from the trees. Moments later, a second figure appeared.

It was the man. The leader of the cult.

His head spinning, his energy ebbing from him, Aaron headed to the lighthouse door. He raised a hand and brought it down on the wood. But not hard enough for someone inside to hear.

He could feel his energy seeping away. All he wanted to do was to lie down on the hard ground and go to sleep. But he couldn't.

Cal was racing towards him.

Aaron staggered to the Range Rover and clawed at the doors. He slipped, landing heavily on the ground. His phone flew away from his hand and under the vehicle. Aaron pulled himself to his feet and tried the doors again. They were all locked.

And now Cal had cleared half the space between them. He would be on him very soon.

Aaron stumbled back, getting closer and closer to the cliff edge.

Cal was coming nearer. His head was down, his dark eyes forward, his arms pumping at his sides.

The world was spinning, the wind all powerful. Aaron glanced over his shoulder and saw the ocean rise like a lion on its hind legs, then come crashing down. He heard the thud of Cal's feet on the ground.

Aaron turned to face him. There was nowhere left to go.

"Cal, wait!" The man's voice was powerful, booming, like the voice of God. Cal slid to a halt. He was a metre away from Aaron, his jaws pulled back in a predatory grin, his eyes glistening with intoxicating bloodlust.

Aaron teetered on the cliff edge, his camera bag clutched to his chest, his blood seeping into the ground. He cast his failing eyes up at the lighthouse, watching the beam turn.

The man came up beside Cal and placed a hand on his shoulder. Cal lowered his head, took a step back. For a while, the man stood very still, staring at Aaron, a strange, unreadable smile on his lips.

Then he said, "I'm curious. Exactly who *are* you?"

Aaron gulped for air. The roar of the ocean was deafening.

"My name," he gasped, "is Aaron Black. What's yours?"

"My name is of no importance. Not to someone like you."

"Someone like me? Someone who knows exactly what you've been doing on your so-called farm." He grinned. "That's right, asshole. I saw everything and I'm going to expose you to the world."

The man smiled. "Is that so? Those are very big promises for someone who's bleeding to death. Someone who probably won't be with us for much longer at all, in fact. Tell me, Mr Black, what is it that you think you saw?"

"I saw you murder that man," Aaron breathed. "I saw all those children. You abducted them. You're brainwashing them, training them to be like Cal. Training them to kill."

The man in front of him smiled.

"I murdered no one. My hands were not on the blade," he said. "And I've abducted no one. Half of those children I fathered myself. Everyone you saw in the barn is there of their own free will. If they wish to leave they only need to open the door and walk out. You see, we're a family, Mr Black. We take care of our own. If one of us is lost, we help them find their way. If one of us strays, we guide them back onto the right path. You may not understand what I'm trying to achieve with our family, but that's because you're not *part* of the family. You're part of the problem. You're what's wrong with this world."

"And you're what? The solution?" Aaron hawked and spat blood on the ground. "Just because you weren't holding the knife doesn't mean you're not as guilty. You made Cal kill that man."

"No one can make anyone do something they don't want to do. If Cal killed that man it was because he chose to."

"Right. So, you didn't threaten to have Cal's mother killed if he didn't do it? You didn't send that van here?"

The dizziness was getting worse. He wasn't sure how much longer he could stand up. Where was the damn lighthouse keeper? Why wasn't anyone coming to his rescue?

The smile had faded from the man's lips. His cold eyes moved down Aaron's body until they were resting on the camera bag.

"What have you got there?"

Aaron clenched the bag. "Mind your own business."

In one fluid movement, the man snatched the bag up and tossed it into the abyss.

"Now it's the ocean's business," he smiled.

The world was growing dark. Time was slipping away from Aaron. Everything was fading. It couldn't all be for nothing. He couldn't die here having saved no one! But he'd tried to call Carrie to warn her and she hadn't picked up. He'd tried to call Nat and she'd ignored him. What else could he do?

His eyes fell on Cal. *Of course.*

"Your mother could be dead while you're standing here," he said to him. The ground swayed beneath his feet. The world turned white, then red. "If she dies then you're just as guilty. If she dies it's because you didn't save her."

A gust of wind blew up from the ocean, knocking Aaron to his knees. He looked up at the figures standing over him and saw Cal stare uncertainly at the man.

"Your mother's safe," the man said. "He's trying to confuse you."

"How do you know, Cal?" Aaron was cold. So cold. And yet at the same time he felt nothing. "Did you hear him call them off? How do you know they're not there, right now, murdering your mother?"

Cal was staring over his shoulder now, at the trees, then back at the man. The bloodlust in his eyes had gone, replaced with something else.

Something that looked to Aaron's fading vision like fear.

"Cal," the man said, holding up his hands. "She's safe."

"You don't know that, Cal. How can you trust him after what he made you do?"

"Cal, I'm telling you she's fine."

But Cal was shaking his head now, his body pulling towards Briar Wood.

"You still doubt me," the man said, his voice wounded. "After everything I've done for you and you still doubt me. Believe me when I say that your mother is—"

Cal turned on his heels. He sprang forward, racing back towards the trees.

Aaron watched him get smaller, then melt into the shadows, then disappear into darkness. Now he could die for something. Now he could die for saving Carrie. Swaying on his knees, he smiled at the man.

"I may not know your name," he said. "But I know who you are."

The man leaned over him, fury burning in his eyes. "I am Jacob. Saviour of the Dawn Children. Protector of innocence."

With the last of his energy, Aaron threw his head back and laughed. "You think you're the Cornish Charles Manson, but your Grady Spencer's son. And you may think you're going to solve the world's problems by killing a few bad men, but really, you're no better than your father."

Jacob leaned in close, his teeth mashing together.

"My father was a monster. A murderer of innocents. He made me help him. He made me kill with him. But I saw the light. I saved Cal from him. I saved all my children from monsters just like him."

"But you didn't stop him, did you? You didn't turn your father in. Because no one can make anyone do something they don't want to do, isn't that what you said? And right now, asshole, I want to make sure you don't hurt any of those kids again."

Aaron lunged out. One hand grabbed Jacob by the front of his shirt. The other wrapped around his neck.

Gravity did the rest.

Terror dawned in Jacob's eyes. His hands shot up and gripped Aaron's wrists. Then they were toppling over the edge of the cliff.

They dropped like rocks; Jacob shrieking at the top of his lungs, Aaron calm and quiet.

The men flew apart.

Jacob's body slammed into the side of the cliff, then went spinning away like a pinwheel.

Aaron looked up and saw the beam of the lighthouse illuminating the sky. He smiled.

I'm sorry, Taylor, he thought. *I'm sorry for everything.*

Then there was only the roar of the sea. Then there was only darkness and light.

48

CAL SHOT through Briar Wood like a demon. Jacob had lied to him. He had never intended to save his mother. He had intended to let her die all along.

And why? So that he could control Cal just like Grady Spencer had tried to control him. It was all anyone had ever tried to do: control him.

But Cal could not be controlled. He was a force of nature. A hurricane. A flood. He was lightning, striking everyone in its path. An erupting volcano, raining death and destruction on all in its path.

All except his mother. Because she was his humanity, he could see that now. She was his last shred of compassion, of empathy and love. He'd been clinging on to it for so long now that only a thread remained.

And now Jacob was trying to tear it away.

Cal ran; down the hill, past the cars, past the houses in which people slept, oblivious to the horrors outside, down past Grady Spencer's house, the final resting place of lost souls, down and down, until he came to Clarence Row.

Cal slid to a halt. There was a police car outside. The house was in darkness. Ducking down behind parked vehicles, he crawled on his hands and feet through the shadows until he was opposite his childhood home.

He reared up, checking the police car. No one was seated inside. He checked the garden. Panic gripped him and refused to let go.

There was a body on the path, lying face down, hand reaching for the garden gate.

Moving quickly, Cal bounded across the road for a closer look. It was a man. A police officer. He was lying in a pool of blood, his eyes open and staring lifelessly at the lawn.

In one fluid movement, Cal swung himself over the gate and landed on the path. He skirted around the body and headed for the front door. It was ajar. He smelled death creeping out in tendrils.

In an instant he was a child again, frightened and alone. In an instant, he longed to be picked up, to be rocked in his mother's arms, to listen to her soothing voice until he fell into peaceful dreams. What if she was dead inside? What would he do? What would become of him?

Shouldering open the door, Cal stepped inside the house. He scrabbled along the wall and found the light switch.

A dark pool of blood lay at the centre of the hall, just in front of the living room door. A duffel bag sat in it. There were signs of a struggle: a broken ornament, an upturned side table.

Cal raced forward into the kitchen, then doubled back and entered the living room. It was empty. The curtains closed.

He ran upstairs, leaving behind a trail of bloody footprints. He checked the bathroom, then his mother's room, finding them both empty. He burst into his own room and stood, staring wildly at his old collection of toys still sitting on the windowsill.

Memories of his old life flooded in. He swept them away.

There was only one room left to check.

His breaths heavy, Cal pushed open the door of Melissa's bedroom. He hovered on the threshold, staring at the wall, where he had spilled his grandmother's blood. He knew there was a body on the floor. He could see it from the corner of his eye.

Suddenly, he couldn't breathe.

He knew she was dead. But he couldn't bring himself to look. He fixed his eyes on the wall, on the blood. The stench of death was all around him, drowning his senses, smothering his lungs.

Cal drew in a breath. Then he made himself look.

It wasn't her.

The body on the floor belonged to another police officer. A woman.

Cal stumbled back, overcome by confusion and rage. He raced downstairs and into the kitchen, throwing open the back door. The yard was empty. His mother was not here.

And now he could hear the wail of police sirens. They were getting louder. Filling his ears until they hurt.

Cal turned and ran along the side of the house. He made it to the gate in time to see the blue and red flashes of police sirens as two patrol cars turned onto the street.

Adrenaline pumping, Cal leaped over the gate and into the road. He hit the ground running, hurtling away from the police cars, away from his childhood home. He didn't know where he was going. He didn't know where reality began and the night-mare ended.

All he knew was that he was going to kill Jacob and destroy the Dawn Children. He wouldn't stop, until they were all gone. Until the world was in ruins. Until there was nothing left but fire.

49

THE SUN PEERED over the edge of the horizon as Cal entered Burnt House Farm. Shadows shifted across the field. Death hung in the air. He stood, staring at the house, hell burning inside his chest. His mother was gone. Now, he would destroy everything.

He would tear it all down.

Moving silently, Cal cut through the yard. The barn doors were shut now. He wondered if the man was still inside. He should have felt guilty, but the fire had burned away the last morsels of his conscience.

Rounding the corner of the house, he came to the laundry room window and loosened the board. A minute later, he was inside, standing in the shadows, listening to the early morning quiet. He used to find solace in this time; the time when the world was still sleeping.

Now, he felt nothing at all.

He exited the laundry room and stole through the hall, past the meeting room, and into the kitchen. Pulling open a drawer, he took out a large steak knife. Then he headed back towards Jacob's office.

Until now, he would never have dared to enter without permission. But that was before Jacob had lied to him. He turned the handle and pushed the door open. The room was empty. Cal moved inside and around the desk. He sat down in Jacob's chair, staring at the book shelves covering the walls. More books sat on the desk, including Hitler's *Mein Kampf*, post-it notes sticking out from the pages, and Aleister Crowley's *Magick: Liber ABA: Book 4.*

Cal swept them from the desk and watched them topple off the edge. He jumped to his feet and flew into a rage, tearing books from shelves, until the shelves were empty and the floor was a graveyard of words. Then he pulled the shelves over, too.

Chest heaving, Cal left the office and went upstairs.

The children's bedroom door was open. He stood on the threshold, looking at the small shapes buried under blankets and sheets, listening to the rise and fall of tiny breaths.

He turned and peered into the adjacent room, where the older teenagers and young adults slept. Sometimes Jacob spent the night, tangled among the women. But he wasn't here now. Neither were Heath and Morwenna. Tightening his grip on the knife handle, Cal stalked to the next room.

Cynthia was awake, the baby nestled in her arms. She looked up with startled eyes, squinting in the shadows.

"Who's there?" she asked, her voice trembling. "Jacob, is that you?"

Cal's fingers twitched. He watched Cynthia set the baby down on the bed, then push back the blankets and get to her feet.

"Cal? What's going on? Where's Jacob? Has he come home?"

He wanted to cut her. To open her up and watch her bleed. And he would. But first, he wanted her to see Jacob die.

Before Cynthia could reach the end of the bed, Cal darted away and headed back downstairs. He heard her calling after him, her voice twisted with fear and worry.

Where was Jacob?

There was one place left to try.

Moving quickly, Cal headed for the basement. Above him, he heard Cynthia emerge on the upstairs landing and head for the stairs. He heard other voices, some of the older ones waking up.

Cal opened the basement door. Familiar cold rushed up to greet him. He descended into darkness. Cynthia was still calling to him, her voice getting louder as she hurried through the hall. Cal rushed forward, until he came to the end of the corridor.

He threw open the door, and with the knife pointed in front of him, he charged inside.

There was light. Electricity. A single naked light bulb hung from the ceiling. The room was large, its walls lined with shelves filled with indiscernible clutter, and sitting against the far wall, half hidden in shadows, were cages.

Cal froze. For a moment, he was overcome with a dizzying sense that he had been here before. For a moment, he wondered if he'd ever left Grady Spencer's basement, if the last few months had been a terrible dream.

But this was no dream.

Heath and Morwenna were here, entwined together on a thin mattress. Cal stalked towards them, the knife pointed at their throats.

The drug-fuelled confidence that usually dripped from their

pores had evaporated. Now, they looked frightened and confused. Now, they looked just like children.

Heath sat up and raised his hands. "Cal, what are you doing?"

Morwenna stared at the blade. "Jacob's not with you?"

She had blood on her clothes. His mother's blood. Cal advanced on them, lips curling back from his teeth.

Heath flashed a nervous glance at Morwenna then turned back to Cal. "Listen, we only did what we were told, okay? We were only following Jacob's orders."

Cal wanted to scream at them, to bellow at the top of his lungs. But it had been so long since he'd uttered a word, he couldn't remember how.

"Where's Jacob?" Morwenna asked him. "Cynthia told us you both went after some guy. What's going on? Why hasn't he come home with you?"

The knife trembled in his hand. The fire in his chest sparked and burned. Cal moved closer.

"Something's wrong," Morwenna said to Heath. "Something's happened to Jacob."

But Heath wasn't listening. His eyes were fixed on the blade. Slowly, he reached around to the back pocket of his jeans. "Relax, Cal. You've got it all wrong."

Cal raised the knife. Slowly, Heath pulled a small torch from his pocket and showed it to Cal. He flipped a switch and a thin beam of light bounced off the ceiling.

"See, Cal?" he said. "Do you see?"

He pointed the torch beam at the cages. Cal followed his gaze. The fire in his chest flickered and died. Curled up in a foetal position, her hair spilling over her closed eyes, was his mother.

She was alive.

He lowered the knife, watching strands of her hair flutter as she slowly exhaled, noticing the bloody bandage that dressed her upper arm.

"Jacob told us to bring her back," Heath said. "He told us that sometimes a boy needs his mother, that *you* needed her so you could lead us along the path to glory."

Cal stared at his mother. He moved over to the cage and sat down on his haunches, watching her sleep. Seconds later, voices filled the air and Cynthia entered the room, followed by a few of the older Dawn Children.

"What is going on here?" she demanded. She turned to where Cal was sitting, to where Carrie slept, curled up inside the cage.

"Who the hell is that?" she cried. "Why can't anyone tell me what's happened to Jacob?"

As the others argued and panicked behind him, Cal reached out a hand and gently brushed the hair from his mother's face. He tried to smile, but he'd forgotten how. But it didn't matter; he was with his mother. They were together again.

50

A DAY PASSED. Police and news crews swarmed over Porth an Jowl, shattering the quiet, sealing the town's fate as forever being known as Devil's Cove. Nat had watched it all unfold with mounting horror. Two police officers were dead. Carrie Killigrew was missing. Aaron Black was missing. His car had been found abandoned on the road just outside Briar Wood, next to another unidentified vehicle. The amount of blood found inside had suggested he would not be found alive.

Now, a large-scale manhunt was underway. A young man had been seen running from the scene of the crime. Bloody footprints had been discovered all over the house. All evidence pointed at Cal Anderson, who had earlier broken into the Killigrew residence and brutally stabbed Carrie's mother.

The press was still unclear as to how the author Aaron Black fitted into the deadly puzzle, and police had so far declined to comment at such an early stage of the investigation. But Nat knew. She knew exactly how he fitted in.

Now, as she stood in the backyard, sucking furiously on a cigarette and fighting the nausea that was clawing at her stomach, she stared at her phone screen. He'd called her in the early hours and she'd ignored him.

But he'd left her a voicemail.

She had almost deleted it. She hadn't wanted to listen to the man who'd treated her like dirt and tossed her aside. But then she'd changed her mind, deciding to wait until the next morning when she was sober. Because maybe, just maybe, he was phoning to apologise. Maybe he was going to admit that he'd been wrong to treat her like an employee and not his equal.

Now, Nat's thumb hovered over the voicemail key. Now, she was terrified of what she might hear. But she had to listen. She had to know what was on there, because Aaron Black was probably dead and there was a chance she could have saved him.

Her body trembling, she pressed the phone to her ear.

At first, she heard nothing, just crackles and static. Then she heard his gasping breaths and what sounded like running.

"Nat!" he said. She heard pain in his voice. Terror. Exhaustion. "Nat, you asshole, pick up!" More ragged breaths. A loud rustling, like branches. Then his voice once more. "I'm sorry. I'm sorry I treated you badly. But you need to help Carrie. They're coming for her. You need—" Crackles. Static. "Oh God! Nat, you need to get her out of there. They're coming! I'm up at Desperation Point. Tell the police to go to—" More static. Pops. The sound of the ocean. Then nothing. Silence.

Nat's body went cold. Tears spilled down her face. He'd called her. He'd begged for her help. She'd had the power to intervene. And now he was dead and Carrie was gone.

The cigarette dropped from her fingers. She stumbled, falling back against the house. Growing numb, Nat glanced across the yard at the tall trees of Briar Wood on the other side of the fence.

She had to do something. Tell the police. Find him.

But it was too late. She had heard it in his voice. Aaron Black had known he was going to die. Barely feeling the cold now, Nat turned to face the house. She could see Rose through the kitchen window, her face grave as she sat at the kitchen table, clutching a glass of port.

Nat turned back to Briar Wood. He'd been at Desperation Point. He'd been metres away while she'd sat upstairs, drunk and high on vitriol, drawing pictures of him being murdered by Cal.

She had to destroy the sketch, before anyone could see it. She had to stop this awful feeling of guilt that was now consuming her from the inside. She had to get out of here.

Before she knew what she was doing, she had crossed the yard. Now she was jumping up, hoisting herself over the fence, and landing heavily on the other side. Now, she was running blindly through the trees, heading for Desperation Point.

She heard voices all around Briar Wood—the police maybe, or a search party looking for Carrie—but she kept running. She didn't know why. All she knew was that Aaron had called her and he'd been up at Desperation Point.

The trees parted. The soft ground gave way to grass and rock. All she could see was the vast, charcoal sky as the afternoon slowly turned dark. Nat stumbled forward until she was metres away from the cliff edge.

Why was she here? What was she looking for? Not Aaron Black, she knew that. Aaron Black was dead.

Movement caught her eyes. Nat spun around to see Ben Ward, the lighthouse keeper coming out of his house, a pipe hanging from his mouth. He paused as he scratched at a dark stain on the door.

Nat ran up to him, caught him by surprise.

Ben was old and salty, his skin lined and tanned from years of coastal weather. He tipped his head towards Nat as he walked to his Range Rover.

"Afternoon," he said, giving her a wary look.

Nat said nothing, just stared.

He reached the Range Rover and unlocked the door.

"Something I can help you with, girl?"

Nat blinked. Shook her head. Then she said, "Didn't you hear anything last night? Didn't you see anything?"

Ben wrinkled his eyes, a look of confusion on his face.

"Old Ben don't hear much these days," he said, tapping his left ear. "Deaf as a post. What was I supposed to have heard?"

Nat stared at him incredulously. "I take it you haven't switched on the news today."

"Why would I do that? The news is all doom and gloom. I get enough of that staring at the sea."

He tipped his head again and climbed into the Range Rover.

Nat stood, numbly watching as the vehicle growled to life, then turned a half circle. Ben Ward drove away, pulling onto the dirt road that led through Briar Wood, back to civilisation. Rain started to fall. Nat looked over her shoulder at the dark, wide ocean that churned and heaved, all the way to the horizon.

I should go home, she thought. *I should tell Rose everything. I should—*

She looked down.

Lying on the ground, where the Range Rover had been parked, was a mobile phone. A shiver ran through Nat's body from head to toe. She stooped and picked it up. She tapped the screen. The lock screen image flashed up. Nat caught her breath. It was a black and white photograph of Aaron Black; a professionally taken shot of his head and shoulders. His hands were tucked under his chin, his eyes staring enigmatically at the camera.

Nat found herself smiling. Then the gravity of what she'd found hit her like a gust of wind. Perhaps there was something on the phone, something that could help the police track down Cal, and whoever else was involved. Perhaps there was something that would help them find Carrie. Maybe even find her still alive.

Running as fast as she could, Nat headed back towards Briar Wood, back towards Rose and her home.

51

CARRIE WOKE from a dream in which she was drowning, pulled under by dangerous currents.

She opened her eyes to darkness. Her head hurt. Her arm throbbed. She felt as if she'd been asleep for a thousand years.

Now she heard a multitude of voices; panicked and angry and laced with grief. She heard furniture being toppled, feet running, jostling. Somewhere at the back of it all, she heard a baby crying.

She tried to sit up. Immediately, a searing pain forced her back down. She waited a minute and tried again. She got up onto her elbow. The darkness pushed back to the edges of her vision. Now she saw light, blurred shapes and movement. The voices grew louder.

She reached out a hand. Her fingers gripped metal bars. She drew in a frightened breath as memories came rushing back. She'd been at the house. She'd been attacked. Instinctively, she felt the wound on her arm. Pain shot up to her shoulder.

Voices became clearer. Snippets of panicked conversation reached her ears.

"What do we do?"

"They'll come for us!"

"Jacob is gone! Gone!"

Carrie brought up her knees and pushed her feet against the bars, manoeuvring herself until she was sitting with her back against the cage. Her vision was clearing. She could see bodies pacing up and down.

"I saw them!" A male voice said. "His car was on the roadside. The police were everywhere. It's only a matter of time before they find us!"

She was thirsty. She needed water. She tried to cough, to clear her throat.

"I say we go. Get everyone in the van and drive."

"No! Jacob may come back."

"Jacob is dead, Cynthia!"

"We don't know that, not for sure!"

"What I do know is there's a body in the barn and the police are crawling all over the countryside. If we don't leave now, we don't leave at all, and everything Jacob's taught us will be for nothing. Monsters like that dead prick in the barn will have won!"

"I don't know, Heath. I don't know—I need time to think!"

"There's no time. I'm gathering everyone up."

"What about the new boy?"

"The boy's one of us now, he goes where we go."

"And *her*?"

"She stays. If we take her with us, she'll only try to escape."

"But—"

"I'll take care of it. Now, go tell Morwenna to start rounding everyone up, then grab what supplies you can."

"But Cal—"

"You just keep him occupied. If he wants to come with us, fine. If he doesn't then I'll take care of him, too."

Carrie's vision pulled into focus in time to see a young man storm away, followed by an older woman with a baby in her arms. Their voices grew quieter, then she heard footsteps hammering on stairs.

Terrified, Carrie leaned forward. She was in a basement. It was cold and damp, a single electric bulb casting light over the room.

She had no idea where she might be and right now, she didn't care. Whoever these people were, they were not going to let her live.

A cry escaped her lips. Fighting back tears, she pushed against the cage door then fumbled with the padlock.

She wasn't going to die down here. She wasn't going to stand by and watch while everything she loved was destroyed.

Pushing herself back up against the wall, Carrie brought her knee up and lashed out, kicking at the cage door. Bars rattled. The padlock flew up and down. But it held fast. Carrie drew her leg back and kicked again and again, channelling all her anger, all her despair. But the lock remained. She hadn't even made a dent in the bars.

And now someone was coming back.

She caught her breath as she heard footsteps moving closer. Panic gripped her throat. They were going to kill her. She was going to die right here, right now.

Carrie turned and saw a figure lurking in the shadows of the doorway. She recognised him instantly, could smell the skin she used to press against her cheek and plant kisses on and shower in soft baby powder.

"Cal?" she croaked. "Is that you?"

He emerged from the shadows; his sinewy frame crouched down on its haunches. He stared at her with wide, dark eyes that were just like hers. He edged closer, then closer still, little by little, until he sat centimetres from the cage.

He looked terrible, she thought. Filthy, malnourished, like an animal. But underneath the feral exterior, Carrie could see her son.

The son who had almost killed her daughter. The son who had stabbed her mother in the chest, narrowly missing her heart. She stared at him, not knowing how to feel. Not knowing what to say.

Cal stared back, his gaze filled with ghosts and demons.

"I missed you," Carrie said, and a tear spilled from her eye. "I missed you so much."

It felt wrong to tell him because he'd almost murdered her mother, and yet it felt so right because he needed to know. Because knowing that he was still loved was the only thing left that might save him.

Cal stared at her, his expression unchanging.

"I never stopped looking for you," Carrie said. She was crying now, her sobs breaking up her words. "You have to know that, Cal. I never stopped looking."

Cal cocked his head to one side, his eyes following the tracks of her tears. He reached through the bars and plucked a tear from her chin. He studied it for a moment, then slipped his finger in his mouth and tasted her sadness.

"Please, Cal," Carrie said, pressing her face up to the bars. "I don't know what's happening. I don't know what you're involved in, but it's nothing good. We need to get away from here now. We don't need these people. It can just be you and me. I can keep you safe."

Cal stared at her uncertainly.

"Think about it—we've missed out on so much in each other's lives, wouldn't it be nice to try again? To have a second chance at being mother and son? All you need to do is let me out of this cage and we can get away. Just the two of us."

Carrie held her breath, watching her son.

Footsteps thundered across the ceiling. A voice, panicked and muffled, shouted out instructions.

"Please, Cal," Carrie said, staring into his eyes. "These people don't care about you. They're leaving and they're going to kill me unless you do something about it. Let's get away. Away from here. Away from the cove. We could go somewhere different. Anywhere you like."

Cal inched closer, until his face was just on the other side of the bars.

"Don't you want that, Cal? Don't you want it to be just the two of us?"

It was like he was trying to see inside her head, to decide whether she was telling the truth.

"We just need a car. There's a van outside, right? We can go. Just drive. You and me, together. But we need to leave right now."

Cal stared at her, his black eyes glittering. He reached out a hand. Carrie took it, gave it a squeeze, turned it over and kissed the bloody palm. Cal watched her, his face pulled into a frown. Then he stood and walked out of the room.

"Cal, please!"

She stared at the empty space he'd left behind, her trembling hands making the bars rattle. Above her head, a cacophony of footsteps and frightened, young voices filled the air. But she was barely aware of them.

Cal was coming back into the room again.

Carrie's heart swelled with relief. Then it missed a beat.

Because it wasn't Cal.

It was the boy she'd seen at her house. He was carrying a jerrycan. The stench of petrol burned Carrie's nostrils.

The boy smiled at her.

"I'm sorry," he said. "We should have left you alone."

He tipped the jerrycan, pouring petrol onto the floor and around the room. He backed away through the door without saying another word, leaving a trail of fuel in his wake.

Carrie shrieked and rattled the bars. She pushed herself back against the wall and lashed out with her feet, over and over, until she had no strength left.

Above her, the house was growing quiet. Footsteps were fading, scared voices turning to distant whispers.

"I'm sorry," Carrie whispered as her body sagged against the bars. Maybe she deserved to die. Maybe she should stop fighting. If she'd kept her eyes on Cal seven years ago, none of this would have been happening. Instead, they'd be at home right now, watching a movie and eating popcorn on the sofa, or they'd be going for a chilly winter walk by the sea, their necks wrapped in knitted scarves.

"I'm sorry," Carrie said again. And then it really was quiet upstairs. Silent, even.

She stared at the wet trail of fuel leading out through the door. How long did she have before the flames came rushing in, until she was a scorched pile of ashes and bone?

Carrie closed her eyes, tried to shut out the stench of the petrol. She gripped the bars with all her strength. And she waited.

And then, after a minute, she felt heat against her skin. At first, she thought the fire had come and she felt a rush of terror. But there was no smoke. No crackle. No singed air.

She opened her eyes.

Cal crouched before her, the tip of his nose almost touching hers. He looked down as he inserted a key into the padlock. Then he hesitated, staring up at her with frightened eyes.

Carrie sucked in a breath. A hole opened in her heart as she swallowed back more tears.

"I promise you, Cal," she said. "I promise that it'll be just the two of us. I promise that I'll keep you safe."

Cal turned the key and tore off the padlock. The cage door swung open.

He held out a hand.

Carrie took it, leaning on him as she staggered to her feet. For a moment, they both stood there, staring silently at each other. Carrie wanted to wrap her arms around him, to hold him to her chest, and yet she wanted to run from him, to escape from this feral creature that had once been her son.

But she didn't run. She followed him as he hurried out of the room and along a narrow corridor, crouched down in the darkness like a nocturnal animal. She followed him to the top of the steps, their feet splashing in wet fuel, then waited as he held up a hand and checked the hallway.

Voices were coming from outside the house. Children were crying. Petrol fumes choked the air.

Then Cal was leading her into a laundry room and shutting the door. Carrie watched him open the widow and remove the board. She watched him climb through. She took his hand and climbed out after him.

It was dusk and it was raining. The ground was icy beneath

her bare feet. They were at the side of the house. Cal was pressed against the wall at the corner, peeking out.

Carrie joined him, saw a flash of a yard with a large van at its centre. She had a vague recollection of being inside that van, of being dragged half-conscious from it. Now she saw young people and children climbing into the back.

Someone pulled on Carrie's arm. She spun around to see Cal. He nodded at her to follow him. They ducked down low in the growing shadows and scuttled past the yard, unnoticed.

Parked behind a large barn was a small, three-door hatch-back that was splattered with mud. Cal held up a car key. Carrie took it.

She opened the door and climbed into the driver's seat. She peered through the windscreen to see Cal was unmoving, his eyes fixed on the barn window, a strange, unreadable expression on his face.

Carrie waved a hand, catching his attention, then Cal was silently climbing into the passenger seat next to her.

Carrie slipped the key into the ignition.

Then she froze.

She had lied to Cal. She had made him a false promise.

It could never just be the two of them. She could never let go of Melissa, and it was only a matter of time before the police tracked him down.

And yet the hope in Cal's eyes had been infectious, filling her with dangerous ideas.

Carrie started the engine. Spinning the wheel, she drove past the barn and then past the van, pushing her foot down on the accelerator pedal.

In the rear-view mirror she saw some of the adults leap out and wave their hands. She saw the man who had attacked her run forward, then a young woman pull him back. She heard them shouting and screaming. They looked terrified.

Then the house was gone from view and they were driving along a dirt track, back to the road.

As they reached the road and turned left, away from the farm, away from Porth an Jowl, Carrie stole a glance at Cal. His eyes sparkled. For a moment, he looked like the boy she once knew.

"Put your seatbelt on," she said.

Cal did as he was told.

Smiling, Carrie drove on.

Her son's life had been stolen from him. Bad men had tried to destroy him then shape him into their own image. Now he would be punished for all the evil that had been inflicted upon him. And even if he'd become too dangerous to be allowed to go free, it was unfair. Because Cal deserved so much more.

He deserved to love and be loved. He deserved to feel safe and secure. He deserved a life that was free of cage bars.

If she could give that to him, if she could show him a mother's true love, even for just a few hours before handing him over to the police, then maybe she could bring him back. Maybe Cal could be a boy again.

Her happy little pirate.

THE DEVIL'S GATE
THE DEVIL'S COVE TRILOGY BOOK 3

The final nerve-shredding chapter of the Devil's Cove Trilogy.

Six months have passed since the horrific events at Burnt House Farm and peace has finally been restored in Devil's Cove. But trouble is on the horizon.

As the town prepares for the annual Devil's Day festival, Carrie is coming to terms with her son's crimes while trying to salvage what's left of her family. Meanwhile, Nat is on a dangerous path of self-destruction as she seeks revenge on the mysterious Dawn Children.

But they are all unaware that a terrifying plan has been set in motion. One that cannot be stopped.

Death is coming to Devil's Cove. And this time, only the chosen will survive...

Available in paperback, hardcover, large print & eBook.

ACKNOWLEDGEMENTS

A huge thank you to my editor, Natasha Orme, whose insight helped to shape this book into a snarling beast with a broken heart; to my team of reader/reviewers: your ongoing enthusiasm and support is greatly appreciated (especially when it comes to spotting those leftover typos!). And lastly, to Xander, for his relentless encouragement, support, and daily doses of sarcasm. Thank you.

Printed in Great Britain
by Amazon

85200754R00192